BENEATH THE ATTIC

Center Point
Large Print

Also by V. C. Andrews® and available from Center Point Large Print:

Bittersweet Dreams
House of Secrets
The Silhouette Girl

**This Large Print Book carries the
Seal of Approval of N.A.V.H.**

BENEATH THE ATTIC

V. C. ANDREWS®

CENTER POINT LARGE PRINT
THORNDIKE, MAINE

PROLOGUE

"Why are you smiling? Are you an idiot?" my mother asked. She was as pale as a faded white rose. Startled, she looked more squeamish than angry, cringing in the doorway.

I was sitting on the floor of my bedroom, staring down at my bloodstained knickers after I had called out loudly enough for her to come running.

My stomach was tight with cramps, but I wasn't thinking about that.

"I'm not a little girl anymore," I told her proudly.

She put her hand over her heart and took a deep breath, her eyes closed. I really thought she might faint. Then she looked at me, my words finally crashing through her ears.

"What? Of course you are still a little girl. Don't leave the room," she ordered, and fled to send for Grace Rose, a nearby nurse, to "deal with the matter."

She had never once discussed this inevitable event with me. It was as if sex didn't exist for her and she still wanted me to believe babies were really brought by the stork. Later, she would accuse me of willing what she called "Eve's curse" to happen too soon and unintentionally revealed that it hadn't happened for her until she was nearly fifteen. By the time Grace Rose

5

arrived, I had fallen asleep on the floor. She knelt beside me and stroked my hair, waking me. My mother hadn't followed her up to my bedroom.

Despite my mother's insistence that I was still a little girl, Grace Rose complimented me on how grown-up I was about the start of my monthlies. I didn't wail; there was no panic. I certainly hadn't done what my mother accused me of doing: I hadn't willed it, but, especially these past few months, I'd been anticipating it. I could feel the changes coming in my body, and from what I understood about the sexual fantasies other girls my age experienced, mine were more vivid and daring.

I was eager to hear everything Grace Rose had to say. She was tall, with light-brown hair and calm green eyes. Although she was too thin, she wasn't unattractive, but she was twenty-three and unmarried and, as far as I knew, not promised to anyone, which I found more curious. There were all sorts of rumors about her, ranging from a terrible early romance that ruined her future hopes to that she simply didn't like boys. People like my mother who wanted to employ her medical expertise overlooked all that. They would never ask her a personal question. But not me. I wanted her to talk about herself.

"To be honest," she told me, "I was far more frightened and frantic about it when it first happened to me than you are. Most girls dread

6

it, but I have to say that your mother wasn't exaggerating." She smiled. "You do look like you're happy."

"I'm happy to be a woman and not a little girl. My mother can't stand it. How old were you?"

"Thirteen and five months," Grace said.

She smiled, remembering. I could feel her honesty. Why couldn't my mother be more like this? Why did I have to turn to a stranger?

"Is it weird that it happened to me so soon?"

"Oh no. It's not that unusual."

"My mother thinks so. You saw that."

She kept her soft smile. There was more in it. She wasn't just trying to be a good nurse. She saw something in me that she really liked. Maybe she saw herself.

"Mothers don't want their daughters growing up too quickly." She tightened her lips. I was confident that she was remembering her own mother's reactions. "I was told to keep it secret, but from the look on my face, all my girlfriends knew what had occurred. We were all anticipating it for ourselves."

"Did boys know?" I wasn't at all interested in other girls' reactions.

"None I told," she replied, "but there were some . . ." She widened her eyes, implying one or two might have realized it.

My mind went wild with thoughts. Could boys really tell? How did your body change? Was there something different about the way you walked, even talked? I nearly overwhelmed her with my flood of questions.

She saw quickly that I was like someone who had crossed the desert of sexual ignorance and even at the age of twelve had tasted the salty flavor of passion. After I was washed and dressed, she sat with me on my bed. It was wonderful to have a young woman explain things, someone who seemed to have had the same need to know more at my age. My mother never would do this, never would tell me anything I really wanted or needed to know. She was a child of the Victorian age, a time, I was told, when people put skirts on curvaceous piano legs because those naked piano legs were too suggestive.

"From now on," Grace said, sotto voce because my mother was nearby, probably hovering and listening on the stairway, "you want to keep track of dates."

"Dates?"

"When you're most fertile. Sometimes we forget or we think we'll slip through safely."

I was pleasantly shocked and excited by just how uncensored Grace was being. Keep track of dates? I was still only twelve. That meant Grace thought I might have sexual intercourse, perhaps in the near future. Otherwise, what was the point of such a warning? From this day on until it stopped, eggs hovered inside me, waiting for the right time to seize a sperm, or was it the other way around? No matter. It all seemed too busy and uninteresting, all that crawling around somewhere within my vagina. It made me think of tiny ants. Ugh.

I refused to reduce love and romance, sex itself, to science, anyway. I didn't want to talk about ovaries and eggs. What could that possibly have to do with romance? I could see Grace understood me.

Actually, why shouldn't she be warning me? I thought. Surely she was wise enough to have seen that at the age of twelve I already had the power to literally hypnotize a man with my cerulean eyes and full, shapely lips upon which kisses would quickly explode into unrestrained passion. If I could dream it so vividly, surely I could do it well.

"Do women always get pregnant if they have intercourse?" I asked.

She smiled as though she had expected the question.

"No, not if they're careful, as I just explained, but . . ." She hesitated, debating with herself about telling me any more.

"But what?" I asked, impatient.

"There are ways if you prepare ahead of time. Think about it and don't just rush into it. Some women practice the rhythm method," she continued, and explained it in detail. "Some are using this relatively new device called a diaphragm, and some insist their lovers use what's known as a rubber condom. There are some other things to do. Some women just depend on men to withdraw in time."

I knew I was sitting there gape-eyed, but I quickly tried to look like I knew more than I indicated and was not really that shocked at her frank talk.

"Your mother might get very angry at me for telling you all this, but I believe in telling a girl who's reached your stage of life everything."

Oh yes, she was right about that, I thought. My mother would be very angry and never use her for anything else.

"I promise. I won't tell her anything you said."

"It's far better than learning it on the street or from some sexually active girl. The key thing," she insisted, "is never rushing into it. Stop when you feel yourself losing control."

Me lose control? That wasn't going to be my problem, I thought. The responsibility was surely something every man who dared to court me would bear.

Probably from the first day I had studied my image in my mother's antique French Regency carved wood mirror, a glass that supposedly had reflected the faces of royals, even princesses, I had realized I was special. Grace Rose knew it, I was sure.

"You're going to be very beautiful, Corrine," she said, pausing in my bedroom doorway on her way out. "But with beauty comes great risk. Don't forget that. Men will lose themselves over you."

She was so convincing that she took my breath away.

But after my talk with Grace Rose and as my body continued its march toward womanhood, I became even more confident of what she had predicted. When I looked into this magic historical mirror my mother had put up in the hallway outside her bedroom, I saw the brilliant faces of femmes fatales, women who had always been in control of their lives and especially their relationships with men. No one else could see it, but I saw it, the tiny, spidery threads that emanated from my face and body. I could will one to touch a boy, a young man, and hold him tightly in my web until I was tired of him and then simply let him go, drifting through the rest of his life frustrated. To make proper love to any other woman, he'd have to be able to superimpose my face onto his fiancée's or his bride's, and even then, he wouldn't be totally satisfied.

Other women would always envy me. Some would absolutely hate me. But alas, I thought, that was the sacrifice I must endure.

Was it a curse or a blessing?

It wouldn't be that long before I knew the answer.

1

"It's easier for you, Corrine," my best friend, Daisy Herman, declared. "You're so pretty that boys flop about like silly seals at your feet."

Daisy was easily what anyone would call adorable rather than beautiful. Shorter than most of us our age, she had diminutive facial features. She was doll-like, someone who would look like a little girl forever, which was nice when you were a child but not something a grown woman would want.

It was midafternoon on a Saturday, and, like some invisible magician, early spring had run her palm over bushes and flower buds to startle us almost overnight with a bright green, rich cherry-red, and corn-yellow world. Daisy, Edna Howard, Agnes Francis, and I were lying on a brown horsehair blanket under the old, spreading oak tree my father had named Henry the Eighth because of the six smaller oak trees around it. He said they represented Henry's wives. Proof, he said, was that two of the six had had their tops blown off in a storm, and Henry the Eighth had beheaded two wives. When I was little, I believed it. My mother thought it was all ridiculous.

This was the first time Edna and Agnes had been invited to one of my so-called womanly talks. Both were rather dumpy and plain, grateful for any attention, especially from me. I left it up to Daisy to issue the invitations. That responsibility made her feel more important and helped her convince anyone that she was my trusted personal assistant.

After Daisy's comment, Edna and Agnes looked at me, anticipating some protestation of modesty, but I wallowed in and often sought compliments more like someone who was far more insecure about her appearance than someone who was confident of her beauty. I even requested praise from mirrors hanging anywhere I went, often pausing to ask, "Am I truly lovely?" I always heard the answer I expected, the answer I deserved.

However, whenever my mother caught me studying myself, she would pounce, declaring, "You're too arrogant and full of sinful pride, Corrine."

I would feel my insides twist and knot so tightly that I couldn't breathe and had to get away from her as quickly as I could. I swear, if she had claws, I'd have been scratched from head to toe.

Why couldn't she see that it wasn't so much my being narcissistic as it was my realizing that anyone who wasn't blind or stupid had no choice but to praise my features, from my unique sapphire-blue eyes with my long eyelashes to my diminutive nose and full, soft, and naturally crimson lips? I had my mother's high cheekbones but a strong hint of character in the way my jawline was just slightly prominent. I had inherited that from my handsome father. I was rarely sick and never pale. My father swore that I had possessed my rich magnolia-white skin from day one, but my mother said that was a preposterous exaggeration.

"Beauty is often not enough," I told Daisy.

I sipped some lemonade and looked past my girlfriends into the woods at the cool shadowy areas. Even from this distance, I could see a swarm of bees madly circling a dead log. For a few moments, I was elsewhere, riding a beautiful white horse beside my debonair fantasy fiancé.

"You mean you have to be smart, too," Agnes said. "Right?" she asked, nodding when I didn't add any other comment. Her highly nasal voice broke my dream bubble.

"Not in the way you're thinking, Agnes," I snapped at her. I was so enjoying my reverie. "I know how much you like to read and pretend you're as informed about politics as any boy or young man our age. But there is a particular book of knowledge that I think belongs with women only."

"Where did you get it?" Edna asked, wide-eyed. "Did you read it?"

"No, silly frog. It's not actually a book. It's something that comes naturally to you when you start to feel more like a woman than a girl. You do things instinctively to water men's mouths with desire."

Now the two of them were smirking at me with skepticism. As usual when I spoke to girls like this, I had to spell it all out.

"For example, there are special ways to look at boys who even slightly attract you. You bat your eyelashes and run your tongue over your lips to signal your interest. There are things you can do with your parasol to make yourself look sexier or indicate to a young man that you have interest in him when walking by. Maybe next time, if there is a next time, I'll bring one to illustrate."

I paused and, like a heart-to-heart confession, added in a suggestive whisper, "I've often tested these suggestions."

"And what happened?" Edna asked quickly. Her eyes reminded me of sizzling egg yolks.

I shrugged. "Nothing in particular, because I didn't want it to go any further. Even though we don't have the right to vote, we can have an influence on what happens in our lives. More women should think like that. As my father says, 'If you act like sheep, they'll act like wolves.' "

Daisy smiled. She loved when I spoke with anger when it came to the rivalry between male and female.

"How do you know so much about how to behave around men?" Agnes demanded with some annoyance. "We're about the same age, and I would never think to do any of that."

"Are we?"

"Well, I was fourteen last week," she said. "Edna is and Daisy is and you are."

I shrugged.

"Years as a measurement of your maturity are . . ." I looked again at Daisy, who had a better vocabulary since her mother was a schoolteacher. She knew instinctively by now when I wanted her to finish one of my sentences.

"Nebulous," she said.

"Huh?" Edna said.

"Vague, unclear. In other words, Edna, time passed pulling up your own knickers doesn't guarantee your maturity."

She and I laughed.

"Daisy is exactly right. We've all learned the science about making love, but when you're an adult, you realize that's hardly enough. You can't learn all you need to know from boring old books in order to conduct a satisfactory romance. Most of what's really important is, as I said, natural instinct. That's how it comes to me and hopefully someday soon will come to you. You grow into it, ripen like an apple or a grape."

"What exactly are we to expect?" Agnes asked. She had small eyes as it was, but when she squinted, they looked like pinholes. "I mean, how would we know when it's come?"

Two swallows flew close to us and then turned off to the right.

"It's like birds," I continued. "Female birds don't go to a school for birds to learn how to attract male birds and create new ones, do they? They do what they must to make it happen. It's in you, in your very female bones," I said. "Things just . . . explode inside you."

"Explode?" Agnes asked.

I raised my eyes and coached myself to have more patience. Then I glared at her.

"Don't you have new and different feelings, Agnes? No tingles, no urge to touch yourself? You have had your period. You shouldn't act like a child and cover your eyes at the sight of a penis."

"The sight of what?" Agnes looked like she had swallowed one of the swallows.

"Some girls are ashamed to admit their feelings. But we've all agreed to be honest with each other. Right?"

"Absolutely," Agnes said.

"Well?"

She looked at Edna.

"Yes," Edna confessed. "I have seen only my little brother's penis, but I've had those feelings."

"There. And there's nothing evil about it, Agnes. One day, the man you love or marry will be touching you in exactly the same places you're touching yourself. And don't deny you do," I quickly accused like a head-on-fire minister.

I thought she would faint. Her face reddened until it was as crimson as fresh-spilled blood.

"I'm sure your father touches your mother there, too. Or if he doesn't, he finds another woman to touch."

Daisy laughed, and Agnes's jaw dropped.

Edna shook her head. I think she wanted to put her hands over her ears, but she was entranced. I smiled to myself. If only my mother could see how infatuated most of my girlfriends were with me, she might appreciate me more. After she had her heart attack learning I conducted these secret womanly talks, of course.

Actually, now that I was older and my loveliness more obvious, my mother's criticism of the pride I took in myself infuriated me. Why would she want to rein in such beauty anyway? Most mothers would be proud, beaming and gathering compliments like a cotton picker.

"Has your mother told you most of this?" Edna asked. "Is that where you learned about it?"

"My mother?" I laughed. "Hardly. It would be too shocking. She would have heart failure, and I would be accused of matricide."

I wouldn't tell them, but in the deepest, darkest, and most secret chambers of my heart, I couldn't help but harbor the suspicion that my mother was simply jealous of me and used her heavy, thorny golden rules of humility to keep me from bursting out of the background in any room or place we had entered together. She knew I would quickly seize all the male attention, not that my mother was looking for any. She was simply drowned in my shadow and practically ignored when she brought me along.

Of course, she wasn't wrong to accuse me of being too forward. I sought to command every smile and all the praise the men around me could afford before their own wives turned their eyes into red-hot embers of disapproval, disapproval that would be directed at my mother for raising such a vamp. That was what it really was for her anyway: concern about her precious reputation.

"My mother would be shocked, too, if she found out we were even discussing such things," Agnes said. "She would forbid me from spending any time with you, any of you."

"Well, don't say anything," Edna warned. "We pledged that everything we tell each other is sacred, didn't we?"

"I won't say anything." She looked more frightened. "My mother would have my father take the strap to me."

"Mothers often forget what they were like when they were our age," I said. I looked back at my house and then leaned toward them to impart a great secret, and the three leaned toward me. "Or they are afraid to confess it. Oh, they might give you a little advice when some proper gentleman asks permission to propose marriage, but until then . . ." I sighed and sat back. "Until then, we're really on our own, aren't we? We have to know how far we can go and what we can do and not do. My best advice is, nibble but don't bite."

"What?" Edna said. "Nibble what?"

"Don't you have any imagination, Edna? Just dare yourself to think about it."

Agnes and Edna stared. They looked quite frightened. I smiled at Daisy.

"Daisy and I know how to do that, don't we, Daisy? We dare ourselves to think about it."

"Yes, but my guess is you'll be the first who attracts a proper marriage proposal, whether your mother likes to admit it or not."

I smiled. She was probably right.

There was nothing my mother could do about all this. Rules, lectures, and pouty faces were useless. It was simply my destiny to draw the admiration and desire, most assuredly the lust, of every man who stepped within the radius of my beauty. I had the power, the glow. To pretend I could stop it or even moderate it was as silly as pretending I could prevent the sun from rising.

"My father would certainly agree when it comes to my attracting the interest of men. I wish it wasn't indelicate for a father to have a conversation with his daughter about a man's sexual needs and all that we must know to be successful at romance. Men know more than women when it comes to the art of lovemaking anyway."

"The art?" Edna said, nearly laughing. I didn't smile.

"Of course it's an art, Edna. That's what I've been trying to tell you. Haven't you listened to anything?"

"You could probably get your father to talk about it," Daisy said, half joking. "He dotes on you."

"Yes," I said proudly. "He does. If I grimace at something my mother says about me, he comes to my defense, and a tear trickling down my cheek would rush along a gift or a promise of one to compensate for my bruised feelings. I know when that will work and when it won't."

"Do you mean to say you do that deliberately? I mean, start to cry?" Agnes asked.

I shrugged. "Whatever works, Agnes. It's called a woman's wiles, a chapter in that book I asked you to imagine. It's part of what you have to learn to do when it comes to men."

"But your father isn't . . ."

"What? A man? Of course he is, and it's good practice. There'll be many other men."

"My father doesn't dote on me like that," Agnes said. "My crying wouldn't matter."

I could practically see the jealousy dripping from the corners of her mouth. She was the youngest of four, and all three older than her were boys.

"Yes," I said. "Men do favor their sons."

"You're an only child," Agnes whined.

"But my being an only child is not the only reason he treats me special."

"What other reason is there?" Edna asked. I could see her mind swirling with sinful and forbidden possibilities now that I had said he was a man.

"Pride," I said. "And not simply because I'm his daughter, Edna. My father is quite experienced and objective when it comes to attractive women. His work and his important responsibilities require him to be a connoisseur of beauty, especially when it comes to the wives of his clients and business associates."

They nodded, but I doubted that they fully understood. Not even Daisy completely understood. Before he had married my mother, my father was already a rising star in the newly formed First United Bank of Alexandria, Virginia, and thus one of the most eligible bachelors in the city. While it was men who were doing the investing in the booming businesses, their elegant wives and daughters were players in a constant parade of social events, wearing the most fashionable clothes and winning the hearts of powerful entrepreneurs.

"I once heard my father say that some men wear their beautiful women like expensive jewelry."

"Wear them? Like jewelry?" Agnes said. She started to laugh. "How do you wear a wife?"

23

"Think about it a moment, Agnes. What powerful man wants a plain-looking wife on his arm? My father greets many of these women and knows whom to bestow his attention on and whom to ignore."

"That makes sense," Daisy said.

"Yes. It's a business thing. He's quite aware of which women are worshipped by their husbands and could order them about, even when it comes to business decisions."

They were all quiet, thinking.

"Gosh," Agnes said with a painful grimace. "There's so much for a girl to learn before she's a woman."

"Precisely, and my father does help and encourage me in little ways."

"What little ways?" Edna asked.

"He's always bringing me presents, trinkets, a pin for my clothes or a new hair clip. Usually, he's observed something one of the more fashionable women is wearing or hears about what she is thinking of buying and then he thinks of me. He thinks of me as more of a woman than a young girl."

"What does your mother say about that?" Daisy asked. Even she was unaware of all my father's gifts.

"What do you expect from my mother? You know her well enough." I paused and then imitated my mother with exaggeration. " 'You

24

spoil her. You'll frustrate my efforts to mold her into a decent, respectable, and humble young woman.' "

"Well, isn't that what we should all want to be," Agnes asked, "respectable and humble?"

"Not me. Is there anything that promises a more mundane life than what my mother calls respectability and humility? It will weigh you down with the most boring days, days devoid of any thrills and excitement. There are no surprises in a life like that. Look at how my mother lives and most likely yours as well.

"She spends most of her free time doing needlework or having tea and gossiping with her few spinster and widowed friends. How droll. For me, it's simply a slower way to die. They all might as well grow whiskers and smoke corncob pipes."

"Some do," Daisy said, and she and I laughed.

"Does your mother know what you think of her, how she lives?" Edna asked, practically breathless.

"Probably," I said. "I've made enough comments about it and even told her she's losing her femininity."

I sat back on my hands and let the sun wash my face.

"I would never say anything like that to my mother," Agnes said, aghast. "Would you, Daisy?"

I opened my eyes and looked at her to see how she would answer.

"Maybe," Daisy said. "I haven't yet, but I could."

"You don't understand, Agnes. A daughter can be different from her mother. Mine hates the wind in her hair, whereas I seek every opportunity to get it in mine. We're truly oil and water. We don't mix well."

"Does your mother think that, too?" Edna asked.

"Let me put it this way," I said, sitting forward again. "If my mother could hire a witch to turn me into an ornament that she could plant in her Victorian sitting room, she would. Although not really above the door, my mother keeps the words hovering everywhere in our house."

"What words?" Agnes asked.

" 'Children should be seen and not heard, but Corrine especially should not be seen until she is gagged, bound, and fitted into an approved marriage,' " I recited. "And I'm sure like all your mothers would say, 'Afterward she can speak only when her husband deems it is proper.' Well, maybe that's how you see your futures, but not me."

No one spoke for a moment. Daisy was looking down, but Agnes and Edna stared at me as if they had just seen a ghost.

"I think I have to start for home," Agnes said. She looked like she was going to get sick.

"Yes, me, too," Edna said.

They both leaped to their feet.

"Remember, I brought you here," Daisy said, "and you swore everything said and heard is sacred."

"We know," Agnes said.

"You'd better," Daisy told them with steely eyes. They looked afraid to swallow.

Daisy turned to me.

"I'll help you bring in the blanket, glasses, and jug of lemonade." She obviously wanted to remain for a few minutes to talk about them.

"Thank you."

We started to fold the blanket. Edna and Agnes said good-bye and quickly walked off together, holding hands and never looking as small to me. Daisy watched them, too.

"They're such children," she said. "*Sex* is still a dirty word to them. A kiss on the neck will seem more like a mosquito bite when and if a boy ever does kiss them."

"If he sucks hard enough, it could have the same result," I said.

Daisy laughed but looked a little astounded at the thought and image. The truth was that Daisy and I pretended we knew so much, but if we were honest, we would have to admit we didn't know all that much more than Agnes and Edna did when it came to actually having sex. Everyone by now had been taught about the birds and the bees, but except for a forbidden kiss Daisy referred to, usually something quite unsatisfactory, neither of us had ventured to do much more.

We brought everything into the house, and Daisy said good-bye. We promised to see each other soon without the other two, or any other girl for that matter, so we could have more revealing discussions.

"I'm amazed at how much I'm still learning from you, Corrine."

We hugged, and she left.

Where was I to get much more to tell her? Despite how wise and mature I appeared to her, I was still forced to live in an asexual world, ignoring every thrilling sensation and avoiding every carnal fantasy. My mother was good at sensing when I had these feelings and erotic illusions, too, especially now that I was older and they came more often. She would take one look at me and say, "Clean up your mind," which brought the blood to my face, a revelation as good as a verbal confession.

Desire and passion were hanging there with all the other forbidden fruit dangling in our home. God forbid I mentioned having erect nipples, and although it was never clearly stated, only vaguely suggested, satisfying the overwhelming urge to masturbate was the same as opening the lid to the hole that dropped you directly into the arms of Satan.

Often I wanted to scream, "I am not made of stone!" Was I to ignore my perfectly shaped, firm breasts that had appeared almost overnight, disregard this smooth curve in my waist, and completely overlook the deliciously formed rear end that Nature herself had designed?

But was it all, this body that Venus herself was sculpting, to be hidden in those awful clothes my mother favored, not only for herself but for me? Maybe my mother wished my hourglass figure would turn into a jar.

No matter what looks my mother gave me at the first sign of flirtation or what waves of ice-cold warnings she declared about the dangers men by their very nature possessed, I couldn't let go of the dream. One day, despite my mother, I would emerge like a dazzling butterfly and lift myself away from her constraining reach. I would hover freely for a while, maybe just to torment her, and then explore the promises that attracted me, each a branch, a leaf, or a soft petal upon which I could land and from which I could shine the beacon of my beauty like a lighthouse of love.

Once I was free, I would bask in the looks of admiration and welcome the wave after wave of compliments unchecked. Men would strain the very limits of their imaginations to outdo each other with flowery praise simply to win my smile. Those who were granted a touch of my hand would struggle to keep themselves from exploding with desire. My beauty was that powerful.

I knew I sounded very brave and sophisticated, which was why my womanly talks had become so famous among my peers, but I felt like a runner who had her ankles chained together or a bird whose mother wouldn't let her try out her wings. What good was my beauty and charm if it was all kept locked up until my parents, like the parents of practically all the girls I knew, decided what man deserved the key?

Maybe that would be their futures, but for me, it was something I was determined I'd decide for myself, no matter what the risks.

And I had no doubt there would be some.

I was just not prepared for how many and how quickly they would come.

2

On my sixteenth birthday, my father presented me with a new, very fashionable cherry-red bicycle, one with pneumatic bicycle tires, top of the line. Especially for young women in 1890, cycling had become the rage. Some wore puffed knickerbockers when they rode, but I saw the gift as a doorway opening me to more sophisticated clothing. I immediately asked for a divided skirt with a shorter hemline so I could ride more comfortably. My mother, so unaware of sportswear, started to object until I explained how the skirt would look like a normal full skirt when I dismounted.

"I must have a new hat and new shoes, too," I declared. "How silly I'll look now wearing a child's bonnet. I should have a new pair of lace-up boots, proper stockings, and pretty petticoats."

"Pretty petticoats! Why does that matter? Who would see you in them when you cycle?" my mother asked, her face lit by lightning.

"Not when I cycle, Mother, but when I dress, I would, and so would you," I said calmly. I was sure she could see defiance swimming in my eyes. "Why can't young women be proud of themselves, proud of how they look, even if it's only in their mirrors?"

"Women proud of themselves? Look what you've started, Harrington Dixon," my mother complained. She waved her right forefinger at him like a hell-and-brimstone preacher. "Pride goeth before a fall. Remember that."

"Oh, it's nothing really that terrible, Rosemary," he said calmly. "All young women are driven by the same fancies. You were simply better at hiding it."

"Fiddlesticks. I never—"

"Rosemary . . ." He smiled. "You'll come along and help choose nice things."

My face soured, even though he hadn't added "proper," which to me was as bad as any profanity. It was one of those "lock and chain" words that restricted you to the point of screaming. I had been hoping to go shopping only with my father, who would stand on the sidelines laughing while I ran wild with my selections.

"Apparently, I have no choice but to do so," my mother said, pursing her lips and narrowing her eyes with frustration. "Now that you've gone and done it."

Despite her ugly faces of disapproval and what I believed were her efforts to hide her natural beauty out of some silly, stern modesty, my mother was an attractive woman with nearly perfect features. She was tall and regal and had hands as pretty as mine. When I would catch her sitting quietly by herself, her face was like one carved in ivory, a cameo, and her blue-gray eyes, not stained with anger or disgust, would be strikingly attractive. Why else would my father have married her? Her family hadn't been as well off as his. As difficult as it was for me to believe, there must have been some iota of romantic love between them.

"What terrible thing have I done?" my father asked, obviously fighting a smile, the smile his eyes betrayed.

"You've opened Pandora's box, Harrington Dixon. That's what you have done."

I hope so, I thought.

"Well, actually, there is something special that would require us to do some shopping for Corrine as well as you anyway, Rosemary," my father said.

"And that is?" my mother asked, tucking in the right side of her mouth. If she only realized how ugly that made her and how it would eventually add more wrinkles in her face, she would stop doing it, I thought.

"Simon Wexler, the chairman of the bank's board of trustees, and his wife have decided to celebrate their tenth anniversary with a gala at their home on May fifteenth. It will be a formal affair, of course. You two will need new dresses. For Corrine, it will truly be like her coming out. And it's time she did."

"Really, Daddy?"

Were my feet off the ground?

His eyes twinkled his yes, which made my heart race with the possibilities. I would be making a grand entrance at a gala attended by the rich and powerful, their wives wearing the latest in fashion. I would finally step onto the stage as a young woman and not a child tagging along behind her parents.

For the past year or so, I had been rehearsing for this dramatic entrance into Alexandria, Virginia's social world, practicing my walk, my posture, and shaping my smile. My mother's busybody friends surely would fan their heated faces harder once they saw me grown and developed, my sexuality revealed, I thought. Men would turn their heads quickly as I passed by. Some would suffer neck strain. All the daughters of other people, especially my parents' friends, would gasp so hard with envy that they might pee in their knickers. My closest friends certainly would. Daisy's eyes would shed green tears, even though we were best friends.

"What's wrong with the dresses I have?" my mother asked. "I don't think it's necessary to put on airs, especially for your board chairman and his . . ." She looked at me and checked herself. "Woman," she added, exploiting the underlying suggestions whispered in the circles of polite society. Everyone my mother knew talked about Lucy Wexler's coquettish ways. There was even substantial gossip about assignations with secret extramarital lovers hovering in shadows. She had two nannies alternating to care for her eight- and six-year-old boys, supposedly so she would have time for all this indiscretion. I thought it was the most exciting topic of my mother's frequent gossip sessions.

"It's really not putting on airs to be in fashion, Rosemary."

"My clothing is still in fashion, Harrington."

"Whatever you think is right to wear, certainly."

"Well, I need a formal dress. I have nothing for such an event, and it's time I did," I said, nearly stamping my right foot for emphasis. I was afraid my mother might successfully stop me. "Right, Daddy?"

"Yes, it's time you had something more in style, more fitting for your age," he said, nodding. "Don't you agree, Rosemary?"

"What's in style today is ridiculous and in some instances obscene," she said, "especially for young girls."

My father didn't change expression or look like he would change his mind. My mother sighed at the sight of another defeat. The words almost appeared on her forehead: *Why bother anymore? Except I still have my own pride.*

"Now that you're determined to do this, yes, I'd better come along and make sure you don't buy her something that would make us look foolish," she added, and left the living room, for a moment taking all the air out with her.

My father gazed after her, shaking his head. Love had become pity, I thought, but I quickly brushed it all out of my mind. That wasn't important now. I had lots of more important things to consider, headed by hair and nails and a new, more sophisticated fragrance.

"Thank you, Daddy," I said, rushing into his arms.

My father was six foot three and broad-shouldered. He had reddish-blond hair with a Vandyke that highlighted his firm, masculine mouth and Romanesque nose. His cheeks were habitually flushed, which served to emphasize the blueness in his eyes, eyes I had inherited.

He looked down at me and kissed my forehead.

"You can break any man's heart you want, Corrine," he warned, smiling and flirtatiously running his right forefinger along the softness of my cheek and over my perfectly shaped lips. "Just don't break mine." He feigned a threatening look.

"Oh, never, Daddy. Never," I said, and hugged him tighter until he laughed and begged to be released.

"You'll crack my ribs!"

We both laughed then.

I was laughing because in my heart, I knew confidently that I could use him to pry open any door locking away anything my Victorian mother and her stuffy friends deemed forbidden.

Later that evening, I moaned and sighed suggestively, turning my head slowly from left to right and back again as I studied myself in my large gilded oval mirror, looking for my most favorable profile when I paused. I envisioned men on my right and then men on my left studying me at the Wexler gala.

Was my face more attractive slightly tilted or with my chin raised? Did I hold my shoulders too stiffly, my nose so high that I looked like I was sniffing clouds? I wanted to move with good posture but not like my mother, who too often walked as if she had an iron rod up her spine. She had perfect posture, but she lacked the grace I had naturally. My body was a finely tuned instrument that played the melody of me. Hers was stuck in a statue labeled *Decency,* judging every sway, every smile, and every turn.

Girls like Agnes and Edna, who still weren't conscious of their habitual moves, were simply dullards. For nearly two years, I had tried to get them to understand a number of times after they had attended my womanly talk, but now they avoided me as if I could tempt them into prostitution or something. Thinking ahead and planning your smile wasn't sinful. I believed that nothing a young woman did regarding her appearance should be accidental. It was preparation and practice that made the difference between success and failure with men, even for someone as truly beautiful as I was. What good was a horse that nature gave the ability to run very fast if it wasn't trained to do so? More important, if it wasn't given the opportunities to do so?

I was not fond of what my mother called "proper understatement" when it came to your appearance. Even with an expensive new dress and shoes, as well as a touch of tinted powder on your cheeks, even someone like me, with all this inherited loveliness, could be ignored and become practically invisible if I behaved like a mannequin and showed no apparent interest in myself, a Modest Mary. That sort of girl was so surprised by a compliment that she became flustered and attracted only clods. They deserved each other.

Once, I had overheard my father tell a business associate that "something moving always has more attraction than something stuck in place." Of course, he had been talking about who would be worthy of receiving a loan to expand his business and who wouldn't be, but I was always thinking in terms of competition for the attention of men. Every day, I thought of and realized more that I could do to be attractive. A gesture that was just a little exaggerated, a shift of a shoulder with a suggestive smile, and a laugh only a trifle louder than most would laugh turned heads toward me. After that, it was my task to hold the gazes of those I wanted competing for my favor, by either dropping my eyelids to send a seductive message or wetting my lips with a swipe of the tip of my tongue before I smiled again.

I wasn't exaggerating during my womanly talks when I suggested some of this as part of a woman's book. Lessons in romance like these were what I intended to memorialize in my diary. There were all sorts of sexy ways to softly close your eyes, hold your head just a little to the side, and sigh seductively. But how was I to explain it so that someone far more naive would understand? As Agnes and Edna and girls like them demonstrated, most girls my age were ignorant when it came to what made them more seductive. I had all this natural wisdom to share, but to talk to them was like trying to converse with someone who spoke a foreign language. Only Daisy seemed to care, to learn from me, but I doubted she would ever reach my level of magnetism and win the man she wanted, even if I got her a personal copy of my book of love.

However, the proper words, words that really captured my feelings and thoughts, were so difficult to write. I was frustrated almost every time I lifted a pen, my diary opened to blank pages, and sat at the mahogany inlaid desk my mother had thought was far too expensive for "a little girl's room." Whenever my mother referred to me that way, my ears would burn, even when I was seven. I was never really just "a little girl."

It was so important to write in my diary, despite my struggle to express my feelings accurately. Most of my girlfriends kept one, but mine would be historic. It might even end up in a museum or be used to teach other young girls how to become fully developed women. Why, someday I could be as famous as Clara Barton or Louisa May Alcott. I was certainly more attractive than they were. And now I would prove it to Alexandria high society.

A new dress, the Wexler gala! *I really am breaking free,* I told myself. I would fill the pages of my diary with memories of this time in my life, memories that would send my mother rushing hysterically into the street, pulling her hair out, even if she had read only one page.

To prepare myself for what I saw as my coming out, I consumed anything I could read about the new dresses and hairstyles. By the time we set out to shop for my new clothes, I was as good as any fashion expert.

Not surprisingly, from the moment my mother had walked into the department store with my father and me, I saw her face droop with disapproval at the sight of the dressed mannequins and hanging garments. She hadn't bought anything new for herself for quite some time. No recent fashion was special enough or good and proper as far as she could see, and it wasn't a case of being deliberately critical of something you couldn't have. My father had never discouraged my mother from buying new clothes and shoes. On the contrary, he was always encouraging her, but carefully, because if he mentioned someone else's wife and how good she looked in something new, my mother would accuse him of lechery.

But with my father's help that day, I had been able to have a dress that clearly marked me as older, mature, a woman and not a child. It was expensive, too. Most important, the colors brought out my rich, magnolia-white complexion, something even the saleslady had to acknowledge, but carefully, especially when she looked at my mother and saw the disapproval sinking into her face. The saleslady came close to making the dress seem too sexy, even though ironically it was vintage Victorian. Most of that had to do with my figure, my small waist and perfectly proportioned hips. She nearly made a tragic mistake for me by saying, "No corset could shape your daughter any better."

"We need something appropriate," my mother inserted. "Not shapely."

"But it is beautiful," I said. "Can we buy it, Daddy?"

I avoided my mother's eyes.

"Buying you something beautiful is what we're here for," he said.

Now that dress hung on my closet door in my bedroom. It was an evening dress of red and white; the underskirt was white satin, kilted in front and trimmed with Mechlin lace and a garland of red roses. The overdress was red silk with a low neck and short sleeves. Of course, I had to have a pair of gloves to the elbow and chose black. Whenever I entered my room after my father had bought the dress for me, I would practically genuflect. Every day until the day of the gala, I would put it on and move around my bedroom, practicing how to turn and sit or simply walk wearing it. I wanted it to look like I'd been wearing sophisticated clothing for some time. This wasn't some little girl bursting out of a shell.

Daisy came over to see me in it one day. Her parents weren't invited to the gala, so she wouldn't be there.

"You are coming out," she said when I paraded across my room. She didn't sound envious, just amazed. We had, after all, practically grown up together, and I could see she felt left behind.

"Soon you'll be just as gorgeous and elegant, Daisy," I said, even though I hardly believed it.

"Right," she said, sounding so sad. It was really as if this was a final good-bye between us, and there was nothing either of us could do about it. I was leaving on a train she had yet to board.

I hugged her. "You will be. Who should know better than the woman who runs our womanly talks?"

That made her feel better, and we sat afterward for hours talking about the good-looking young men I might see at the gala.

"Promise to tell me all about it as soon as you can," she said.

I assured her I would remember every important detail. "It will be like you were there."

That was enough to put a smile on her face when she left.

I returned to perfecting my appearance. I preferred her not being there when I concentrated on all this. Despite everything I had taught her, she wouldn't know what to emphasize and what not, and I would have to spend and waste time explaining why little things mattered.

My mother was adamant about me not tinting my cheeks, but that was fine. With my youthful complexion and a little trick pinching them before I entered the gala, I was confident it wouldn't matter.

When it came to preparing my hair, I was already far better at it than my mother was at doing her own. I wore it in a high coiffure. My mother wasn't going to lend me any of her jewelry, but when I asked her again in front of my father, he insisted that she should.

"I won't have her looking underdressed,

Rosemary. Either lend her what's appropriate, or I'll buy her what's appropriate."

Seeing he was serious, my mother reluctantly offered me a double row of pearls for my necklace and a gold brooch with pearls to wear at the center of my neckline. However, she didn't give me any of it until the day of the gala, claiming I might dare to wear something away from the house and lose it, especially if I wore it riding my bicycle.

I didn't argue. I concentrated on my complete appearance without the jewelry daily, however. Right after they had bought my dress, they had bought my shoes. I loved the gold satin slippers with pointed toes trimmed with rosettes of mousseline de soie, very large and full. Even my mother was impressed when I told the saleslady exactly what I wanted. My father first thought my mother had explained that much about fashion, but he quickly understood I knew it all myself.

"Maybe I'll start having her choose my clothes," he said, half kidding.

Now overwhelmed herself, my mother quickly volunteered to give me one of her evening cloaks. My father would have told her to anyway. I asked for her velvet full shoulder cape.

"I was going to wear that," my mother said, almost wailed. I didn't change expression. "Oh, well. I'll do something else."

I smiled. Seemingly, there was no stopping me now, and I knew I just had to take advantage of every opportunity.

When I stepped out of her room and joined my parents in the study the night of the gala, my father broke into the proudest, warmest smile I could recall.

"Who is this young lady?" he said, pretending he really didn't know me. He turned to my mother and growled, "Why do you surprise me with strangers in my own home?"

My mother raised her eyes toward the ceiling. "Please, Harrington," she said.

"What, 'please'? I do believe she'll steal the evening from Lucy Wexler."

I beamed, but my mother shook her head and scowled.

"What dreadful thoughts are you stuffing into her already swollen ego? It is quite, quite impolite to steal away the evening from Lucy Wexler on the occasion of her anniversary, Harrington."

"I thought you weren't that fond of her."

"I'm not, but it is their anniversary, and I wouldn't want any woman, even a Lucy Wexler, to be mistreated."

She turned to me, her eyes too familiarly cold and angry.

"You mind your manners, young lady, and remember what I told you about being modest, especially in the company of unmarried men.

You make sure you are properly introduced to strangers and always by an adult."

"Oh, yes, Mother. Thank you. I certainly wouldn't want to make a terrible social faux pas and embarrass you and Daddy after you've taught me so much about social etiquette from your own experiences," I said. I was dripping so with sarcasm that my father risked a smile. My mother ignored it.

"Shall we go, then?" my father asked my mother.

My mother nodded, looking more like she was about to attend a funeral than a celebration, while I could barely contain myself.

Even if I hadn't had new, more sophisticated clothes and believed this was my coming out, I would have been excited to attend a gala at the now-famous Wexler mansion. The nearly 15,000-square-foot house was built on 180 acres that featured a half-mile-long lake. The mansion had grand Doric columns and a triangular pediment that resembled a temple. There were over fourteen grand-sized rooms and a ballroom. It had originally been built and owned by a large slave owner. The rumor my father told me was that Simon Wexler had outmaneuvered another bank that had foreclosed on the property to buy it all for almost half its value.

Although the gala had been advertised as a gathering of close friends and relatives, it was quickly apparent from the line of carriages as we approached that this was no small gathering. The moment my father turned into the long entry drive, over which grew very old oak trees creating a dramatic green tunnel, my mother gasped.

"There must be over a hundred people!" she exclaimed.

"Most likely close to two hundred, Rosemary," my father said. He turned to look at me. "Lots of cousins."

I smiled at his laughter. We were only halfway down the long entry when we heard the music. It sounded like a very big band with more than three banjos.

"They're playing 'Oh, Them Golden Slippers,' " I cried. "And that's my shoes!"

What a good omen, I thought.

The entry drive curved at the front of the mansion. As we drew closer, we saw it was swarming with carriages unloading and men and women in the most elegant clothes stepping out. There were dozens of servants taking care of the horse-drawn carriages. As we drew even closer, the music was louder, and I could see that people were being greeted at the front entrance by help serving glasses of champagne as they entered. The festive atmosphere was explosive.

"May I have a glass of champagne, Daddy?" I quickly asked.

"Of course not," my mother said.

"Oh, I think one is appropriate, Rosemary. Corrine's old enough to toast the Wexlers."

My mother shook her head but said nothing more.

My eyes went everywhere, evaluating the dresses other women wore, searching for someone who was young and pretty enough to be my competition. I was heartened by how many girls my age were still dressed like young girls, some still looking more like bleary-eyed children, too unsophisticated to be anything but bored, even here with all this.

My father held out his right arm. My mother was on his left. We'd do the stairs that way. My father looked prouder than a peacock with me and my mother at his side, and he looked more like a Roman emperor surrounded by an adoring crowd. I could feel the eyes turning our way and thought most were looking at me. For many who knew my father and mother well, there was an obvious moment of curiosity: was I their young daughter?

I froze my soft smile the way I had practiced before the vintage mirror, to be another *Mona Lisa*. In a moment, everyone, especially the men, would realize that I was miles past being a child.

Simon and Lucy Wexler were just inside the front entrance. Simon was stout, with a small potbelly, graying dark-brown hair, and a graying brush mustache. Lucy was an attractive woman with chestnut hair that complemented her strikingly green eyes. I thought she looked at least a decade or so younger than her husband. She was so bedecked with jewelry that I thought she resembled a walking Christmas tree with all those diamonds twinkling in the light.

Simon Wexler might have ten times the wealth my father had, I thought, maybe even twenty times, but he was nowhere near as handsome and as distinguished-looking. My mother, although prettier than Lucy, was so plainly dressed in comparison that she looked like she would quickly fade into the background and become more like a party favor than a guest.

But not me, I thought.

"Rosemary," Simon Wexler said, taking my mother's hand. "Thank you for coming to celebrate with us."

He spoke to my mother, but his eyes were on me.

"Harrington? Is this who I think she is?"

"Yes, my daughter, our daughter. Corrine," my father said, stepping back so I could step forward to take Simon Wexler's waiting hand.

I saw Lucy Wexler's arrogant expression fade into curiosity and then envy. I wasn't surprised. What woman her age didn't want to be as pretty and as young? Beauty for such women faded like an aging rose. But not for me, I thought, not for me.

49

"Welcome," Simon Wexler said. He was practically drooling. "You'll certainly help dress up our gala, young lady."

"Thank you, Mr. Wexler. Congratulations, Mrs. Wexler," I said, and nodded ever so gently, with a slight curtsy, keeping my eyes down. *That's enough poise to please my mother,* I thought.

"Please, enjoy yourselves," Lucy said. She turned instantly to a dashing young man who had arrived alone.

My mother rolled her eyes, and we moved forward to pluck glasses of champagne off one of the trays. My father handed me one.

"Drink it slowly, my dear."

"So it lasts all night," my mother added with warning.

I barely let my lips touch the bubbly and then followed them into the mansion as they greeted people, my father constantly introducing me and wallowing in the praise I captured and the compliments both he and my mother were being given for having such a beautiful, poised young woman. We moved toward the ballroom, where the musicians were playing and the food was laid out on long tables. There were tables and chairs everywhere and dozens of servants.

I want to live like this, I thought. *I deserve to live like this.*

Everything in the ballroom was decorated, from the chandeliers to the chairs at tables, colorful crepe paper, balloons, and, streaming from one side of the ceiling to the other, a pair of white and red drapes. *Just like my dress,* I thought. It was all serendipity. As I panned the room, studying other women, noting how some clumped together to chatter while the men gathered in smaller circles, I turned and suddenly, ironically, faced Emma Lawrence, whose birthday was a day after mine, although no one would believe it. She was with Elsie Daniels. Both wore simple cotton dresses that looked two sizes too big on them. Probably hand-me-downs, I thought. Emma's was light blue and Elsie's a chocolate brown. Neither wore any jewelry, and both had the ugliest black shoes, footman shoes.

"How fancy we are," Emma said. She was tall, nearly five foot ten, but far too plump. The features of her face were almost swallowed by her ballooned cheeks. I thought she still moved more like a boy and wondered if being so overweight smothered sexual development, especially in a girl. Elsie was only about five foot four but had stunning strawberry-blond hair. Her freckled cheeks and moss-green eyes made her cute but not really pretty in my judgment.

"Is that a compliment?" I asked.

"You look very pretty," Elsie admitted, somewhat reluctantly.

"Thank you."

"The best thing to eat is the roasted pork,"

Emma said. "And they have wonderful cupcakes."

"I'm not going to eat a thing," I said. "I'm just going to drink champagne."

I held up my glass. Both girls eyed it as if I held a valuable diamond in my fingers.

"My mother wouldn't let me take one," Emma said.

"My father said absolutely not before I could even ask," Elsie added.

"They simply don't think you're old enough," I said, smiling. "You've got to convince your parents that you're an adult. You've both attended one of my womanly talks, haven't you?"

"A year or so ago," Emma said. "We've never been invited back."

"You learned enough back then. Put your little-girl faces away, and don't let them treat you as if you were still a child. Parents love to keep their children as children. It helps them to feel younger, remember?"

They both looked stunned. It was as if they were listening to a woman years and years older, with the wisdom of the ages on the tip of her tongue.

I turned slowly to look at the guests and noted one man was staring in my direction with a slight grin on his face. I was sure he was looking directly at me. He was wearing a custom-fit gray suit that looked more modern than any suit the other men wore, including my father. I shifted my gaze as if he held no interest, but then I was unable to continue ignoring him. When I glanced back, he was still looking at me with that same tantalizing grin. I imagined him to be at least six foot one and could see he was broad-shouldered, quite trim, and athletic-looking. If I ventured a guess about his age, it would be somewhere in the mid-twenties.

Now aware of how I was caught staring back at him, I suddenly felt very nervous. It was not how I usually reacted when it came to how a man looked at me, but there was something unique about this man that caused me to suddenly feel insecure. He widened his smile, obviously laughing at me. Had my hair fallen? Was I standing awkwardly? Did I look ridiculous with Emma and Elsie beside me? Could he tell we were the same age? Was I holding the champagne glass wrong?

"We're going to talk to the Howard twins," Elsie said. "Even though they're twins, I think Jesse is better-looking. Emma and I have a bet whether or not you would think so."

"At this moment," I said, "I can think of nothing less interesting to think about."

I turned and walked away from them, heading in the direction of my parents, who were talking to people who hadn't seen me yet, including the Franklins. I was looking forward to their reactions. Halfway across the ballroom, I heard a man ask, "Where have you been all my life?"

I paused and looked to my right. It was the man who had been staring at me.

"Excuse me?" I said. "Were you addressing me, sir?"

His laughing smile reappeared, which seemed to light up his deep-blue eyes. "Addressing? Yes, I think so," he said.

There was delicious danger in the way he looked at me, so clearly undressing me with his eyes and his imagination that it brought a blush up from my neck and through my face.

I glanced quickly at my mother, who at the moment was in an intense conversation with Margret Elliot, the wife of my father's bank's chief fiscal officer, Leroy Elliot.

"Let me properly introduce myself," the gentleman said, stepping closer. "Garland Neal Foxworth."

He held out his hand. I saw the stunning emerald pinkie ring.

"I don't bite. Much," he said when I hesitated.

"I do," I said, and he laughed and quickly took his hand back as if he thought I literally would nibble off a finger.

"I'm sorry we are not being formally introduced, but I'm afraid I'm at a great disadvantage here," he said, glancing around.

"And what would that be, pray tell?"

"No reason to pray. I'll tell. I'm a stranger. I

don't know a soul except our hosts," he added with a wink.

I looked at my mother, who was now looking disapprovingly at me. That, perhaps more than anything, encouraged me to keep talking to him.

"And where would you be from, then?"

"Just outside of Charlottesville. And you?"

"Here," I replied in a tone that suggested it was as close to the worst place to be than anything.

He laughed. "Can I know your name?"

"Corrine," I said. "Corrine Dixon. My father works for the bank for which Simon Wexler serves as chairman of the board."

"Ah, yes, Harrington Dixon. I met him at the bank," Garland said. "A very nice gentleman, and now that I see you, I can see his finer features. Your mother must be very beautiful."

"She is, but she doesn't care to be," I said. The sarcasm brought more laughter.

"Mothers and daughters often compete," Garland said. He looked at my still quite full glass of champagne and nodded at it. "Not very good?" he asked.

"What? Oh. I just arrived, Mr. Foxworth."

"Please. Call me Garland, even when you're vexed at me."

"I don't know you well enough to be vexed at you, sir, but I can see where if I did, I might be. And often," I said, my eyes on fire.

He looked like I had just confirmed I was the goddess he had been searching for all his life. His eyes brightened, and his lips stretched into a wider smile. "Maybe that's why I haven't found the right woman to be my wife, or the right woman hasn't found me."

"Most probably," I said, and glanced away as if I was losing interest in him, which I was certainly not.

"Can I get you something to eat?" he asked quickly. "That might guarantee my sitting with you. I live only for one thing now."

"And that is?"

"Your getting to know me enough to be vexed at me," he said.

I looked at my mother, anticipating her starting in my direction.

He saw my hesitation and where I was looking. "Have to sit with your parents, do you?"

"No," I said emphatically, so clearly that he stopped smiling and just widened his eyes. "I'm not on anyone's leash."

He nodded, his appreciation deepening. "Then, please," he said, "permit me to be your loyal servant for a fleeting hour or so. I'd gladly be on your leash."

His words nearly took my breath away.

He froze, his hands up and turned outward, looking as if a no would shatter him.

I shot my mother a look of defiance and then

turned to him. "Actually, I am a little hungry, Mr. Foxworth," I said.

"Garland."

"Yes," I said. "Garland."

He held out his arm. "Onward to the food, then," he declared.

I laughed and took his arm.

What a scene. In minutes after arriving, I was on the arm of who I thought was by far the most handsome man at the gala. Even though I had thought that might happen, I couldn't help being a little surprised, a little giddy, that it actually had.

I tried not to look left or right. I hoped he was really unmarried and unengaged. Otherwise, the gossip surely would send my mother into a closet, shutting the door behind her.

3

Apparently, my father had vouched for Garland Foxworth's integrity, because my mother didn't come rushing over to the table to drag me off and rescue me and the Dixon reputation from some playboy who had pounced on an innocent young girl.

"Would you prefer the beef or the chicken or the pork, Corrine?" Garland asked after escorting me to a seat at an empty table and helping take off my cape.

"The beef tonight, please," I said. As he turned to go, I cried after him, "But not much."

"Oh, I know. A proper lady always leaves the dinner table hungry," he said. "One of the things my mother taught me so I would know exactly how to behave in such company."

"She wanted you to be with a proper woman only?" I teased. I was aware of how quickly I had become comfortable enough with this stranger to do so. He looked impressed. Really, what a beautiful smile, I thought.

"Oh, absolutely only," he said. "Let me fix you a plate the way our cook used to fix my mother's."

Our cook, I thought, as he walked toward the food. How rich would he be? I wondered. And why did he say "used to fix"?

When I scanned the guests at other tables and groups of them talking off to the sides, it seemed every one of them was looking at me and talking about me. Emma and Elsie were standing with the Howard twins, all of them staring at me with childish expressions of surprise splattered like spilled milk over their pale faces. Emma started to wave, so I turned away from them quickly.

The band was playing "Where Did You Get That Hat?" and people nearby were laughing and moving to the melody. More of the invited guests had arrived. Some of the women were wearing dresses that I knew were imported from France or England. I had seen them in magazines and stores. There was enough jewelry displayed to buy the state. I thought that this was the biggest and most festive event I ever had attended. The music renewed my excitement, not that it had diminished even an iota. I was just frustrated and annoyed by how careful I had to be with my every smile and gesture, knowing my mother probably was watching me like an eagle by now.

Garland returned carrying two plates of food. He nodded at a waiter nearby as he put my plate before me.

"Madam, as you wished," he said, and sat across from me. "You haven't drunk much of that champagne. Want something else?" he asked.

I looked at my glass and thought how ridiculous

to spend the whole night on one glass. I gulped most of it and nodded.

"Another, please," I said, perhaps too enthusiastically. He laughed and ordered another for me and one for himself. I chastised myself. A woman shouldn't laugh so much and should rarely giggle. *You know that, Corrine Dixon.*

"Hope that is not too much to eat," he said, nodding at my plate.

"It's perfect. I thank you, sir."

"I've had a good start, then," he said.

"Good start?"

"Winning your affections."

I looked at him deliberately suspiciously. "Is that really your goal?"

"I'd have to be half dead for it to be otherwise," he said.

I felt my face glisten. "I fear you might be having fun with me, sir," I said, looking down as would someone who suddenly had turned quite bashful, which was difficult for me but not impossible. I knew it to be a chief tool of a coquette.

He feigned immediate indignation. "*Moi?* Oh, far from it, Corrine. I mean every word I say to you. I might as well have a Bible in my hand."

"Until proven otherwise, I will believe you," I said.

When he smiled, his eyes really did lighten. There was a positive energy about him, difficult to ignore but maybe difficult to trust.

60

The waiter brought us two additional champagnes.

"Shall I make my first toast in your presence, then, to prove my sincerity?"

"Please do," I said, raising my glass. I was actually terrified that any moment my mother would appear and reprimand me for having a second glass in front of this handsome stranger. She'd rip it from my hands and embarrass me to death. I held my breath.

"To Destiny that gave me a special gift of beauty and Southern elegance tonight," he said.

He held out his glass to tap and looked surprised at my hesitation. What, I wondered, would he say when he discovered how old I really was? Would he accuse Destiny of deliberate deception? I expected he would be drained in disappointment if I were in any way beyond his reach.

Until then, enjoy the moment, I thought.

I smiled and tapped his glass.

We drank, not taking our eyes off each other.

"So," he said, getting into his food and gazing about, "how is it that these young Southern gentlemen aren't hovering around you like pigeons hoping for a crumb of a smile? Is something lacking in the water here?"

"Maybe they're afraid," I said, nibbling at my food. My stomach was in knots of nervousness now. This was the first time I was eating alone at a table with an older, unmarried gentleman.

"Afraid? Of what?"

"Being pecked," I said, and he leaned back to laugh.

"Fools," he said. "They'd never enjoy anything as much. Anyway, I'm certainly not complaining. The moment I saw you, I was afraid you were already tethered and tied to someone."

"I am most certainly not."

Did I say that too quickly? I wondered.

"Then I am truly blessed tonight," he said, sipping his champagne and smiling at me through those beautiful and sexy eyes. "It makes me wonder how even a kiss could bring me more pleasure than simply sitting here and gazing at you."

Was I blushing?

No man, of course, no boy, had ever complimented me like this, I thought. A kiss? Tethered? His words were full of sexual suggestions. If I even had an ounce of doubt whether I could compete with the young, unmarried women who were years older, that ounce was gone. I had read enough social instructions and paid enough attention to older girls to know how to carry on a conversation confidently with a young, handsome man I had just met. Even if he learned my age in the next ten minutes, he would express his disbelief.

"What is it you do, Mr. Garland Neal Foxworth?"

"Oh, a little of everything these days. I've

opened two additional cloth factories in Richmond, bought a lumber mill in Fishersville a few months ago, and"—he hesitated and looked around to be sure no one was listening to our conversation—"invested in your father's bank. That's why I am here, why I was invited. It's not my first bank," he added. "But I've put enough money in it to have a seat on the board."

"You look too young for all that."

"Yes, I do, don't I?" he said, smiling.

Could I have met someone more conceited than I was? I had to laugh as well, but he didn't know, of course, that I was laughing more at myself as I thought, *I might have met my match.*

Suddenly, we heard a loud "ah" from the crowd and turned to look toward the musicians. They stood and stepped aside as an upright piano was wheeled in. It looked brand new. The pianist appeared on the right and took his seat. He began with a waltz. Four couples began to dance immediately, and others started to join them.

"Oh, I love this," Garland said. "I recently had a Steinway Victorian C delivered to my home. We have a ballroom, too, and my parents once hosted many galas as big as if not bigger than this one. Do you dance, Corrine?"

I shook my head. Dance? In the Wexlers' grand ballroom, with all these people watching? *How do I get out of this?*

"I've never attempted a waltz."

"Oh, the waltz is easy. Will you permit me to show you?" he asked, and stood as if he wouldn't take no for an answer.

I immediately turned to look for my parents. My mother could literally charge across the room and drag me off the floor if I rose. I saw them way to the left with some other executives and employees of the bank and their wives. Their attention was fixed on the pianist and the dancers in front of the piano, however. Should I chance it?

"Really, I've never really danced the waltz."

"How surprising, but don't worry. It's easy," he said again, crossed to me, and held out his hand. "You'll see. Please. It will be the highlight of the evening for me."

What made me hesitant was the fear that we would surely attract attention. Someone, one of the younger girls, perhaps, would approach us and either accidentally or enviously mention how young I was. What kind of a scene would that be? My outrage could easily bring my mother.

But really, what was I to do? Any more hesitation might get him suspicious anyway.

I rose, and he took my hand and led me to a clear space that was really away from most of the others dancing. Then he placed my left hand in his and raised it. He turned so we would face each other.

"Put your right hand on my shoulder," he said.

"Go on," he urged. "I'm not that hot to the touch . . . yet."

Out of the corner of my eye, I saw Emma and Elsie smothering a laugh. How childish, I thought. *Don't look at them and encourage them,* I warned myself.

"Keep your elbow up like so," he said. "Perfect. Now, just follow what I do. We're going to do the basic box step."

He announced each move just before he did it, and I followed, holding my breath. I felt like his eyes, this close, were exploring every inch of my face, fixing on my lips.

"Yes," he said. "I knew you'd be good at it. Just bend your knee a little more as you step."

The music continued.

"See? You're dancing the waltz," he declared. I was afraid to look anywhere but his face. I sensed there were lots of eyes on us, but hopefully not my mother's.

When the music stopped, the audience applauded the pianist. Everyone but my immature friends had their eyes elsewhere. I breathed relief.

"They're really applauding us," he whispered, leading me back to our table.

Simon Wexler and his wife were announced and walked to the front of the ballroom as the applause began again. The pianist started a new waltz, and they took to the floor. Lucy was very graceful, but Simon looked uncomfortable and awkward.

Garland remained standing after he had pulled out my chair for me. He stood just behind me, his hands on the back of my chair, and watched the Wexlers. After a few moments, he leaned over to whisper, his lips touching my ear.

"We're already better than that," he said. The guests were clapping. He still made no effort to return to his seat. Was he done with me? "It's a bit stuffy in here suddenly. Care for some air?" he asked.

Again, I looked for my parents, but they were dutifully glued to the Wexlers. Did I dare walk out with a complete stranger unchaperoned and without asking permission? If he realized that was a concern, he'd surely withdraw the invitation. But shouldn't he realize how daring that was, and was he even a true gentleman to ask it?

The chance that he wasn't actually excited me. I quickly swallowed back any hesitation and nodded.

He helped put on my cape before he took my hand. While everyone's attention was on our hosts, I and Garland Neal Foxworth slipped out of the front of the house and stepped down to walk along the path to the right that twisted around the variety of beautiful flowers, including common yarrow, red columbine, and swamp milkweed. There was a whole section of yellow wild indigo and marsh marigold. To the right was white turtlehead.

"It's a regular botanical garden, isn't it?" he said as we continued down the path.

Enjoy this while you can, Corrine, I told myself. As soon as my mother and my father discovered that I had left the gala with a stranger I had barely met, my mother would surely send my father to fetch me. It could be even more embarrassing than I had imagined inside. But the champagnes, the dance, and the excitement had me ready to risk anything.

"Yes. Far more than we have at our home," I said.

"But not far more than I have."

"Really?"

"Currently, I have two full-time gardeners."

"You live alone or with your parents?"

"My parents are unfortunately deceased," he said.

"I'm sorry. Both?"

"My father had heart failure when he was in his mid-forties, and my mother suffered consumption."

"And what of brothers and sisters?"

Was I being too forward asking so many personal questions?

"A younger sister who died giving birth. Her husband remarried and moved to England with their child. I have some cousins on my mother's side. They used to visit us, but we don't see each other very often now. Family . . . family is a drifting memory."

"I'm sorry."

"No reason to be. Perhaps being alone so young is why I'm so driven to be successful," he said. "When your parents entered, I saw only you. Are you an only child, or is there an older brother, sister living away from Alexandria?"

"I am an only child."

"We have so much in common," he said.

"Do we?"

"Oh, I think so, and I think we'll discover much more."

He paused. I wondered if he sensed how nervous I was. Was he toying with me? Discover much more? When? How?

"Do you smoke?" he asked.

"No," I said, shocked at the question.

"That's good. I know some women who think it makes them look sophisticated, but to me, there's nothing more revolting than the stench of tobacco on a woman's lips. Turns my stomach," he added.

How forceful he was with his opinions, I thought. I wasn't sure I liked that. What if I had said I did smoke secretly or something? Would he have still been so critical, maybe turned us around to return to the ballroom instantly?

"I think the same is true for men," I countered. "Thankfully, my father doesn't smoke, or if he does at some meeting, he changes his clothes before he confronts my mother, who would let him know if he didn't. I would do the same, sir."

Garland laughed. "So you've inherited your spunk from your mother, then?" he asked, or really concluded.

I paused. Had I? Funnily, I rarely thought about what I might have inherited from my mother besides her high cheekbones. I was too busy confronting her or avoiding her.

We turned when we heard peals of laughter off to the right, definitely coming from a young woman. We saw the couple hurrying deeper into the garden.

"Apparently, we're not the only ones who have taken air," he said. "Do you have many friends attending?"

What would I say? I would practically die on the spot if Emma or Elsie, looking like they did, approached me when I was with him.

"No," I said quickly, and then thought, what did that say about my friends that they weren't here at such an elegant and important affair? "I mean, there are some acquaintances, but I don't have very close friends at the moment. Most are . . . too immature."

"For you? I bet so," he said, and paused. He looked at me and then up. "Magnificent sky tonight. Cloudless, splattering constellations everywhere. Have a favorite?"

"Aries," I said too quickly. I knew what question it would lead to.

"Ah, because your birthday is?"

"April tenth." I held back the year.

"Yes, I might have guessed Aries."

"Why?"

"Aries people are ambitious, like to be number one. You might like to be popular, but I venture to guess you also like your independence and don't cater closely to the opinions of others. It's in your sign."

"Surely an ambitious and successful man doesn't really believe in all that," I said. "*You* have a lot to do with who you are."

He shrugged. "I don't read horoscopes, but I do have faith in significant coincidences. Luck, as you might have it, but luck," he added, stepping closer, "is only valuable if you have what it takes to exploit it."

He was inches away.

"Luck has come my way again. To meet you and to treat it as just a delightful moment, nothing more, is to throw back a fish not really too small."

"Am I a hooked fish?" Usually, I was the one casting the line.

"Not yet, but hopefully soon," he said.

"And how do you intend on exploiting your present luck, sir?" I asked.

"Like this," he said, and then astounded me by bringing his lips to mine, gently but with determination.

It was a moment of possible fateful decision.

Kiss him back, instantly retreat, or just stand there like one of my childish friends, shocked and nothing else.

I had made my decision months, maybe years, ago. There was no exploration more exciting than my own sexuality. Yes, I wanted boyfriends, but I wanted them to be grown men, and here, with his hands on my shoulders and his lips on mine, was my first real man, perhaps the first of many. Maybe it was evil for me to think it, but I believed that a woman could have more than one sexual partner, too. I was no Susan B. Anthony or Elizabeth Cady Stanton. Nothing was as boring to me as politics and this whole debate about a woman's right to vote. No, the equality I sought was in the bedroom.

I kissed him back as strongly and as passionately as he was kissing me, perhaps surprising him. He did look speechless and then smiled.

"For a moment there, I thought I might have been lifted to the stars."

"Who says you were not?" I asked.

How he roared at that.

When he stopped laughing, he looked at me more seriously. He could see that I had self-confidence and wasn't afraid of being touched, being kissed, but perhaps he also saw that there was something about me that did not support simple promiscuity. Maybe I was convincing myself or maybe being too hopeful, but he

71

looked like he was quite smitten with me, and I so much wanted him to be. My first real test in the sophisticated social world, I thought, and I was doing so well he'd never know how innocent I really was.

I glanced back at the mansion's front entrance, anticipating my mother shooting out from the doorway like a cannonball and ruining all this with a few sharp phrases, some directed at him.

"Perhaps we should return," I said. "My parents might grow frantic."

"Oh, then, perhaps we should. I don't want to get on the wrong side of them now." He took my hand and started back.

"You'll have to be careful, then, when and if you meet my mother."

"Oh? Why is that?"

"She's old-fashioned, too formal. That's my kindest way of putting it."

"Not necessarily a fault," he said.

"In her case, it is. She was born old-fashioned. My father says she threatened the doctor who slapped her rear when she was born. He calls me 'her handful.' "

He laughed so hard that he had to pause a moment. "Something tells me you are more than a mere handful."

"I should hope so," I said.

We continued to the steps.

"Do you ever get to Charlottesville?" he asked.

"On occasion. I have a great-aunt there, Nettie Lloyd. She's a widow who lost both her sons in the war."

"Ah, yes, the stupid war," Garland said. "Many lost so much, but some exploited it. I'm ashamed to say my father was one. He was quite the clever importer." He leaned in to whisper, "And sold to both sides discreetly."

"Ashamed, you said. Did you give all the money to charity?" I teased.

He laughed. "Haven't you heard? Charity begins at home."

I smiled. It wasn't something I didn't believe; it was simply something I'd never say.

We started up the stairs. Before we reached the entrance, I let go of his hand. My mother could be just inside the doorway.

"About Charlottesville," he said. "Any chance you'd visit your aunt in the near future?"

"Yes, I'm sure I will," I said. "I am expecting an invitation from her any day now."

"Please, then," he said, reaching into his pocket to produce a card. "Do write to me to warn me so I can anticipate your coming. I'd very much enjoy taking you to lunch and perhaps, if your great-aunt permits, showing you my home, Foxworth Hall. She would come with us, of course."

"Foxworth Hall? Sounds impressive."

"Oh, it is. I promise you."

"My great-aunt is quite old. She doesn't venture

about much, from what I understand. However, I might find a way to visit your home unchaperoned. It doesn't have to be in the social columns."

"I do avoid that quite well," he said, maybe warned.

"Something I'd prefer, too," I replied.

It was as if there were fireworks exploding. I saw light flashing in his eyes as they would reflect it. Had I turned him speechless?

I looked at the card. "We'll see," I said. "I don't want to make promises and then disappoint you."

"Not very possible," he said.

"What?"

"Your disappointing me."

I wanted to respond, but I thought I had already said too much. Primarily, I had no such invitation from Great-aunt Nettie Lloyd, not yet at least. I put my hand on his arm and leaned toward him to whisper.

"I'd better see to my parents," I said. "Be sure my mother is having a good time. My father depends on me to help him with that burden."

He glanced at my fingers lingering and then nodded as I rushed toward the ballroom. Had I gotten away with it all? Was my mother truly distracted enough to miss everything I had done?

I glanced back before I entered the party, but he wasn't there. Did I commit a faux pas by not bringing him to meet my parents? Did he turn and go? Was his deep interest in me mostly in my imagination? How could he leave such a gala? Then again, I thought, maybe being with me was quite enough. No one else here interested him.

I scanned the ballroom and saw that my parents were at a table having coffee with the Elliots. As casually as I could, I approached their table.

"Where have you been?" my mother instantly asked.

"Just getting a little fresh air, Mother," I said, smiling at Leroy Elliot. His wife looked amused.

"Everyone was talking about how pretty you look, Corrine," she said, "but I didn't see you until now. You do look so grown-up."

"Put her in chains!" Leroy cried. There was brandy beside the coffee the men were drinking.

"I'd like to," my mother muttered.

My father's eyes were twinkling with delight and maybe a little too much brandy.

"Where's our young Mr. Foxworth?" he asked. So he had noticed it all.

"I really don't know," I replied. It was the truth. "He was here one moment and gone the next."

"It was longer than one moment," my mother said.

"Was it? Time goes so fast when you're having fun, and this is such a wonderful gala."

"Yes, it is," Leroy said. "Enjoy everything you can while you're young."

My mother gave him a look stern enough to sober him instantly.

"I think I'll get a cupcake," I said. "They look so delicious."

"Indeed, they are," Leroy agreed. "Sweets for the sweet." Despite my mother, he was flirting with his smile. I pretended to be oblivious, but I could see his wife was not. It was something I was sure I would get used to and casually ignore.

I hurried off. Apparently, I had somehow escaped more critical notice, and there was no feeling quite like the uplifting sensation that came with the knowledge I had gotten away with something right under my mother's eyes.

But not Emma's and Elsie's, I quickly learned. They made a beeline for me the moment they saw me.

"Glad you left some cupcakes for other people," I said, not looking at them as I put one on a dish.

"Where's the gentleman you were with?" Emma asked.

"You went outside with him," Elsie said.

I bit into the cupcake and turned to them. "Did I?"

"We saw you. We went to the entrance, too, and we saw you walk off into the gardens. You were holding his hand," Emma added, as if she was accusing me of murder.

"So that's what it was," I said. "I knew there was something in my hand."

Elsie laughed, but Emma kept her disapproving face.

"So where is he?" she asked more insistently. She could look just like my mother when she twisted her lips like this, I thought.

I leaned toward them as I would to give them a secret. Both leaned toward me.

"I killed him, smothered him with kisses, and left his body in the garden," I said, and walked off laughing at the expression of shock on both their faces.

I tolerated more than enjoyed the gala after that. My parents' friends were as dull as usual, and my face felt sore from all the false smiling I had to do. My eyes were continually shifting toward the doorway of the ballroom, hoping Garland Foxworth would reappear, obviously looking for me as well. But he didn't, and time, which had become annoying for me sitting there and looking as interested as I could in my parents' and their friends' discussions about politics and financial matters, seemed to go ever more slowly. A cloud of boredom floated above and around me, so when my father declared it was time to say good night to the Wexlers, I practically leaped to my feet.

"I saw you dancing earlier," Lucy Wexler said when I and my parents were saying good night, thanking them, and wishing them ten more years. I glanced at my mother, who looked surprised. "You dance well."

"My first time waltzing," I said.

"Really? Well, some of us have a natural grace." She looked at my father. "I believe your daughter does."

"Thank you, Lucy," my father said. "I think so, too."

My mother looked ready to burst a blood vessel at her temple.

"Your gentleman was quite graceful, too. First time you met Mr. Foxworth?"

"Yes, ma'am," I said, not sure how I should react to the words *Your gentleman*.

"Perhaps not the last time," she replied.

I saw the sly look and smile. Maybe she had hoped to corral the dashing young Mr. Foxworth, or maybe, worse, she already had and was disappointed he had drifted toward someone else so quickly.

"Really, your first time waltzing?" Mr. Wexler asked with a suspicious smile. "I saw you, too. Young women do have their little secrets now and then these days."

"Oh no, sir. I do have secrets, but that's not one. It was my first time," I said. "With the waltz," I pointedly added.

He laughed. "My wife is right. One would never have thought so," he replied, and nodded at my father in a way that I thought sent a subtle warning.

My mother, of course, needed none.

"How is it that I didn't see you dancing with that man?" my mother asked as soon as we stepped out of the Wexler mansion and started down to the carriage.

"It wasn't very long, Mother. He was simply showing me the basic steps, and there were far better dancers perhaps commanding your attention. We were a bit off to the side, too."

My mother swallowed back her short grunt, and we boarded the carriage.

"A proper gentleman would have asked our permission first, at least your father's."

"Well, that was a pretty penny spent on a gala," my father remarked as we headed away, ignoring her. "Did you enjoy yourself, Corrine?"

"I did. Thank you, Daddy."

"From the reception you received, I believe you've been properly presented to our local society," he added, and looked at my mother. "Rosemary? Remind you of your first gala?"

"Hardly," she said. "I certainly didn't dance with a stranger."

"Oh, he's not all that much a stranger. As I told you, he's now involved with our bank and in a big way, too."

"He's a stranger to our family, Harrington."

"Maybe not for long," my father said, casting a look of amusement at her.

I sat back, smiling and thinking, *Yes, maybe not for long*.

"I'd like to visit Great-aunt Nettie soon," I announced a few minutes later.

"Why?" my mother instantly demanded, spinning around to look at me.

I shrugged. "She's always invited me, and I think I need to strengthen my ties to family, seeing how important it is to most everyone, especially you, Mother."

My father smiled conspiratorially. "You do think that, Rosemary, and she is your mother's sister."

"I don't know how well she is these days," my mother said. "Visitors might be too trying. That woman has suffered far beyond what's reasonable in one life."

"More reason for Corrine to visit her and provide some amusement and joy, Rosemary. We should leave it up to her," my father said. He looked back. "No harm in writing to her to see how she would receive you."

"Of course, Daddy."

"I'm not interested in such a visit," my mother said sharply.

"I'm just going to see my great-aunt, Mother. You don't have to accompany me everywhere I go."

My mother was silent.

In fact, no one said another word until we were home. I made sure to hide Garland Foxworth's card in my desk drawer. Then, as soon as I was undressed and ready for bed, I dug out my personal stationery and began a letter to Great-aunt Nettie.

Dear Great-aunt Nettie,

I know I haven't written in a long time, but I've been thinking about our family and how far apart we all are. I'm sixteen now, and I went to my first real gala at the Wexler mansion. Mr. Wexler is the chairman of my father's bank. It was his ten-year anniversary. My father and mother bought me a beautiful new dress. I wish you had seen me in it.

I was sitting here wishing all that when I suddenly thought it would be wonderful to visit you. Perhaps I'll bring along my new dress to show you. Years ago, when you were here, you told my mother she should let me come visit you. I have time to do so now, especially in the next two weeks. Would you like that?

Please let me know as soon as you can so I can make plans.

Your loving great-niece,
Corrine

I checked the letter three times to be sure there were no grammatical or spelling mistakes. Great-aunt Nettie had been a schoolteacher before she had met her husband, Clyde Lloyd, when she was in her mid-twenties. He was in shipbuilding and eventually became a part owner of the company. Unfortunately, he died at fifty-eight, and with their sons dead, Great-aunt Nettie was left alone with her lifelong housekeeper, an African woman named Hazel Waters, whom Nettie's husband had brought back with him from England not long after they married. Hazel was still with her, but other than that, I knew little more, and she probably knew next to nothing about me now.

Nevertheless, she'd surely be surprised and happy to hear from me, I thought, and I gave my father the letter in the morning to post. I did it when my mother wasn't around so we wouldn't have to go through her multiple questions and negative comments. He looked at it, tapped it on his palm, and smiled.

"Now, this sudden interest in family doesn't have anything to do with a certain Mr. Foxworth who happens to live in Charlottesville, does it?"

"Why, Daddy," I said, batting my eyelashes. He laughed. I paused to think. "How old is he anyway?"

"He's twenty-three. He inherited a great deal, but he's made smart use of his money. But my advice is don't take a bite of the first apple that falls off the tree into your lap, Corrine. You have many good years before you get yourself tied down in a marriage. I know you. You want to enjoy those years," he added, and pinched my cheek.

"I certainly do, Daddy," I said.

He laughed and left to go to work.

Despite his warning, I was barely able to do anything but think of Garland Foxworth. In fact, I ran back upstairs after my father had left and began constructing a letter to Garland. I took out his card, handling it as if it were a precious stone. *I can't sound like a lovesick young girl,* I thought, and began writing, tearing up one opening sentence after another until I decided the best way to do the letter was to sound quite formal. I even referred to the business-letter form my father used. When I looked at the letter after that, however, I thought it was too cold and impersonal. What if it discouraged him enough for him not to answer or care? What, indeed, would I do at boring Great-aunt Nettie Lloyd's home then? I decided to permit myself some words that would certainly build his ego and confirm I was not looking for a mere acquaintance.

Dear Mr. Foxworth [in a formal letter, I just couldn't call him Garland],

I am anticipating visiting my aunt, indeed, sometime within the next few weeks. As I promised, I am informing you of such a possibility. I am not that familiar with Charlottesville, so I do not know if my aunt's home is indeed close enough for you to consider a visit or not.

I would like to thank you for spending

your time with me at the Wexler gala and especially for having the patience to teach me the waltz. I so too enjoyed our little getaway to the gardens.

If I hear back from you before I confirm my visit to Charlottesville, I will give you the date.

Sincerely yours,
Corrine Dixon

I had read about women putting a scent on their stationery but was afraid to do it on a first letter. I kept it out and read and reread it at least a dozen times before finally getting it into an envelope. I was tempted to seal it with a kiss for good luck but quickly considered that something most of the childish girls my age would do. This had to be lifted out of the realm of a young girl's crush.

If Garland received it a day or so after my great-aunt received her letter, I would hope he would respond immediately.

All my life, at least my years since I considered myself no longer a little girl, I dreamed of having just such a romance as this. That it had come so quickly and with a man this handsome and accomplished almost made me swoon with excitement. The trick now was to keep all that away from my mother's inquisitive and critical gaze. If she knew what I really intended to accomplish by visiting my great-aunt Nettie, my mother would surely forbid me to take a single step toward the journey.

It wasn't until the letter to Garland was mailed that I paused one night before I went to sleep, looked up at the constellations I and Garland had viewed together, and asked myself, as if I was another person, *Really, what do you hope to accomplish with all this, Corrine Dixon?*

"I don't know," I whispered. "Maybe I just wanted to keep looking at the stars the way I did that night. Is that so terrible?"

Oh, you want more than that, Corrine Dixon. You want far more than that.

4

Late in the morning of the following day, Daisy appeared on our doorstep. I had just risen, sleeping later in the morning than usual even though my mother had come up to wake me earlier. I had groaned and fallen back asleep. Now, dressed in my robe, my hair a mess, I answered the door and faced my grinning best friend, who had cycled over. From the way she was smiling and how perspiring and flushed she was, I knew gossip had run uphill to her this morning, uphill because it came from Emma and Elsie.

"You'd better tell me everything," she said, her eyes blooming with expectations.

"There isn't that much to tell, but come in. I'm just having breakfast."

"Just?" she said, entering.

"Keeping up appearances wears you out," I told her, deliberately sounding like a sophisticated socialite. She widened her eyes, and I laughed. "Come on, but don't say a word about anything to my mother."

My mother stepped out of the pantry just as we entered the kitchen.

"Oh," my mother said, running her hands over her hair. "I didn't hear anyone at the door."

She wasn't dressed in anything much more than her robe and was still in her slippers.

"It's only Daisy," I said. I started to fix myself some eggs.

"Well, I expect *you* had your breakfast at a decent hour," she said to Daisy.

"Yes, Mrs. Dixon."

My mother nodded at me as if she had driven home a terribly important point and then left us, probably to get better dressed before Daisy left.

"So what did they tell you?" I asked as I broke the eggs and began to scramble them. "And how did they get to you so fast?"

"They cycled over about an hour or so ago. Their faces were so bloated with excitement that I thought they would explode, especially Emma."

"Not so unlike yours right now."

"Forget me. So? Who was he?"

"Who was who?" I teased, putting the eggs in the skillet.

"C'mon, Corrine. You know who I mean. The man at the gala, the man you ate with and wandered off with?"

"Oh, him." I shrugged. "Just one of my father's business associates," I said. "Do you want some coffee?"

"Coffee? No. Well, was he someone you had met before the gala? I mean, how did you get so close with him so quickly?"

"Is that what they told you?"

"Yes," she said, getting frustrated.

I returned to my eggs, slipped them onto a plate, buttered some bread, and poured my coffee. She sat across from me.

"I didn't think it was that quick. My parents took forever introducing me to everyone, and when they wandered off, he approached me."

"And?"

I ate and thought.

"I don't usually meet my father's business people. I usually avoid them. Generally, they are as exciting as dripping molasses at the corners of their mouths, talking about profits and losses, margins and capital expenditures . . . honestly Greek to me. I smile and slip away before they give me a headache."

"But not him?"

I paused to look like I was giving it great thought again. "No, not him." I continued to eat.

"Stop it!" she squealed. "You're teasing and tormenting me. You know exactly what I want to hear."

I smiled and sat back, my excitement now boiling over like overheated milk.

"He's quite good-looking and apparently, from what my father tells me and what he told me himself, very wealthy."

"How old is he?"

"My father said he is twenty-three."

"Twenty-three! And he doesn't know you're only sixteen? I mean, couldn't he tell?"

"Do I behave like a typical sixteen-year-old?"

"Oh, no, of course not. They said you ate with only him."

"There were a few hundred people around us, so it wasn't exactly dining alone."

"You know what I mean, Corrine. They said you danced with him, too?"

"If you can call it that. He showed me the waltz. It lasted only a few minutes."

"And?"

"And I need practice." I continued to eat.

She stared at me, her eyes filling with anger and frustration.

"What?"

"I thought I was your best friend. I thought we were going to travel when we were eighteen and have lots of romantic adventures. I thought you trusted me with all your deepest secrets. I trusted you with mine, and now this, this making me pull teeth," she said, throwing up her hands and pouting.

"Did I teach you how to be this dramatic? I think so. You were quite the shy thing when we first started planning and plotting together." I put my fork down, sipped some coffee, and smiled again. "You are my best friend, Daisy. That hasn't changed. All right," I said. "I'll tell you the rest of it. He asked me to go for a walk, and we went out to the Wexler gardens."

"Alone?"

"My parents didn't see me go, but apparently,

our little spies did. Yes, alone. He was . . . quite charming, describing his mansion, his property, and then we both admired the stars . . ."

"The stars? And?"

"And he wanted to kiss me, of course."

"And?"

"I didn't let him. You don't want ever to appear too eager, remember? I think that was womanly talk three. The more he longs for you, the more control you have. Once you surrender, even a little, they seize the reins. As I suspected, he wasn't upset about it but not turned away from me because of it. He is wise enough to know that I'm a woman of character who is full of self-respect."

"They said you said you kissed him a lot."

"I told them what they wanted to hear. Besides," I added, sipping the last of my coffee, "he disappeared after that, and I didn't see him for the remainder of the gala."

"Oh. Then maybe he was too disappointed."

"I wouldn't come to that conclusion, no," I quickly replied. It was my own stabbing fear. "Actually, I might see him again, and soon, matter of fact."

"How? Where?"

"I'm going to visit my great-aunt Nettie, who lives in Charlottesville, and he lives just outside of the city in his family mansion. I mentioned that I would write to let him know, and he was quite happy to hear that. He gave me his card so I would do so."

She looked thoughtful and then unhappy.

"What's bothering you?"

"I just knew one day you'd find an older man and leave me behind."

"Maybe he has a friend. I could arrange a blind date. You could sneak off and join us."

Her eyes widened. "I couldn't do that. I mean . . . do you think I could?"

"You never know until you do," I said. "Come on upstairs. We'll talk as I put on my cycling outfit. I think I need to ride a little and clear my head. When you get this close to a real romance, you have to be extra careful, and that means constantly alert, reconsidering, reviewing, and questioning your own feelings."

She nodded as if she had the experience.

I rose and put the dishes in the sink. When my mother saw them and chastised me for leaving them there, I would tell her I had planned to do it later, as I always told her. She would accuse me of knowing that she wouldn't wait, she wouldn't leave a dirty dish for someone to see. Of course, she was right about me, but it was her own fault that she was so obsessive about it. Besides, washing dishes and clothes damaged and aged your hands.

As I changed, I described Garland a little more, stressing how attentive he was and how polite. She sat on my bed, clinging to my every syllable.

"It's nice to experience a mature gentleman. I doubt I'll ever give boys our age a second glance again," I said. "Being with someone older forces you to act older, too. But I think I told you most of this one time or another."

"Probably," she said. "But I like hearing it all again." She was hanging on my every word.

I continued to describe the gala and Garland, even after we were on our cycles and pedaling through the streets, making sure to go by Emma's house. When we parted at the corner that veered off right to her house, I promised to keep her up to date on anything that occurred between me and Garland Foxworth. She rode off thinking she had been admitted to the most secret romance of the age.

My father arrived shortly after I had returned. He received all our mail at the bank and brought home anything personal. I wasn't anticipating anything yet, but to my happy surprise, Garland's reply to my letter came faster in the mail than Great-aunt Nettie's response. Anticipating my mother's horrified reaction to my starting a relationship with a man in his mid-twenties, a man I had met only at a gala and a man who had not been formally introduced to her, my father smiled and winked like a fellow conspirator when he handed Garland's letter to me. I hurried away to read it privately.

At first, I thought Garland might have just decided to write a letter hoping I would see him again. Maybe he had written it immediately after the Wexler gala, even on his way home. That was an exciting thought, but when I opened the envelope, I saw this was not a letter full of compliments and eagerness for us to meet again soon. It was so disappointingly short and curt I almost crumpled it up and threw it away. I wanted to have something I could read repeatedly, perhaps memorize, or at least receive something from him that was filled with flowery, emotional comments suggesting his hope for a longer relationship. I even was considering letting Daisy read it.

I had received notes from boys who had crushes on me, but this was really going to be my first love letter. At least, that was what I had dreamed I would receive.

Instead, his first letter was scratched quickly on the back of some billing form, looking like it was done as an afterthought. Why would I ever show this to Daisy or press this into my book of memories?

> Dear Miss Dixon,
> Do let me know your arrival date whenever it is determined. Maybe I'll continue teaching you the waltz.
> Garland Foxworth

That was it? No description of what he would propose we do in Charlottesville? No reference to the walk we took at the Wexler gala, the stars, or our kiss? Just a tongue-in-cheek comment about our dancing? Was it all so matter-of-fact to him? How many women was he courting at the moment? How many did he hold in his arms and kiss since we had met? Was there someone he thought prettier, perhaps? Why bother writing back to him? Was I making a total fool of myself?

I fumed, sulked, and then, days later when my aunt's reply arrived inviting me as I had expected she would, I broke down any resistance quickly and wrote to him but made sure to sound far less formal than he had sounded.

Dear Garland,

My great-aunt has invited me to her home anytime, so I will move up my plans and prepare a visit in two days. I intend to stay in Charlottesville for a week, perhaps a day or two more. I am including my great-aunt's address in this letter. It's only two houses east of the People's Bank on the corner of Court and Market. I do look forward to seeing you again. You made the Wexler gala quite enjoyable for me.

When I arrive at my great-aunt's home, I shall tell her about our meeting each other at the event and your investment in my father's bank, so she will know you are no stranger. I am bringing the dress I wore to show her.

Perhaps you can send a note to her address to let me know when you might appear on the doorstep.

Warm regards,
Corrine

Once again, I debated scenting the letter. This time I decided to do so. When I gave it to my father, he looked like he detected the sweet aroma even before it was in his hands. Had I overdone it? There was that little smile on his lips and an impish glint in his eyes.

"What?" I asked.

"I'll get your train ticket," he told me.

It would be the first time I would be on a train by myself, sitting in a passenger car with strangers. I had never thought of it as a joyful experience. There was soot and noise, and the seats weren't all that comfortable. Every time we were on a train, my mother would force me to stay seated, and I often got off nauseated.

Nevertheless, I was having so much trouble containing my excitement during the next two days that I thought it best to avoid my mother as much as possible, and whenever I did confront her and my mother asked about or mentioned my visiting Great-aunt Nettie, I tried to avoid looking at her or making any part of it sound interesting.

"I'm sure I'll be bored in two days and come home," I muttered.

It was clear my father had still not mentioned Garland Foxworth, and for some reason, my mother, who was usually suspicious about anything I did or wanted to do, didn't make the connections or ask pointed questions. Instead, she talked about my great-aunt and Hazel, warning me I would be shocked at how they lived now, cooped up and dependent on so many others. She assured me I would come away thankful for the privileged life I had.

"Sometimes we have to lose something, even for a short while, to know how important it was. Now that I think on it more, I realize this trip is a good idea. Maybe you'll take less for granted."

Oh, how I hated her lectures. However, she still didn't even hint about Garland. Perhaps, I thought, she didn't know how close to Charlottesville was the Foxworth home, and of course, she had not seen enough of me and Garland at the gala to realize there might even be a chance of a real romance.

I occupied most of my two days of waiting with choosing what I would take to wear. I should have been smart enough to get my father to buy me more clothes that day we went for my evening gown. Why didn't I envision what would follow? You can't be a young lady one night and a child the day after, but I feared that was how I would seem. All my clothes looked juvenile and inadequate when it came to highlighting my maturity. And I hated every pair of shoes I owned. I actually coveted some of my mother's clothes despite how uninteresting they were. At least I wouldn't look so young, I thought, and wished we were the same size.

The morning I left with my father to go to the train station, my mother had not yet risen. We practically tiptoed out of the house.

"This is, in fact, your first trip alone, Corrine," my father began before I boarded the train. "I hope you will enjoy yourself but also maintain decorum, mind what you're told, and give your great-aunt Nettie only a pleasant experience."

"Of course I will, Daddy," I said.

He tilted his head and narrowed his eyes. "Be careful, Corrine. A man in his mid-twenties is not a boy."

"I know that, Daddy." I wanted to add that was the point, but I didn't.

"I'd like you to send me a telegram in two days and tell me how things are. Send it to my bank."

"I will, Daddy."

I kissed him good-bye and took my seat by the window, holding my breath almost until the very moment the train started away. The train jerked so hard that a little girl fell off her mother's lap. The sound of the steam engine pumping was drowned out by the sound of my own heart thumping in my ears. I paid no attention to anyone else on the train once we were on our way, even though I felt the eyes of every man drifting toward me. I was sure they wanted to start a conversation, but I avoided all smiles and eye contact. All I did was think about Garland Foxworth. There hadn't been enough time for him to respond to my second letter, and that little voice inside me that always challenged my dreams and hopes began to ask the dreaded questions.

What if he was only toying with you? What if he never responds? Are you going to sit by your great-aunt's front windows all day waiting for his appearance? Will you feel like a fool? How long will you wait to be disappointed?

Shut up, shut up, shut up! I screamed inside myself. I imagined that those on the train who continued to look at me thought I was a little touched in the head, because I was pounding my knees and muttering under my breath occasionally, not the typical behavior of one as young as I was. Eventually, I calmed myself and sat back with my eyes closed.

I dreamed that somehow he would have learned about the train's arrival and would be there waiting for me, his hand clutching a bouquet of beautiful flowers or a box of chocolates. He'd be sharply dressed, maybe wearing a top hat, and he'd have a fancy carriage with a driver waiting to take me to Great-aunt Nettie's house. When we were pulling into the station, I opened my eyes to search for him, but he wasn't there, and I had to get a taxi carriage.

The city of Charlottesville was busier and more crowded than I remembered. There were people everywhere I looked. Seeing so many strangers, most looking through me or past me, made me feel small and lost. *What a fool I'm making of myself,* I thought. I didn't know another soul here. What was I going to do with myself staying with two elderly women? How long could I wait, and wouldn't I look foolish if days and days went by and he ignored me? I would not send another message. That I vowed.

Great-aunt Nettie Lloyd lived in a black-and-white two-story Georgian Colonial. I had been there twice before with my parents and always found it bland and dull, colors fading, siding cracking and chipping, and the porch floor quite worn. When I was younger, I saw that Hazel usually did a good job of keeping the house clean and tidy, but my mother recently told me that as Hazel aged alongside my great-aunt, her work became erratic and slow. Her eyesight was failing. Little care was given to the areas not used very much, which, unfortunately for me, I would discover included the one guest bedroom.

When I arrived, both of them at the doorway to greet me. My great-aunt looked like she had shrunk. She was never heavy, but at five foot five or so, she had always looked robust, her gray hair pulled up into a tight bun. I remembered her as someone who took great pains to look as perfectly put together as possible. Not a strand of hair was out of place. Her dresses had narrow skirts with only slight padding at the rear. The gathered material had perfect pleats, but above everything, her clothes looked well cared for, immaculately clean.

I was surprised to see how disheveled she was now, her hair bun falling apart on both sides. There were little hairs growing on her chin. Couldn't she or Hazel see them and pluck them? Her socks were slipping over her reddened ankles, and her shoes looked scuffed. The dress she wore was stained and should have been taken in at the bodice and waist. Her hands were almost all bone, too. How could she step out of her house looking like this? I would never let this happen to me, I thought, no matter how old I was.

Hazel, wider in the hips than I recalled, was nevertheless dressed better than my great-aunt. She wore a dark-green Basque bodice with a high-standing collar and much nicer shoes, too. Her face was round and full, with barely a wrinkle. She also had what looked like a red ruby pinkie ring and a bracelet of small pearls. In contrast, my aunt had no jewelry on, not even a marriage ring, which had probably become too big for her thinning, bony finger. If it weren't for Hazel being African, one might wonder who was the owner of the home and who was the servant. Hazel's hair, although peppered throughout with gray, was still curly black, and those black-opal eyes were bright and cheery. Thank heaven for that, I thought.

"A real lady she is," Hazel said, gazing out at me.

"What?" my great-aunt asked, leaning toward me to see me.

Hazel repeated what she had said but a lot louder. In fact, I thought she was shouting, and I looked behind me to see if anyone walking by had stopped, wondering what was happening.

"Oh," my great-aunt said, nodding, but there was a look in her eyes that told me she had no idea who I was. If she did remember I was coming, I think she was expecting to greet a much younger version of me.

"Hello, Aunt Nettie," I said, making sure to say it louder than I normally would. "Hello, Hazel."

"Rosemary?" Great-aunt Nettie said. I looked at Hazel, who rolled her eyes and smiled at me.

"No, I'm Corrine, Aunt Nettie."

"Oh?"

I saw she was struggling with my name. Who was this Corrine?

"I'm Rosemary's daughter, Aunt Nettie. I've been here before with my parents years ago. I think I was eight or nine. I'm the one who wrote to you recently."

"What she say?" Great-aunt Nettie asked Hazel.

Hazel leaned forward a little. "I read your letter to her, and then I wrote you back for her," she said. "She forgets more'n she knew these days. Come on in, darlin'."

She reached for my suitcase. I held my large handbag, a silk metallic my mother had let me borrow. She didn't use it much.

"I don't remember all that much myself," Hazel continued. "They say you forget what you want to first, and the rest just trails behind it like a herd of sheep crying to be remembered."

Herd of sheep? My great-aunt was practically deaf and blind. What was I stepping into?

I followed her through the short entryway, Great-aunt Nettie trailing behind me as though she was the visitor and needed to be the one told what was where. The living room was on the right. The only way to approach the kitchen was through it. The small dining room was on the other side. There was a short stairway that led up to the three bedrooms.

It wasn't simply the worn floors, rugs, and furniture that immediately depressed me; it was the redolent odor of age and dampness. The house was slowly dying alongside its inhabitants. I had forgotten how small it was as well. My mother was so right. She knew what I would confront, and now I understood why she was so amiable about my going. She wanted me to be put off, depressed, and unhappy. She believed that disappointment and unhappiness were the best teachers. I had no idea how bad it was and what

I would be confronting, despite her warnings. In its day, this house had probably been quite nice and impressive, but now . . . I'd never even step into it if it weren't my great-aunt's home.

"Don't look around too closely," my mother had warned me with a smile, trying to puncture any balloon full of excitement I might have floating in my dreams. "Not that you would, being oblivious to anything that displeases you."

Oh, how self-satisfied she surely was, gabbing about it today with her friends. "She'll come rushing home as soon as she is able to," she most likely was telling them. And they were nodding like pigeons.

When I paused and studied the living room, Hazel saw where my eyes were going. There were cobwebs in the corners of the ceiling and what I feared might be evidence of mice in the far corner of the living room. An attempt had been made to cover the worn areas of the small sofa with pieces of lace and cotton. I saw a pair of slippers just under a chair and what looked like a pile of yellowed old newspapers on the small table in front of the sofa. The faded light-blue curtains were partially open, and the windows looked like they hadn't been washed for decades. The house did face what had become a far busier street than I remembered, so maybe neither of them cared much about looking out at the scenery.

"It's a mess, I know. With all that traffic

outside, the horses and carriages, the dust seeps in everywhere. But pay it no mind. We'll get you settled in, darlin'," Hazel said, "and then, after you rest a bit, we'll have tea."

I remembered that tea meant dinner for Hazel.

She turned to Great-aunt Nettie. "Then Corrine will tell us all about the family back in Alexandria," she added much louder for Great-aunt Nettie. "Won't that be nice, Nettie? You remember Alexandria, don't you?"

"Oh yes," Great-aunt Nettie said. "I had a sister who lived there. I think she died," she added. Her uncertainty about the death of her own sister, my grandmother, and the casual way she said it was quite surprising. I looked at Hazel.

"We forget what we don't want to remember first," she repeated. "Here, let's go up to the guest room. I put our best comforter on the bed, and I'm sure you want to unpack your things."

"Thank you, Hazel."

I won't last here two days if Garland doesn't appear, I thought as I followed Hazel up the rickety steps. The thick walnut balustrade rocked a little, advising me not to put my weight on it. I looked back at Great-aunt Nettie, who stood watching us as if she had already forgotten who I was and why I was going up her stairway.

Thankfully, Hazel had opened the window in the guest room, so there was at least some fresh air to chase away the odor of a room long shut up and unused, but there was all that dust swirling around just outside. The bed was half the size of mine, and the old wood floor was bare, with not even a rug to step down on in the morning.

"You remember that there's only the loo downstairs," Hazel said.

"Loo? Oh, bathroom. Right."

"You can't depend on the hot water for the bath all the time," Hazel warned. "Best to take yours in the mornin'. The piping is a bit old now. We've had some troubles with the burner. A good handyman named George Thomas helps out from time to time."

"Oh," I said. "I was hoping for a soak before tea. Travel and all. When you get off the train, you feel like you've been riding through a chimney."

I was really thinking, dreaming maybe, that Garland would show up, and I wanted to look the best I could after my journey.

"Well, you can try it. I can put up a few kettles in case," she said. "The drawers in that old armoire stick a bit now and then. Just give 'em a good tug. They haven't been opened for years."

She smiled.

"Don't worry about breakin' anything, darlin'. Most everythin's broke one way or another in this tired old house, includin' us. Best to think of a visit like this as a travel experience. Like going to Africa or somethin'."

She laughed. When she smiled, I saw how many of her back teeth were gone.

I thought again of my mother back home, laughing to herself. She and my father had been here not much more than a year ago, but just to pass through. My father had mentioned nothing negative. I wondered if he thought that warning me would seem like he was discouraging me from having anything to do with Garland Foxworth. From time to time, even he would admit that the way to get me to do something was to tell me not to do it, and vice versa.

"I got quite a nice ham cooked and made some of my bread. There's collards I made with crispy bacon, sautéed onion, ham, and garlic. You probably don't remember my collards. Oh, and we have some very nice potatoes, too. And then later, we'll visit in the parlor and have some of my golden rod cake. Your great-aunt is quite fond of it, but I only make it for a special occasion."

"Thank you, Hazel."

"Sure, missy. You go on and unpack your things, and I'll put up some hot water in case." She squeezed my hand gently. "It's so nice of you to think of us old folks. Most young folks don't," she said, and left me.

I stood there for a moment wondering if I would laugh or cry about what I had gotten myself into. When I opened the top drawer of the dresser, I jumped back. Even though they were harmless, two spiders harvesting ants and moths in their webs shocked me. I decided I would leave all my things in my bag. Gingerly, I peeled back the comforter and top sheet to see what might be living in the bed. There was nothing there now, but who knew what might be crawling in with me later?

Despite the clouds of dust I saw outside, I tried to open the window a little more, but it was quite stuck. Oh well, I thought, getting a comfortable sleep was not why I came here. I took out the clothes I thought I'd wear, now wondering if I would ever show my gala dress to my aunt. It would be a waste of time, I thought, and went down to take my bath. Hazel and my great-aunt were sitting in the living room. The instant Hazel saw me, she rose.

"Let's see about the water," she said, and led me to the bathroom.

I did remember the deep zinc slipper bathtub with the hand-painted marble on the exterior. My mother had given me a bath in it, and the image of it was stamped on a wall in my house of memories. Hazel ran some water and shook her head.

"Just as I feared," she said. "Got to get George Thomas back to fiddle with the burner. I have two kettles cookin'."

I felt a small panic. What if Garland came soon? He probably knew the train schedule between here and Alexandria and imagined I'd be here by now.

"I'll start with a washcloth," I said, and began to take off my clothes.

"That's all we really do," she said in a whisper, and left.

She returned a while later with the first kettle. I saw she was struggling to carry it, so I helped pour it in.

"A quick dip will be enough, Hazel. Don't bother with the second kettle," I said. She looked relieved.

"You leave your clothes, and I'll get them washed later tonight," she promised, and left me.

A quick dip it was, and then I dried and dressed myself. I fixed my hair, brushing it back and tying it. The mirror they had was faded in spots, but I saw enough of myself to be content. When I stepped into the living room, my great-aunt was so surprised to see me that Hazel had to reintroduce me.

"You look a lot like my sister," she said.

We had only one good photo of my grandmother, and I didn't think I looked anything like her. She wasn't ugly by any means, but her face was rounder, her eyes smaller, and her mouth not as feminine as mine. Luckily, my mother looked more like her very handsome father, who had been a colonel in the Confederate Army. I loved the picture of him in uniform. He died before I was born and remained a debonair ghost.

As I sat across from the two of them, I wondered what I could possibly talk about that would make any sense to these two. I found myself babbling about our house and my cycling and then decided to tell them about the Wexler gala. They both sat transfixed as I described the size of the estate, the decorations, and the food. I was tempted to go up and get into the dress. Hazel remembered I had mentioned it in my letter.

"We'd love to see you in it, wouldn't we, Nettie?"

My aunt nodded but looked like she had no idea why she should.

"Maybe later," I said.

Finally, I thought I would mention Garland.

"I met a fine gentleman who lives outside of Charlottesville," I said.

"Oh, did you now?" Hazel asked.

"What?" Great-aunt Nettie asked, and Hazel repeated what I had said.

"She met a fine gentleman," Hazel said. "As pretty as she is, that's no surprise, is it, Nettie?" She smiled and nodded at me. "I bet you have quite the full dancin' card whenever you go to one of those fancy dos."

I didn't want to say the Wexler gala was my first big event. I wanted to appear as grown-up as possible so they'd be less concerned about my seeing someone while I was here. I decided to mention it now.

"He might come calling. I told him where I would be," I said.

"Well, won't that be somethin'?" Hazel said. "He might come callin'," she told my great-aunt.

"Who?"

"Yes, who, dear?" Hazel asked.

"His name is Garland Foxworth," I said. "He's in business with my father's bank."

"Foxworth," Hazel announced.

"Neal Foxworth?" Great-aunt Nettie asked after a moment of thought.

"No, Aunt Nettie. His name is Garland."

"Foxworth Hall," she said. "That's the grandest mansion in Virginia, right, Hazel?"

"I never saw it myself, mind you, but I did hear a great deal about it. My, my. Will wonders never cease? Well, I should set the table," she decided, and stood.

"I'll help," I said. That wasn't something I often volunteered to do, but the prospect of yelling back and forth with my great-aunt seemed worse.

"Oh no, missy. You spend the time with your auntie. She doesn't have many visitors at all these days. That's why I was so happy to receive your letter."

Before I could offer another argument, she was gone. I looked at Great-aunt Nettie. What would I tell her now? She was looking at me, but I could see she was thinking of something else.

"My husband didn't like Neal Foxworth," she said. She didn't look like she was talking to me especially. It was more like someone reciting as she remembered. "He said he'd sell his mother for a silver dollar."

"I never knew Neal Foxworth, Aunt Nettie. I know only Garland, his son."

Her eyes seemed to click like the eyes of someone who had just woken.

"My mother had hair your color," she said.

"Did she?"

"So did my sister, but I took after my father. My father died, you know. He fell off a horse and broke his neck. He was only twenty. My grandfather shot the horse. Granger was the horse's name. What's your name again?"

"Corrine," I said.

What would happen to her if something happened to Hazel? I thought. Maybe my mother and father would look after her or see that someone did. It wasn't a responsibility I'd want.

"Time to have our tea," Hazel announced from the doorway, as if it were the doorway of a grand ballroom.

"Is it?" Great-aunt Nettie said. "Then come to the table with me, Rosemary," she said, rising and holding out her hand. I looked at Hazel, who smiled and nodded. It must surely be exhausting telling Great-aunt Nettie the same things all day, I thought, and looked toward the front door.

Oh please, please, come knocking, Garland, I prayed under my breath.

I hadn't realized how hungry I was until I began

to eat. Despite her age and I was sure her failing eyesight and hearing, too, Hazel was still a very good cook. While we ate, Great-aunt Nettie often paused to stare at me, obviously trying to remember who I was every time. Hazel kept me occupied with her memories of when the house was grand and my great-uncle was still alive.

"I made fine dinner parties back then. The best of Charlottesville society came here. I know that's hard to imagine now," she added sadly. "You take your time enjoyin' your youth, missy. It doesn't last as long as we all hope it will."

You don't have to tell me that twice, I thought. I was sure my mother hadn't intended it to be, but that was the biggest lesson I'd have swallowed and digested when I left this house and went home. I offered to help clean up, thinking that would get back to my father somehow and he'd be very proud of me, but Hazel insisted I take my great-aunt back to the living room and wait for her to bring in tea and her golden rod cake.

Time dripped by like a slowly melting icicle. Every time I heard the sound of people talking on the street or the sound of a horse and carriage, I stared hopefully toward the front door, but no one came knocking. Great-aunt Nettie fell asleep a few times while we had our tea. The golden rod cake was delicious, but soon they were both drifting off. Hazel woke with a start and began to clean up.

"We'll be goin' up to sleep soon, Nettie," she told my great-aunt, who was already half asleep again.

Everything inside me felt tied up with frustration. I began to think up different reasons for why I had to cut my visit short.

"You don't have to go to sleep with us old birds," Hazel said, returning.

It was only a little past twilight, and from the view I had of the street outside, I could see there was a full moon.

"I might sit a while," I said. "Maybe take a short walk."

"Just be careful. The way they go by with their horses and carriages these days, a pedestrian takes her life in her hands crossin' the street, especially after sundown.

"Come on, Nettie," she told my great-aunt, and reached for her arm to help her stand.

It was just then that we heard the knock on the door. Of course, I heard it first. I was hearing it in my otherwise silent prayers and for a moment thought I might have imagined it. But I heard it again.

"Someone's at the door!" I cried, standing quickly, my face full of hope.

Hazel paused to listen. There was another, louder knock.

"Well, I do declare. You're right," she said. "It might be some panhandler," she warned.

"I'll go see," I said, and started for it, but I quickly slowed down and pulled myself up. *Don't dare look so anxious, Corrine Dixon,* I told myself.

I opened the door slowly and looked out at Garland Foxworth, whose smile was bright enough to light the whole house. He immediately took off his black derby hat. He wore a suit, a tie, and high black leather boots. The splash of moonlight turned his hair a yellower gold than I remembered.

"Why, hello there, Corrine," he said. "I do hope I'm not calling too late on you fine ladies. I just returned from a business trip and thought I'd stop by on my way home."

Hazel and my great-aunt Nettie appeared in the hallway.

"Good evening," he said, nodding at them. "I'm Garland Foxworth."

"Yes, we heard you might be callin'," Hazel said. "I'm afraid I have to get Mrs. Lloyd up to bed. Might be a good idea for me as well."

"I apologize for the lateness. As I was just telling Corrine—Miss Dixon—I'm on my way home from a business trip and had to go by your home."

"Yes, well, you can offer him some of the golden rod and make some tea, if you like, Corrine," Hazel said.

My great-aunt was simply staring at him.

"I know you," she finally said. "Neal Foxworth."

"Oh no, ma'am. That was my father. I'm Garland Foxworth."

"Foxworth's Foxworth," Great-aunt Nettie replied. She was actually scowling.

"Oh, it's time for bed, Nettie," Hazel insisted. She turned her toward the stairway.

"I know him," Great-aunt Nettie told her as they started up the stairs. "That's Neal Foxworth."

"You haven't said a word," Garland said, smiling at me as soon as they were gone.

"Well, come on in, and we'll see what you get out of me then," I said.

His smile nearly exploded off his face. "A better invitation I never had," he said, entering.

I closed the door and nodded toward the living room.

"It's not quite the house it was," I said. I was actually embarrassed by it.

"With you here, I'm sure it's more than it ever was," he said.

It was as if his smile and his words were the magic I had been dreaming really existed. I was so stirred that I could have been stark naked and not a bit more excited.

But of course, I'd have to wait to find out if that would be true or not.

And there wasn't a teaspoon's worth of doubt that I soon would.

5

"Don't fuss over any tea and cake," Garland said immediately after we had entered the living room. Without waiting for me to sit first, he dropped to the sofa, leaned back with his arms across the top of it, and looked up at me. "I ate more than any man should today. Wined and dined, as they say. Everyone wants some of my money, including, of course, your father's bank."

"Well, I don't," I said sharply, and sat across from him. "I don't worship money."

"That's because your family has it," he said. "Although you might become converted for other reasons."

He smiled, but I wasn't sure I liked it. Sometimes when a man smiles at you, you can tell that he merely thinks you're cute or adorable, some sort of compliment that belongs tagged onto a little girl, not a woman. A woman is attractive, beautiful, pretty. That's the smile I wanted, more of a look of wonder and, most important, desire.

The look on my face changed his expression instantly. "No offense. Actually, you are surprising. I'm impressed," he said.

"Why?" I asked sharply.

"It's very nice to see a young woman who cares enough to visit old relatives and not simply put them off on some shelf to be forgotten." He squinted. "Or am I seeing something that is not?"

Did he want me to come right out and say I came here mainly to see him?

"Do you doubt that was my intention, sir?" I asked instead.

"Long ago I decided not to ponder too long on the way a young woman thinks. Too many forks in that road."

"So you've had a number who confused you? Now I'm the one truly surprised. Something like that happening to a man of worldly experience."

He threw his head back with a laugh and slapped his knees. "I do say you are the most challenging young woman I've met, Corrine. Are you a good student? Do you intend to be a teacher, a nurse, or someone's secretary?"

"Hardly," I said. "I don't intend to work. I'm not one of these radical women looking to establish a career. And I'm not a good student. I despise being forced to do numbers, even though my father would appreciate it. History bores me, not to mention science. I simply don't have the patience for lectures and taking notes, as well as reading assignments."

"Well, that's not a tragedy for a woman these days."

"Maybe. But I do pride myself on being a good student in the world. In that way I am more my father's daughter."

"Probably so," he said, nodding and looking more thoughtful. "Are you free tomorrow? May I show you and your aunt Foxworth Hall? I promise to go easy on the history."

"I am not sure my great-aunt's up to it," I said. "You saw her. To be honest about it, I am not sure she'll notice if I'm here or not. In the morning, I expect Hazel will have to reintroduce me to her."

"I see. And your parents gave you no restrictions, instructions?"

"I do not think of myself as someone who still needs her parents to give her instructions," I said. "I thought I demonstrated that at the Wexler gala."

His eyes took on a new intensity, his face almost vibrating with delight and exhilaration. He looked at the doorway and then toward the kitchen like someone afraid to be overheard. For a moment, he tapped his derby against his leg as he pondered. I don't know why, but my anticipation of what he would say next kept me from taking a breath.

"I imagine, then, that they wouldn't notice if you were gone now," he said.

"Gone now? You mean go to Foxworth Hall now?"

He took out his pocket watch, snapped it open, and then nodded. "It's not that late. You must have had your dinner early, which makes sense considering your aunt's age." He paused, smiled, and sat back. "You're not Cinderella in disguise, are you? If we should violate midnight, my carriage won't turn into a pumpkin, will it?"

"No, I am not Cinderella, and I don't have a curfew, sir."

"Not that I won't get you back by midnight. Do you want to see Foxworth Hall now? You should see it both at night and during the daytime. It's a mansion with its own special personality. It changes when the sun goes down. Sometimes I think of it as being alive. It's well over one hundred years old, but between some of the improvements my father had made and ones I've been making, it's . . ." He looked about the living room. "It's not suffered like this, although there are rooms, places, that no one's paid much attention to for some time, decades, in fact.

"Let's just say it will be an experience to remember, night or day," he concluded.

The idea of sneaking out of my great-aunt's house seemed thrilling. This was just the sort of excitement I had hoped to have.

"With such a promise, how can I refuse?" I replied.

His smile burst like a firecracker on his face.

"You don't need anything. There's just a slight chill in the air, but I have a new horsehair blanket, specially made for me recently. I'm experimenting with emblems for the Foxworth family. I'd love your opinion of this one. Shall we go? I have a driver waiting just outside."

He stood.

Now that I had bragged so much about exercising my freedom, actually doing it took on another meaning, however. I listened for any sounds indicating that either Hazel or my great-aunt was still awake. It was very quiet. They really wouldn't know I had left, I thought. There was no danger of that.

"Very well," I said, standing. I was trembling a little, knowing how upset both my parents would be when and if they learned about this evening escapade unchaperoned. I smiled immediately to prevent him from seeing the fear and hesitation in my face, but he was apparently good at reading me.

He put his right hand over his heart and recited, "I promise I'll get you back well before midnight, and no one will be the worse for it, including you."

"Then we should get started if I'm to have the time to see anything," I said, washing away any hesitation. The longer we talked about it, the more frightened I became.

He nodded. "Absolutely," he said, and went to the front door, holding out his arm.

I took it, and we stepped out. I had never seen a carriage like his, parked in front of my aunt's house. It looked like it belonged in a fairy tale. It was no wonder he had referred to Cinderella. There were four beautiful large horses, each at least seventeen hands, all coal black. The carriage had an enclosed black body with gold trim. There were two doors and a glazed front window.

"It's beautiful," I said.

"It's imported from England," he said. "I have four different carriages. This one is a brougham. You'll see that I had the seats re-covered in new leather."

The driver, who had been waiting, leaped down and opened the door. There was one unfolding step.

"This is Lucas," Garland said. "Lucas, this is Miss Corrine Dixon. You might see quite a bit of her over the next few days, if we're both lucky."

Lucas was a slim man with dark-brown hair, the strands going every which way. I didn't think him to be much older than I was and not much taller.

"Evening, ma'am," he said, touching the brim of his hat and bowing slightly. He glanced at me and looked away quickly, as if a glance was all he was permitted. Getting into this carriage made it easy to feel like royalty.

Garland held my arm firmly as I stepped up and in. The seats did smell new.

"Open it up when we're out of the city, Lucas. Miss Dixon likes to go fast," Garland told him, and got in smiling. He sat beside me and unfolded the rose-colored blanket that had a lion embroidered in black at the center. It was captured in motion as if it had just leaped to seize its prey.

"What do you think?" he asked as we started away.

"Striking," I said. "Beautiful work."

"Yes, I have someone from New York City working on this, a true artist. I like the sense of movement, power, and confidence in the lion's face."

"Is that how you see the Foxworths, see yourself?"

"As reflected in the faces of the people I meet," he said. "Am I overstating?"

"I'll let you know," I said.

"I imagine you will."

Looking through the front window, I could see that the streets of the city were still quite busy. Like Alexandria's, Charlottesville's streets were increasingly lit by electric rather than gas lamps. They were brighter and for me gave the city more excitement at night. There was wave after wave of voices, people shouting and laughing, and music spilling out of bars and restaurants along the way.

"Busier than usual tonight," Garland said, nodding at other carriages. "Kind of festive, don't you think?"

"Yes." My eyes were going everywhere, seizing on the women in scant clothes who were openly flirting with men, and men drinking from bottles of whiskey. I saw even women doing that here and there. Children who struck me as orphans were scurrying about offering to do favors and begging for change.

"My mother would call it Sodom and Gomorrah. She'd be absolutely overwhelmed by it now."

"My mother would be in a faint if she were in this carriage," I said, and he laughed.

The carriage picked up speed the moment we left the city streets. It bounced over the rough road. Garland put his arm around me.

"For your own protection," he said, smiling. "Just call me insurance."

He held me firmly, his handsome face closer to mine. If I turned completely, our lips would surely meet. My mother's eyes would widen with such astonishment that she could tear her lids. But truthfully, I liked his being this close, liked the sense of strength I could feel in his arm. Some women, especially my mother's close friends, complained about how domineering men were, but I would gladly bathe in this warm, firm protection.

After we had left the city, I saw houses occasionally, but there were mostly trees and empty fields. As the twilight sky darkened, Lucas slowed the carriage. The half-moon cast a wide amber glow over everything in front of and around us. I didn't question Garland's comment about Foxworth's personality changing when the sun went down. I always felt that night changed the world in subtle but occasionally startling ways. An ordinary maple tree looked more spidery. Sometimes gaps between leaves with some stars behind them resembled eyes. As a child, I always wondered where the birds went at night. There were night birds and often bats, but where did the other birds go to sleep, and why was it so hard to see them? My mother fled from such questions, but my father smiled and made up answers, saying things like "They flew to the other side of the world where there was light. Where else would they go?"

However, at the moment, I worried about whether nighttime was best to see Foxworth Hall for the first time. Maybe I wouldn't like its evening personality. Even houses, especially large ones, were often gloomy, washed in deep shadows, looming rather than looking majestic and regal the way I had imagined Garland's family home to be. I had told myself I was on my way to see a castle gleaming with gold and light, a romantic place in which a young prince lived.

The road wound upward. As we drew closer to the hills, I noted how the trees paraded up and down between them. I mentioned it to Garland.

"The Foxworths planted many of them," he said, "to serve as windbreaks. They also hold back the heavier drifts of snow." He smiled. "It's as if we had the power to control nature itself, don't you think?"

Once I set eyes on Foxworth Hall rising against the night sky as we drew closer, I understood Garland's arrogance. His home sat above and looked down on the far smaller houses splattered almost randomly beneath it. For a part of the day, Foxworth literally blocked the sun and cast long, seemingly ever-creeping deep shadows over so many of these homes and their residents. Even my father would be intimidated as he approached and then entered this mansion. *How powerful and rich must be the man who owns all this,* he would surely think. I know I did.

"Do you live by yourself in such a house, Garland?" I asked.

"I have servants, of course," he said. "But since I lost my immediate family, I have lived alone. One can get used to it if one has grown up amidst the echoes rolling through the hallways. You will see that I have many rooms to wander in and out of. I am never bored with my home. It seems like every day when I'm there, I discover something to change, something to add, and something to, shall we say, retire. The vast attic is more like a cemetery filled with discarded furniture, portraits of relatives I never knew or even heard of, and old toys, antiques, as well as closets of clothes once thought to be elegant. There are coats and shoes, busts and mannequins. It's a virtual gold mine of relics. It wouldn't surprise me to find actual skeletons.

"When I was a little boy, maybe not that little, I'd go up there and explore. My mother worried about rats and spiders and even ghosts. Once you spend time in Foxworth Hall, you'll understand why I often think it's alive. Somewhere in some dark part of it, its heart beats."

When he spoke, he seemed hypnotized, talking like someone dreaming. Although his arm was still around my shoulders, I could almost feel him drift away. I was speechless, of course, maybe even a little shocked. I looked closer at Foxworth Hall and thought I had never had even an inkling of such a feeling for my house. I could move out of it tomorrow and not miss a corner, a step, or a window. My father talked about houses in the same way he spoke about investments. The only emotion he seemed to have was joy when its value rose.

And yet I would have to admit that it was intriguing to think of a house as central to who you were, to your family's identity. Only a Foxworth could feel it in this one, perhaps. Garland certainly seemed to.

"How many rooms are in the house?" I asked, more to bring him back to earth than to educate myself about it.

"Thirty-six, but there are closets in some rooms as big as rooms in other people's homes. I have

126

my favorite ones, of course, and I'll be interested to see which rooms you like the most. Of course, you'll love our ballroom and that new piano I described."

"Do you play?"

"No, but it's easy to hire someone who does when I want to, when I want the music in the house, when I have a reason to use the ballroom."

He smiled but did so facing the mansion more than me. It was as if he believed the house could hear him talk about it in such favorable terms.

"You'll see that the Wexlers' ballroom is closer to a closet compared to the one in Foxworth Hall."

"And servants?"

"I have a very good cook, Mrs. Wilson, a few gardeners, as I told you, and a maid, Myrtle Steiner. She's plain-faced, with what I call a roly-poly figure, but she runs the place like it's hers."

"Only one maid in so big a mansion?"

"Obviously, I don't use all the rooms on a daily basis. The doors are closed. No need to dust them until just before they'd be used. However, to be sure, there's my bedroom, a guest bedroom, a living room I frequent, the kitchen, dining room and bathrooms, all seen to daily."

"When did you use the ballroom?"

"Truthfully, I've had no reason for a gala, but I expect I will soon. Right now, it's been just a big private party room. Whenever it was used for that, which I haven't for some time, I bring in a half dozen or so to clean and wash and polish before and after.

"Lucas, who is quite handy for a man his age, serves as something of a house manager, looking after lights and pipes and such. Once we're inside, he'll run ahead and light candles and torches so you can have your first tour. It is spectacular to see it at night, isn't it?" he asked, nodding.

We were pulling up to the large double entrance doors with gaslit sconces.

"Yes," I said, but tentatively. I hadn't yet really seen it. To a stranger, it might not have the magic he believed it possessed, but it was obviously very important to him that I be more than impressed, perhaps overwhelmed.

We stopped.

"There, that wasn't too long, was it?" Garland asked.

"No."

"And the ride was fine. Of course, being beside someone as charming as you, time flies anyway."

"Not too fast, I hope. I don't want to be left behind."

He roared. "A wittier young woman I have yet to meet."

"And hopefully won't," I added.

He laughed again. Lucas opened the door for us and waited to help me step down. He then hurried to open the front doors, which were so thick and tall that it seemed he was opening the portals to some netherworld.

"M'lady," Garland said with an exaggerated bow, "my humble home is at your disposal."

And we entered Foxworth Hall. The entryway was well lit, but the lights were low inside. Seemingly out of the shadows, a small woman, perhaps five foot four at most, approached us. She wore a dark-blue dress and black shoes that looked more like men's. They had a thick heel and sole, probably to add a half inch or so to her height. Nevertheless, I felt like I towered over her. Her plain face told me who she was before Garland had stepped forward to introduce us. She had patches of redness on her cheeks and forehead and dull dark-brown hair pinned back.

"This is Mrs. Steiner," he said.

Mrs.? I thought. Because of the way he had described her and how she looked, I couldn't imagine her being married, and if she was, where was her husband? There was no mention of him.

"Mrs. Steiner, Miss Dixon."

"Good evening," she said. "Welcome to Foxworth Hall." She turned to Garland. "I thought you might want a fire in the living room, Mr. Foxworth. It seems a bit chilly tonight."

"It's always a bit chilly to you, Mrs. Steiner," Garland said, smiling. "But thank you. I'm going to be giving Miss Dixon the two-cent tour of

Foxworth Hall. The dollar tour will occur in the daytime."

"Would you like some tea or . . ."

"Nothing, thank you, Mrs. Steiner."

He turned to Lucas.

"Light some candles for us upstairs, Lucas."

"Yes, sir," he said, hurrying ahead.

I gazed up at the high ceiling. Scattered along the walls were portraits of people I assumed were Foxworth ancestors. I was surprised at some, because the men looked so austere, cold, and not at all like Garland. But then I thought they might have wanted that look, believing it made them appear more powerful, authoritative. The women I saw weren't attractive and weren't portrayed as happy. Their faces were pinched and tight like the faces of women who had been forced to pose perhaps for hours.

"I'll introduce you to some of them at a later time," Garland said, seeing how I was studying some of the paintings. He leaned over, smiling coyly, and said, "I like to tease them. They're all dying to know who you are."

"What?"

He laughed, took my hand, and led me to the end of the long foyer, where there was a pair of elegant staircases that wound upward to join a balcony on the second floor. From the balcony, there was a second single staircase rising to another flight. Three giant crystal chandeliers hung from a gilt carved ceiling some forty feet above the floor of mosaic tiles.

"Impressive," I said in a whisper. Somehow I thought I shouldn't speak in tones any louder. It was as if I had entered some temple.

"Oh, you haven't seen anything yet, Corrine."

As we approached the stairway, I gazed at the marble busts, the crystal lamps, and the antique tapestries. There were museums that didn't have as much as this house, I thought. The wealth displayed along the walls and on them would take anyone's breath away. I hadn't been in a home this majestic. Garland didn't rush me through it, either. I thought he was relishing the way I reacted, wide-eyed, to everything I was seeing.

"My father believed that Foxworth Hall could charm any woman more than any Foxworth man could. 'Bring the woman you love here, and she will love you,' he would tell me."

"Was he right?" I asked coyly.

"I have yet to find out," he replied. Few men I had met could hold their smile in the glint of their eyes as well as he could. Was he telling the truth? I doubted it, but I liked the fact that he wanted me to feel special.

"With all due respect to your father, a woman doesn't marry a house," I said.

"Maybe," he replied. "You have yet to feel all its magic."

We walked on, Mrs. Steiner remaining close

behind as if she was there to catch whatever new request Garland tossed over his shoulders.

Before we reached the stairway, he nodded to his right. "That's our library," he said. He paused. "Turn up the lights a bit, please, Mrs. Steiner."

She charged into the library and increased the illumination. Garland led me to the doorway, and I gazed at the walls lined with richly carved mahogany bookshelves crowded with leather-bound volumes. The ceiling was at least twenty feet high, the shelves of books almost meeting it. A slim portable stairway of wrought iron slid around a track curved to the second level of shelves, and there was a balcony from which someone could reach the books on the top level.

"I have something of an office in the rear. I can show you that later, perhaps in the daytime tomorrow if I can steal you away again. There's a nice view of the property from the windows there."

"It's the most beautiful home library I've ever seen," I said. "Have you read any of these books?"

He laughed. "One or two. I don't sit still long enough these days to finish a book. Are you a reader?"

"Of volumes I like."

"I'll have to learn what those are and get more of them for you if they are not here now. You can spend hours checking titles, but many have to do with history and legal matters. It would take months to peruse all this. But I think you'd enjoy every day."

I loved to hear him say things that foresaw a future for us, for me.

"Our bedrooms, the family's," he quickly corrected, "are upstairs in the southern wing. There's warmer exposure. There are fourteen rooms in the northern wing, all various sizes. My parents had frequent guests."

"And you don't?"

"Occasionally. Who knows? This house is so large there might be some still left from months ago."

"You're kidding."

"Of course," he said. "But we'll see."

He turned me to the stairway, and we started up. As I walked, I ran my hand over the smooth rosewood balustrade. Lucas came hurrying toward us when Garland turned us toward the south wing. Right there stood a suit of armor on a pedestal. Now I really thought I had entered a castle.

"Oh. Another relative?"

"Still inside," he joked.

Lucas had softly lit the hallway ahead, giving me the sense that he had done this before when Garland had brought in a young lady for a tour. I caught a quick smile. He was more like a fellow conspirator.

I looked to my right and down. "I've never

been in a house with bedrooms so high up."

"Yes. My father used to say our stairways either conditioned us to live longer or killed us off younger than expected. There were definitely a few heart attacks up here," he added.

"Really?" I said with nearly a gasp, even though he didn't sound upset.

"Have you heard about elevators? I'm seriously thinking about getting one installed."

"Yes. I heard my father mention them when he was talking about investments in new commercial buildings, but I had never heard of a house having one."

"Exactly. I'd probably be the first in Virginia. Shall we continue?"

We walked a little farther before stopping at the open doorway of a large room.

"Take a peek," he said. I stepped in through the doorway.

There were at least a dozen heads of various animals on the walls.

"Not much here yet. I haven't been at it as much as my father, but I intend to add to our collection in the foreseeable future. Hunting," he added when I didn't respond.

"Oh."

"It's sort of a trophy room." He studied my reaction to some of the heads, the eyes frozen in what I thought was anger. "You don't look like you approve."

"They look like they're all staring at us with rage."

He laughed. "Who could blame them?"

He took my arm again, and we continued until we reached a set of open double doors.

"This is my room."

It was at least two, maybe even three, times as large as my parents' bedroom. An ornately carved cherrywood bed was at the center. It had hand-carved posts topped with a white canopy. The bed was covered with a spread of quilted satin. There were two large white pillows with hand-crocheted pillowcases.

The bed was set between two large paneled windows, which were draped in light-blue pleated antique silk curtains. The room had a polished hardwood floor, but there was a thick light-gray wool rug beside the bed.

"The bed is a little oversized for a bachelor," he said, "but we Foxworths have our superstitions."

"And what is this one?"

"Since I've slept in this bed so long, the babies made in it will inherit our best features and health. Looks like a wasted pillow right now." He leaned closer to whisper, "But I alternate nights with each."

He laughed at my expression of surprise. Was he serious?

There was a large mirror to our left, and beside it was a dressing table of cherrywood. Everything on it was neatly organized.

Beside the dressing table was a large dresser and what looked like a very large closet next to that. There was one blue cut-velvet chair oddly facing the bed as if someone sat there to watch him sleep, perhaps watching something else as well. On the right were another closet and another small dresser. The room had a fireplace, which was now unlit.

"Where do your few servants sleep?"

"Their quarters are above the carriage garages in the rear."

"You called your maid 'Mrs.' Is her husband here as well?"

"I'm afraid not. He died of smallpox seven years ago. They had no children, which might be a blessing. He wasn't very good-looking, either."

He smiled widely. I poked him.

"You are a terrible man, Garland Foxworth. Do you know that?"

"I've been told so on occasion, even by my own mother," he said, laughing. "Shall we continue? There is another bedroom to show you. It's never really been used. My mother had the bed made on a whim, according to my father, and after it had been constructed, she was embarrassed to use it. It is something special."

He paused at the closed door.

"You could count on the fingers of one hand how many people I've shown this room, but somehow, for some reason I can't explain at the moment, I think you will appreciate it as much as my mother hoped she would. She was a little too . . . shy, perhaps," he added, and opened the door.

At the center of the room on a dais was a bed with the sleek ivory head of a swan, turned in profile, looking like swans do when they are just about to plunge their heads under the ruffled underside of a lifted wing. I'm not sure if I gasped or not, but I had never seen anything like it. Although Garland didn't move forward, standing back almost as if he was afraid to enter any farther, I did.

Looking at it more closely, I saw that the swan had one sleepy red ruby eye. Its wings curved gently to cup its head on an almost oval bed. The wing-tip feathers were like fingers holding back the delicate transparent draperies that were in all shades of pink and rose and violet and purple.

"Your mother wanted this?" I asked.

He stepped up beside me. "She designed it herself. It was sort of a hobby of hers. My father never thought much of her talent or vision when it came to designing things. He made fun of it, actually, sometimes bringing her to tears."

"How cruel. Anyway, he was quite wrong. This is beautiful. The swan was a perfect choice because of its grace."

"Somehow I knew you would say that."

I gazed around. "The whole bedroom is unique."

There was a thick mauve carpet and a large rug of white fur near the bed. There were four lamps four feet high made of cut crystal and decorated with gold and silver. Two of them had black shades, and placed between the other two was a chaise longue upholstered in rose-colored velvet.

"What a shame that it's gone unused."

"My father hated all this color. He wouldn't come into the room after she had it completed. If he could have, he would have nailed the door shut. Even though she didn't sleep in that bed, she spent lots of time in here. It was sort of an escape for her, escape from my father and even from me."

I nodded.

"You don't have to believe that so fast."

"I'm sure you don't lie," I said.

He laughed.

I looked at the walls covered with opulent silk damask in a bright strawberry-pink and then stepped up to the bed to feel the soft, furry coverlet.

"Sleeping in this bed would be like sleeping on a cloud, I imagine."

He pressed his lips together and nodded. "It doesn't look the same in the daytime."

"Probably not," I said. "Nothing does, including most people."

He laughed heartily again and reached for my hand. "Come on. I have the most interesting new drink to share with you, something I discovered in Italy. I brought back the recipe and have it made for me here in Charlottesville now."

"What is it?" I asked.

"They call it limoncello. Some say it began with monks; others say fishermen. Every part of Italy seems to take credit for its origin. I'll venture to say you won't find it anywhere else right now in all of Virginia, even all of the United States, but here. I do like discovering new things and bringing them to Foxworth Hall, delicious and beautiful things. I'll show you what I can tonight."

What he could? Was there a surprise behind every door?

We stopped at the one just past the Swan Room.

"Another little hideaway of mine," he announced. "The house lends itself to secrets."

"Do you have so many that you need so many rooms?"

He laughed. "We'll see," he said, and opened the door.

It was just another bedroom.

Lucas was a conspirator, I thought. He had gone ahead and lit the lamps, which burned low, casting an enticing glow over the bed and the thick, white, furry rug in front of the fireplace. It looked like the material I had felt on the swan bed.

On the table beside it was a bottle of lemon-colored liquid and some glasses.

"You're in for a treat," he said, smiling.

My heart was pounding. I was lost somewhere in this great house and captured by that smile. It was a little frightening, but even that was something I had sought. Passion without danger seemed incomplete, even false.

He was still holding my hand. His look was more intense.

"You're even more beautiful here, Corrine, but that's another proof of Foxworth's magic. Diamonds twinkle brighter within its grasp. I can feel it," he said, gazing around. "The house likes you. You glitter in its light. I can only imagine what it would be like to have you here all the time. You'd fall so in love with it I'd be jealous."

All the time? I thought. Jealous?

If my body wasn't craving it, I might not have taken a breath.

6

After my second glass of his delightful liquid, Garland's laugh seemed to grow thinner and a little longer every time he did laugh. He had poured me my first glass after he had us lie down in front of the fireplace where he then proceeded to describe his travels in Italy and how he had fallen upon this drink in a small inn near the Amalfi coast. It was like listening to someone spin a tale of wonder and make-believe, and I was a little girl again, willing to be enchanted by his words.

"From my first sip, I knew that this was something very special. I had gone thousands of miles to find it after I heard about it at a dinner in Rome," he said, making himself sound like Marco Polo. He held his glass up, looking through the yellow liquid as if he was judging fine wine. "This batch is perfect. I'd have never discovered it had I not been enamored of pleasure journeys."

Travel was always to be part of my future. My best friend, Daisy, and I imagined ourselves in many exotic places, but no one described the sights, the views of the seas, and the quaint little villages with the enthusiasm Garland did, which made me want to do it so much more. From what he was relating in one tale after another, he had been over much of England and had visited

France, Germany, Spain, and Italy. Now he was planning on trips to the Middle East and Asia.

His descriptions were vivid, always stressing the romantic aspects: the piazzas in Italy at sunset with musicians playing and singing, the patios in southern France overlooking the Mediterranean with views that could take your breath away, the pebble-stone streets in Greece with their small shops and restaurants, and the seaside on the Costa del Sol in Spain where he said he ate tapas and walked miles on the beach barefoot.

"I can still feel the warm sand between my toes. Have you ever walked on a beach?"

"No," I said sadly.

"You'll walk on one with me someday."

"Will I?"

He tossed out his predictions for me with such assurance. Anyone hearing him would think he had a crystal ball that revealed every day of my future, and every day included him.

While he spoke, I drank more and more of his delicious lemon drink. He poured me a third and kept describing details of his most recent travels. Many of these places Daisy and I had seen pictures of in books. At home, I voiced a desire to actually see them, be there, even before I was eighteen, but my mother was not fond of real traveling, and my father always seemed to be too busy for long holidays.

"Did you always travel alone?" I asked, fishing

for more information about his romantic life. After all, how does a man alone enjoy such beauty, the music, and the wonderful dinners he had described?

"Yes," he said quickly. "I like to go about when I feel the need, move on a whim and a wish, and not have to discuss it to death," he added, but he didn't deny that he might have met women at these places. I sensed he might have left broken hearts trailing behind him. From what he described, a wife, at least back then, when he started his extensive traveling, was the last thing he had wanted.

"What about your parents? Did they ever go along?"

"My father was too tethered to my mother's moods and looked forward more than anything to his hunting expeditions, because she would never go on one. He took me on a few when I was older, which is how I acquired the taste for it. I try to do at least two a year."

"But how do you do these trips and keep up with your businesses?" I was really thinking about my father, who had much, much smaller responsibilities than Garland did and took almost no holidays.

"Good managers. Although I'm away, it doesn't mean I don't keep track of things. Besides, most of my investments take care of themselves. Cash cows, my accountant and I call them. Moo, moo," he added, and laughed.

Although I didn't think it was all that funny imagining a cow being milked for dollars, I laughed, too, but at this point, I felt I might laugh at anything. It was truly like doors opening and restraints weakening. I felt so light that I thought I might just start to float.

He poured me a little more limoncello when he saw my glass was almost empty.

"You do like it, don't you?" he asked when I hesitated. He sounded like it would break his heart if I said otherwise. He waited anxiously for my answer.

"Oh yes, it's . . . quite wonderful. Like you said, 'It's like drinking a spring day.' "

He stared at me a moment, holding his smile.

"What?" I asked.

"You don't forget anything I say. Perhaps you'll write my autobiography," he added.

"I doubt it. I have enough trouble trying to write my diary."

"Oh, I'd like to have a look at that."

"Never," I said, and he laughed.

"Am I in it yet?"

"Maybe."

That obviously pleased him.

He continued to talk about his trips, describing a recent one to England on business. I was listening, but his words were beginning to flow together, and I was hearing the cadence of his voice more than I was hearing what he was actually saying.

Suddenly, he paused, his eyes so fixed on mine I couldn't look away. I had heard about hypnotism but had never seen it performed or met anyone who claimed to have been hypnotized. However, from the way I felt myself drifting, swimming, in his strong focus, I thought it might just be happening to me right now. I wasn't panicked or afraid. The warmth that came with every sip of the lemon drink was washing through my body. It made every part of me feel like it was softening. I liked the feeling, but soon the room began to spin. I felt myself sway and turned quickly to lie on my back and close my eyes.

As I did so, he took the glass of limoncello from my hand before I spilled it on myself and the rug.

"Can't waste a drop of this," he said with a laugh.

Even though my eyes were closed, it still felt like the floor was tilting and turning. I wasn't frightened as much as I was a little embarrassed. I had had wine and even rum and never felt this way. I had thought his drink was nothing much more than lemonade. I tried to laugh, but it was as if I couldn't move.

"Corrine," I heard him whisper. And then I felt his lips on mine.

I didn't want to open my eyes. My body seemed to be sinking into the soft rug. He said my name again and kissed me on the neck, unbuttoning my blouse so he could move his kisses to my shoulder and then down between my breasts. A tiny streak of lightning shot up my legs, into the small of my stomach, and up to my breasts.

His lips were nearly touching my ear when he whispered, "You are so beautiful."

Was I smiling? My face felt as if it was drifting away. I think I wore a silly grin. I heard him chuckle.

"I'm floating away," I said. "Hold me down before I disappear."

I laughed after I said it, and he laughed, too.

"No, you're not disappearing. You're dreaming. I just happened to slip into your fantasy, which is now mine as well."

His lips were on my neck again, moving like silk over my cheeks and my closed eyes, pressing softly and then pressing harder to my lips. While he kissed me, his hands were moving all over my body. I wanted to lift my arms to bring a moment of hesitation to us, but they were so heavy I didn't get them an inch off the rug. I felt his fingers undoing all my clothes, and all I did was moan. I'm sure that only encouraged him.

When his hand caressed my uncovered breast and his lips closed on my nipple, I finally opened my eyes. He went from one breast to the other, muttering how perfect I was and how much he wanted me.

"You want me too," he said. "Just as much, if not more. Am I right?"

Before I could speak, he was pressing his mouth

on mine, and his hands were softly lowering my chemise and then my drawers.

I wondered if this was really happening or if I was, as he had said, in a dream.

"Oh, Corrine," he whispered. "Oh, Corrine, you're like a goddess come to earth."

I knew what I was feeling between my legs. I wanted to warn him, to stop him from thinking I was so easily willing to do this, but he pressed on, grunting and pushing until he was in me.

It was a little more painful than I had anticipated. I uttered a small cry.

"I thought you were a woman of the world," he said, not whispering now but sounding more like someone complaining. "You had me fooled."

Nevertheless, he continued. I started to cry but at this point offered not even the suggestion of resistance, because I felt some pleasure building, too. It was like kissing someone wonderful in the middle of a raging storm. I lifted my arms and grasped his shoulders, digging my fingers deeply into him. If I was hurting him with my fingernails, he didn't care. I remember thinking pleasure could overcome pain for us both.

The room was spinning again. I think I was clinging to him out of fear I would faint, but the harder I grasped him, the more encouraged he was. He said so many things, but I couldn't hear him. There was thunder in my ears, his groans and grunts and cries of delight almost drowning it out.

When he throbbed inside me, matching my own throbbing, he cried out, "Yes, yes!" dropping his face against my breasts. A long moment passed, and then, to my surprise, he laughed. He turned over on his back. I didn't move. There was so much warmth between my legs.

"Well, there goes a good rug," he said. "But you're definitely worth it."

I had yet to speak. My whole body felt as though it was still vibrating. I had just done the most intimate thing a woman could do with a man, but it hadn't been how I had imagined it would be. It was too quick and too rough. Where was the fantasy I had designed for myself in so many daydreams? Where were those magic chimes? Why didn't I feel lifted and free, wanting more and more?

I heard the snap of a match and turned to see him light up a cigar. He crossed his legs. He was still wearing nothing below his waist. The strong odor of the cigar made my stomach churn. I groaned. Smoke streamed out of his mouth.

"Oh, I'm sorry. Does this bother you?"

"Yes!" I cried, swallowing back my urge to throw up. Didn't he remember what I had said in the Wexler garden?

"It's a pretty expensive one," he declared, turning it in his fingers. "But . . . for someone so pretty, I'd burn and waste a dozen."

He snuffed it out on the wooden floor, as if his massive home was simply a big ashtray.

I realized I was still naked and reached for my underthings.

"Oh, don't do that," he said, seizing my wrist. "The night is young."

"I should be thinking of going back to my great-aunt's home."

"You said they wouldn't know if you were there or not, and I saw what that house is like. Why rush back to that when you have all this to enjoy here?"

I reached down to feel the warmth between my legs and then looked at my fingers.

Blood!

"Oh my God," I said. I saw there was some on his rug.

"Don't worry about it. I won't even bother having it washed. Maybe I'll pin it up in that trophy room I showed you."

"What?"

He laughed. "Just joking. I'll have it burned up. But they say the first man a woman makes love to is the last man she'll forget. How do you feel about that?"

"I feel a little sick," I said.

He laughed again.

"I do!"

"It'll pass. Just relax. Everything will be better for you this next time. You won't have to wait long. I'm loaded for bear tonight."

"What does that mean?"

"My father's expression. Now that we've opened the door, tilled the soil, let's return to where we were," he said. He took a long sip of his glass of limoncello, and then he looked at me and smiled. "This never disappoints," he said, holding up the glass. "And you liked it, too."

Liked it, too? Right now, I felt I had been hypnotized and drugged with a sweet-tasting arsenic. I was on the verge of crying, bawling uncontrollably. I think he saw my lips tremble and moved quickly to lie beside me again.

"Now, now, Corrine. Don't blame yourself for making things more difficult for us tonight. All of it had to be overcome eventually anyway. It's all part of growing into a woman. My own mother told me that, not that I was old enough at the time to understand a word of it."

I grimaced. What kind of a mother would discuss such a thing with her son? Her daughter, yes, but tell him a woman's deepest secrets? I couldn't get my own mother to do it. Why didn't he go to his father for that sort of information anyway?

He stroked my hair.

"Don't despair. You're a woman who simply can't look anything but beautiful before, during, and after great lovemaking."

Normally, I would have wanted so much to hear those words, but right now I felt nauseated. He was actually starting to annoy me with the odor of the cigar on his breath and his fingers traveling over my shoulders and breasts like a spider.

But if he saw any of this in my face, he ignored it. He leaned over and began to kiss me, starting from the small of my stomach, but not, as I was anticipating, moving up my body.

I tried to shift away, but he held my hips and kept me from moving.

"Another man might run, but most don't know there is so much pleasure in satisfying all your senses at once when you have the opportunity to do so. Besides, I like the smell of you."

He inhaled as if I was made of some perfume and then brought his lips to my thighs. He nibbled on my skin and lifted himself over me again, sliding his hands under my legs to hold them firmly as he moved me forcibly to make his entry easier and more comfortable for himself.

"Let's try it with your eyes open the whole time this time," he said. Before I could protest, he was at me again.

Maybe it was the cigar, maybe it was the lemon drink, or maybe it was the way he rushed at me this time, not smoothly and lovingly but hungrily, more like ravaging me, but it all combined to explode inside me. He wasn't quite done before his precious lemon drink came up and out of my mouth, splattering on his chest and my breasts. However, it didn't stop him; he didn't pause until he was satisfied, groaning and then laughing.

"Not the most romantic time I've had but most interesting," he said, rolling over onto his back.

Interesting? How could all that have been interesting?

He rose to his feet. "Just lie there. I'll bring in a pan of warm water, a washcloth, and a towel."

He walked out half naked and unconcerned that he'd be seen.

I groaned, closed my eyes, and lay back, turning on my side. I think I was just as sickened by how disappointing all this had been as I was from the lemon drink. My fairy-tale prince had taken advantage of me. Foxworth Hall didn't seem like much of a castle now, either. I started to cry, sobbing quietly to myself. Everything had begun so beautifully and had come to this point so quickly.

I heard him return. He slapped the cool, damp washcloth over my forehead and eyes.

"You'll be fine," he said, and kissed me on the neck. "You just need some sleep. I have an idea. Why don't you just sleep here tonight? I'll have Lucas take you back early in the morning before your aunt and her housekeeper awaken. How's that sound?"

"No."

I seized the cloth and wiped off my chest. Then I reached for my clothes.

"Take me to a bathroom," I ordered. "Take me!"

He nodded and slipped into his leggings quickly.

I put the towel around myself and embraced all my things. He led me out and down to a bathroom on the right, moving in first to light a lantern.

"Perhaps you'll reconsider my offer once you're more comfortable," he said, and then left.

I cleaned myself up the best I could and dressed. When I stepped out, he wasn't waiting. There was no one in the hallway. The candles were dim, some having gone out. Shadows seemed to be growing right before my eyes, all growing toward me. I was still quite dizzy.

"Garland?" I called.

I waited, but he didn't appear, so I continued down the hallway. I was feeling very tired, battling to keep my eyes open, in fact. When I reached the stairway, I called for him again. I waited, looked back down the hallway, and, still not seeing him, started to descend.

It wasn't until I had stepped down from the balcony onto the next set of stairs that I saw him below talking softly to Lucas. They both turned to watch me continue my shaky descent. Not very gallant of either of them, I thought. They should be rushing to my side, seeing how unsteady I was.

"Feeling better?" Garland asked when I reached the bottom steps.

"No," I said petulantly.

I longed to see my father and his look of concern and love even when I was merely in a dark mood. How could Garland have just left me up there fending for myself?

Lucas stepped forward to take my arm when I stepped down and swayed.

"As I told you, I think all you really need is a good night's rest," Garland said. "You can probably get up whenever you want at your old aunt's house. Of course, you could do that here as well, and in quite an elegant bedroom. Changed your mind about it, perhaps?"

"No. Please, I want to go back now."

"Oh, absolutely. Lucas will take you. I have some paperwork to review, so I can come by about noon and bring you back to Foxworth Hall to see it in the bright sunlight. How's that sound?"

"Nothing sounds good right now except sleep, and plenty of it."

He laughed. "Lucas, get her home as quickly as possible but as comfortably as possible. Avoid every bump you can along the way."

"Yes, I will," Lucas said.

Garland stepped forward and kissed me on the cheek.

"Good night, m'lovely," he said, then turned and headed for the library, strutting like some conquering hero.

"This way, miss," Lucas said. He took my left arm gently and led me through the long entryway and out to the carriage. After he had helped me get inside, he closed the door. I lay back on the seat, and when we started away with a rough jerk of the carriage, I lowered myself and closed my eyes. The rocking of the carriage and the sound of the horses galloping put me in a daze. I know I fell asleep, because when I looked out again, we were in Charlottesville. Sleep had been a blessing for sure.

The streets were very quiet and much darker because it was so late. After we reached my great-aunt's home, Lucas hurried to open the door and lower the step. He didn't let go of me when I stepped down, and he escorted me to the front door.

"Are you all right now, miss?" Lucas asked.

"Yes," I said. "Thank you."

He touched the brim of his hat and returned to the carriage. I entered the house slowly. It was very dark, and the living-room window curtains were still closed. I paused. Hazel hadn't left a light burning. Of course she wouldn't, not knowing I had left. Like a blind girl, I reached out and made my way to the stairs. There was some candlelight at the top, at least. Clinging to the shaky banister but trying not to put too much weight on it, I ascended, hoping it wouldn't shatter. I found my way to my room, but when I got there, I didn't pull back the comforter. I simply fell forward, almost diving into the bed, and almost instantly was in a very deep sleep.

I remained asleep until I felt someone touch my leg. For a few moments after I opened my eyes, I didn't know where I was. Then I heard Hazel ask, "Are you all right, dearie?"

I took a deep breath and turned over to look up at her. How much did she know? Did she hear me come up the stairs late at night? Did she realize I had left the house?

"Oh, hi, Hazel," I said, quickly putting my hand over my eyes. Bright light stung.

"My, my, you must have been tired. You didn't even take off your clothes or prepare your bed," she said. "How long did that gentleman caller keep you awake?"

I rubbed some life back into my face and sat up. She obviously hadn't realized I had left. Thank goodness for that, I thought.

"I don't remember," I said. "What time is it?"

"Oh, it's noon, at least," she said. "I made some hard-boiled eggs and have some nice bacon and my homemade bread for you." She leaned over to whisper, "Your great-aunt forgot you're here. She hasn't asked after you, so don't be surprised she's surprised when you come down."

"I know," I said. "Noon?"

"Maybe a little after."

"No one's come to ask about me?"

I remembered Garland had said he was coming by at noon. I imagined he was going to propose a lunch, maybe even a picnic. I envisioned him doing all that he could to make up for the terrible time I had experienced at Foxworth Hall. Now that I could think more about it, I realized I might have shared some of the blame. In any case, I thought I should give him a chance to apologize.

"No, missy," Hazel said. "I've set out some fresh towels for you in the loo. I mean bathroom," she quickly corrected. "Your aunt and I will be havin' lunch while you have breakfast. Think of it this way. She'll be delighted to see you all over again." She laughed and left.

I rose slowly, went to the window, and saw it was another beautiful day. Looking down at the street, I did not see Garland's beautiful carriage parked in front. The street looked as busy as it had when I arrived. My stomach felt as though I had swallowed pebbles. I racked my brain to remember the details of what had happened the night before. So much of it seemed vague, lost in the ether of my crippled memory. Rather than struggle with it further, I took out clothes to wear. As I had feared, it all looked so juvenile for me, especially now. But what else could I do? I couldn't wear *these* clothes. I didn't care to smell them. They were drowned in the odor of the limoncello and Garland's cigar. I was surprised Hazel hadn't noticed. Maybe she had but was too polite to ask about it.

I went down slowly, hearing my great-aunt

and Hazel talking in the living room, and went directly to the bathroom to wash. I stripped completely naked to clean my whole body. But no matter how hard I scrubbed, I still felt unclean. There was a spot of blood near my right knee. I could never claim it had all been a dream.

I dressed and brushed my hair. When I stepped out, my great-aunt and Hazel were sitting at the table.

"Everything's ready," Hazel said. "Know who this is, Nettie?" she asked my aunt.

"Is it . . ." She stopped and shook her head.

"It's Rosemary and Harrington's daughter, Corrine, here to visit. This is your great-niece, Corrine Dixon."

Great-aunt Nettie nodded. "Rosemary was always so shy," she said, probably misunderstanding and still thinking I was my mother. She looked at her food.

Hazel smiled and shrugged. "I made coffee. You like coffee?"

"Like it or not, I need it," I muttered, more to myself. My eyes were still aching. I pinched my temples between my thumb and fingers and pressed.

Hazel went into the kitchen to bring out the pot of coffee. Right now, that was all I wanted.

My great-aunt looked up at me. "Is my sister here, too?"

Her sister? My mother's mother?

"No, Aunt Nettie. Only I am here."

"No one comes here anymore," she said. "No one wants to see you when you're old. Do you know why?"

I shook my head. Somehow the sight of me was bringing back the power of whole sentences and thoughts for her.

"It reminds them of what they'll be. My mother told me that." She paused. "You ever see my mother?"

"No, Aunt Nettie. I'm too young to have seen your mother."

Hazel brought me a cup of hot coffee. "I heard her talking. That's the most she's said in a long time," she added, smiling. "Very nice that you've come to see her, dearie."

I sipped my coffee.

"There's a nice hard-boiled egg and some bacon."

How could I tell her I had no appetite because I had drunk too much of some European lemon drink full of alcohol? I nodded and began to nibble on the food. We heard a knock at the door.

He's come for me, I thought. How should I act? Should I be angry? Or forgiving?

"Now, I wonder who that could be?" Hazel asked me with a smile. "I'll go see, dearie. You eat," she said when I started to rise.

I sat again but turned to hear. The words were mumbled, and the door was closed quickly. I waited, holding my breath, expecting to see Garland, but Hazel returned alone and held out an envelope.

"A young man, the driver of a very fancy carriage, gave me this for you," she said.

"Thank you."

I took it slowly and opened it. There was a short note inside.

Dear Corrine,

I'm so sorry, but pressing business has called me away. Perhaps in the near future, you will return to Charlottesville, and I can show you Foxworth Hall in all its daytime splendor.

Until then . . .

Yours very sincerely,
Garland Foxworth

I read the note twice, because my brain would not accept the meaning of the words the first time. Then I folded it up neatly and put it back into the envelope.

"Good news or bad news?" Hazel asked.

"I'm not sure," I said. It was the best answer I could provide, both to myself and to her.

Right now, I didn't want to think about it.

I didn't want to think about anything.

7

The hours that passed after I ate as much as I could and excused myself from the table seemed to tick away more with the length of days instead of minutes. I returned to my closet of a bedroom and lay there staring up at the ceiling, with its chipped paint and cobwebs in the corners. Street sounds mixing the *clip-clop* of horses with people talking and shouting to each other, pans and tools clanging on the backs of wagons, and hawkers calling out their wares floated up and through the windows. I never realized how much I cherished the quiet interrupted only by the music of birds back home because our house was outside of the city proper.

Minutes continued to drip like leaky faucets from the roof's edges. I could hear Hazel downstairs, busy with my great-aunt, making her comfortable. Apparently, according to what Hazel had described, Great-aunt Nettie spent most of her day with bleak, dark eyes sinking deeper and deeper into her earliest memories. She sat in the living room, occasionally working her fingers to do what to anyone else would be her invisible needlework. Hazel told me that from time to time, she would ask questions about people who were long dead or talk about her husband as if he had just left for work. Sometimes she stood by the window, waiting for him to appear. It seemed like she was caught in the echo of time. The present didn't exist, and the future was as empty as another false promise. I would have had more sympathy for her if I wasn't feeling so sorry for myself.

I heard it grow silent downstairs, and then, moments after, Hazel came up to ask me if I wanted to go with her to do some shopping.

"Yes, I'll go. I promised my father I'd send him a telegram."

I was still undecided about what I would write, and I didn't want to tell Hazel what I was thinking yet.

"Oh, I'll take you right there. It's near the fish market," Hazel said.

Downstairs, my great-aunt had fallen asleep on the sofa, her head back against the cushion and her mouth open, resembling the mouth of someone suddenly amazed. Her chest lifted and fell like a fireplace bellows.

"Is she all right?" I asked.

"Oh yes. She'll be like that for hours," Hazel told me. "I lock the door behind me just in case she wakes and has some thoughts about goin' out. She'd get hit by a horse and carriage for sure or lose her way."

I was still feeling quite tired and depressed, probably just as much from my disappointment as from the amount of limoncello I had consumed. If I never saw another lemon, that would be too soon, I thought, no matter how wonderful Garland thought his discovery was.

Hazel and I left the house. As we walked through the streets, she talked about the old days, when my great-uncle was still alive and he and my great-aunt were such prominent people. She was obviously used to the noise and the dust. Anyone seeing her would think she acted like someone walking in a field of wildflowers, serenaded by a chorus of sparrows, robins, and bluebirds.

"If your uncle and aunt had lived in London, he'd have been knighted," she said. "Believe me that."

As she went on about it, I was surprised and amused by how proud of them she was and how honored to have been their housekeeper. I guess I shouldn't have been amazed. After all, how else would someone who came from her station in life have touched so much of the upper class? Even though it was difficult for me to imagine the house as busy and bright, hosting important dinners and visitors, she spoke of the Lloyds as if America did have royalty.

She described the time the governor of the state had stopped to visit and how, because of my great-uncle's influence and success, she had stood with my great-aunt to listen to a speech by President Grant.

"We were only twenty feet away. I never was that close to Queen Victoria. I can tell you that, dearie," she said.

She paused to point out the Western Union office.

"I'll be just down here," she said, nodding at the farmers' market.

"Thank you, Hazel."

I stepped in and went to the table where I could write my telegram. The moment I lifted the pen to write, I felt the tears welling up. There was no way to sugarcoat it; I was fleeing from romantic disappointment, something I had never dreamed would happen to me. I looked at the clerk, who was staring at me. He had a thick black mustache with almost no chin. He was nearly bald but, from the look of everything else about him, probably not a day over thirty, if that.

"Would you know the train schedule?" I asked.

He brightened with the opportunity to help me. "Where ya goin'?"

"Alexandria."

"Oh." He sifted through some papers and looked at a card. "Today?"

"Yes," I said.

"There's a train at four thirty and nothing else until tomorrow."

"Thank you," I said, rewarding him with one of my best smiles.

I turned back to my telegram and pondered

how to say this. I didn't want to write anything that would even hint about what had happened. Of course, there would be lots of questions. As far as my mother was concerned, I had made such a big thing of my coming here to visit my great-aunt Nettie that my immediate return would sharpen her curiosity but feather her suspicions. My father, of course, knew my real reasons. One way or another, I would have to face him with something of the truth. But not now, not in a telegram. *Just say it,* I thought, *as simply as possible.*

Dear Daddy,
    I'll be coming home on today's four thirty train.
                             Corrine

I handed it to the telegraph operator and paid him. Of course, he had to read it to send it, but he tried to make it look like he wasn't thinking about the words.

"You can watch me do it," he said after he took my money. "They'll be reading it on t'other end almost as soon as I send it."

Maybe he thought I was thinking he'd take my money and not send it or something, or maybe he just wanted me to be standing in front of him as long as he could get me to do it. I didn't think I looked particularly pretty today, but then again, I was probably one of those women who couldn't look unattractive to any man. He smiled, and I watched him.

"You coming back to Charlottesville, I hope," he said as he tapped out the words.

"Maybe for a funeral," I said, and his smile leaped off his face.

"Oh. Sorry about that," he said.

Not as sorry as I am, I thought, and walked out to find Hazel. I found her choosing some fish for dinner. She was talking so quickly and excitedly about how she was going to make it and her special mashed potatoes that I almost didn't have the heart to tell her what I was doing.

"And I'm doin' a pie for us, my apple pie with a secret ingredient. I brought that recipe from England," she added in a whisper, as if she thought someone would overhear it and claim it for her own.

"Don't buy too much or do too much, Hazel," I said. "I'm leaving on the four thirty to go home."

Her face seemed to regain years and lose every speck of hope and joy. "Why is that? You just arrived. After another day or two, your great-aunt might remember you without me introducin' you again and again. And she has so much stored up that she can tell you about your family, your mother's side, of course. She knows things no one else does, and there's nothin' as valuable to you as your own history, dearie."

I didn't want to tell her that my mother's family history held little interest for me. In fact, for me, nothing in the past mattered. It was only the future, my future, that commanded my thoughts and dreams. Right now, that future looked bleak again. It wouldn't be long before my mother would convince my father I should be married to this man or that. She cherished the idea that she would put me in the direction she chose. It was almost as if marriage was a prison sentence, and she, influencing my father to help make it happen as she wanted it to happen, was the judge and jury.

"The girl's not sensible enough to find the proper husband on her own," she'd say. I was like a playwright constructing my own drama, dialogues and all.

But I could say none of this to Hazel. My mother might contact her with a letter and ask horrible questions. Poor Hazel would be forced to write things she never would say.

"I know. And thank you for making me as comfortable as you could, Hazel."

Her face twisted with frustration. She tossed back the bigger fish she had chosen and nodded. "I don't need much, then," she said sadly, and finished her shopping quickly. She was quiet until we had started back to the house. "That man disappointed you?"

I was silent, but she heard my thoughts.

"Let's just say it hasn't turned out as I thought it might."

"Your aunt's maybe lost her wits, but her memory of the Foxworths might have done you good service," she said. She nodded to herself. "Probably a good thing you came and heard her, even if you haven't stayed much more than a day."

I wasn't going to make her feel better about it by saying I'd be back soon. I had no doubt Hazel would see through a false promise better than I could. She had probably lived through tons of them, growing up poor and being someone's servant from the moment she could lift a washcloth. I wondered what would become of her the day after my great-aunt's funeral, which was probably a day rising on the horizon like the morning sun.

"Do you have any family left in England, Hazel?"

"I have a younger sister who works for a Lord Appleby in Oxford. He and his wife live in a large manor house with ten bedrooms. We have an understandin' that I'd return when the time came and help her with her duties. You young people don't put as much value on it these days, but family is the best gold you'll find. It takes some almost all their lives to realize it," she added. "And by then, it's usually too late. Worst thing on God's green earth is dyin' alone."

My abrupt leaving obviously had opened the door to dark thoughts and memories for her. I felt more guilty about that than anything.

My great-aunt's house came into view. Maybe because of what had happened, it looked more dilapidated and run-down than it had when I arrived.

"If you want, you can leave your clothes for me to wash, and I'll have them shipped home."

"Oh no," I said, maybe too sharply, but I was worried about a bloodstain.

She didn't say anything until we reached the front door. "While you're gettin' your things together, I'll send a boy to fetch you a carriage taxi to take you to the station," she said.

"Thank you, Hazel. I will miss you."

She glanced at me with a face full of skepticism, a face that said, *Don't bother with that. I've swum my way through lies of every kind.* I wondered how long it would be before I added her expression to my own catalog of telling looks. I was that miserable about myself. It clung to every part of my body like honey would if I had bathed in it, but there was nothing sweet about this feeling, nothing at all.

Without much to pack, I had my bag ready quickly and started down the stairs. Hazel was sitting with my great-aunt, who had just woken but was still dazed from her sleep. When she looked at me, she wasn't surprised, but she didn't show any signs of recognition, either. It was as if she was looking through me.

"Your carriage just arrived," Hazel said. She was holding my great-aunt's hand. "I just started to tell her you were leavin'."

"I'm sorry I have to go so soon, Aunt Nettie. I'll try to come back."

"Rosemary's daughter's leavin', Nettie."

Her eyes widened as she became more fully awake. "When Rosemary was a little girl, she broke her finger climbing a tree. My sister wanted to give her a whipping, but her husband wouldn't hear of it. Rosemary loved her daddy, but she didn't have him long, and she was as jealous as a Barbary pigeon."

Hazel smiled. "She does that on and off these days, remembers things way back and spins them out and then doesn't talk for hours. You gotta be around to scoop them up. She can't hold a pen long, or I'd have her write some of it down."

"Who was she jealous of?" I asked, now truly curious.

Hazel looked at my great-aunt, who was just staring at me now. "Who else," Hazel asked me, answering for her, "but other girls who had their fathers to love and have them love them?"

It was as if a curtain had been opened a little. Hazel was right. Family history was important. It could help you realize who you were and who your parents really were. But right now, I

170

didn't want to think about it. I wanted to forget I was here. Nevertheless, I put down my bag and hugged my great-aunt, who looked at me with surprise and delight.

"She'll talk about her sister all day now," Hazel said, rising to walk me to the door and then out to the waiting taxi. The driver had taken my bag and started to help me in when Hazel reached out for my arm.

"When you have a bad memory, Corrine, you think of dippin' a spoon into the ocean. Don't hold the memory long. Drop it back in, and tell yourself you'll never find that spoonful again. That's what my daddy taught me."

She hugged me, and I got into the carriage. As we pulled away, she nodded, waved, and then turned to go back into my great-aunt's house, where my great-aunt waited to spin her memories like pieces of a puzzle, a puzzle she would never finish. Even so, I was still feeling sorrier for myself.

Once I was on the train and looking out the window, I couldn't help my wishful imaginings. In my fantasy, Garland, realizing how upset I was, went to my great-aunt's house and found out I had just left. He whipped his horses and came running to the train station. As soon as he set eyes on me, he apologized and begged me to stay, offering to buy me new dresses and shoes. Of course, I would get off the train. He'd have a wonderful dinner for us at Foxworth Hall. He'd hire musicians to play for us while we ate and the piano player to play his new piano in the ballroom afterward. Everyone would be working harder to please me. I'd be treated like a queen.

When the train jerked and started forward, I was still imagining my romantic scene. I didn't look back, however, and soon my eyes were closing, and I was feeling tired again. I fell asleep quickly. At one point, the train rocked harder than usual, and I woke. Other passengers looked concerned and frightened, but whatever had caused it passed, and the remainder of the ride was uneventful.

My father was waiting for me at the station in Alexandria. I knew from the expression on his face that he was upset. He took my bag without saying hello or hugging me and walked out to his carriage. I got in quickly, and he started away. It wasn't until then that he began to speak.

"What turned you around so soon?" he asked.

I quickly decided to blame it all on the house and Great-aunt Nettie's condition.

"Hazel had to keep reminding her who I was. The guest room was disgusting. There were spiders in the dresser drawers. I didn't take my clothes out of my bag. They have no hot water most of the time. The ceiling in my room looked like it might fall in on me."

"What are you not telling me, Corrine?" he

asked sharply. "It's better you tell it all to me before we get home and your mother starts asking you questions. She may look oblivious at times, but she's keen."

"I didn't like Charlottesville. It's too busy," I added.

He shook his head. "You saw Garland Foxworth, didn't you? We both know that was your chief reason for going there. Well?"

"Yes. He came to see me late yesterday, and we talked in the living room. It was embarrassing to bring anyone in there, much less a man as wealthy as he is who lives in what's practically a castle."

"So you went to his home?"

"No," I said, probably too quickly. "He promised to come by at noon today to take me there and give me a tour, but he sent a messenger instead to say he was called away on business and wouldn't see me while I was at Great-aunt Nettie's. He wrote that maybe he could do that some other time," I added, not hiding my bitterness. At least, this part was true.

"Is that all of it?"

"Yes," I said.

I wasn't fond of lying to my father, but I couldn't tell him about the night before. I certainly couldn't tell my mother. I had no one to tell, no one to confide in who would sympathize. I wouldn't even tell Daisy, who would be shocked and worried that if something like this could happen to me, what would happen to her? Any of my other girlfriends would luxuriate in my discomfort. I knew how jealous of me they were and how happy they would be learning I had been seduced. *Drugged* was more the way I saw it. Drinking all that limoncello was as damaging as smoking opium, not that I had ever done that. I had just read about it and heard stories about young girls who were sexually assaulted in those dens of sin. How was it any different for me? Where had I been if not in a den of sin that just happened to be located in a great family mansion?

My father glanced at me and then looked forward, silent all the rest of the way home. I couldn't remember a time when I felt more miserable. As I anticipated, my mother practically pounced when I walked in the door. She came flying out of the living room, ready to pin some crime on my chest.

"Well? What did you do to upset my aunt?"

"What? I didn't do anything to upset her. Who said that?"

"No one has to say it, Corrine. You were so determined to visit her and made light of any of my warnings about her condition, Hazel's, and her home. So what happened if they didn't ask you to leave after spending only one night? Did you make fun of them, criticize them, mock the condition of the house, and make them feel terrible?"

My father stood behind me, waiting to see what I would say to her.

I put down my bag and started to cry. He didn't come over to hug me or save me from my mother's burning glare, however, so I took a deep breath and wailed through my words, hopefully putting on the most convincing act I could.

"You were right. I should have listened to you. It was worse than you described. The guest bedroom was more disgusting than . . . than a woodshed. There were spiders and cobwebs and mouse droppings. I couldn't bathe because they were having trouble with their burners, and my great-aunt . . ."

"What?"

"She doesn't know where she is. Without Hazel, she would starve or wander off and die in a ditch," I added. "It wasn't any sort of holiday for me. I was afraid to breathe. The room I was in probably hadn't been used for years and years. I opened the window, but I couldn't get rid of the smells, and all the dust from the street came flowing in. I think maybe something died in that room recently," I added. "How would they know? Why didn't I listen to you? I promise, though, I didn't say anything about any of that. I think Hazel assumed I was just bored. I'm not used to old people."

She looked satisfied, especially since she was

being proven right. She took a deep breath and nodded. Now she was feeling sorry for me.

"I told your father not to let you go, but no one listens to me in this house. Go give yourself a nice bath and rest," she said. It felt like any moment she was going to bless me like the pope because I had confessed.

I picked up my bag and started for the stairway.

"You can leave your clothes to be washed. Bugs could have crawled into that bag and will escape into this house."

"Oh no, I don't think . . ."

She put her hands on her hips. "Harrington?"

"Do as your mother asks, Corrine. I'm going to see to the horses."

It was difficult to look at him, because I could see he knew I was holding something back from him as well. Who knew me better than he did? I nodded and dropped the bag.

"Have you eaten anything?" my mother asked.

"Very little."

"Then maybe you should come down after your bath and have something before you go to sleep. Wash your hair," she added. "Bed bugs can burrow into your head."

I wasn't thinking of all this, but now that she had brought it up, I felt even sicker. I had passed out last night. Anything could have crawled through my hair without my having realized it. Wash my hair I would, and vigorously, too.

My father left, and I started up the stairs. I glanced back to see my mother pick up the bag, but holding it away from herself as if touching it would contaminate her. That was good. She would probably close her eyes, pinch my clothes, and drop them into a basin to wash them. An hour later, I was drying my hair. I was still not very hungry, but for now, I didn't want to disobey anything my mother had told me to do.

When I went down to eat, she had more detailed questions to ask me. My father was already retired to the living room to read his business news.

"They weren't living like paupers, were they? There was enough food and such?"

"Yes, and Hazel is still a very good cook. She baked us a golden rod cake."

"I remember. My uncle was well-to-do, but like most women unschooled in the value of things, my aunt let most of their fortune slip through her fingers after my uncle died. Your father did his best to help her. Frankly, I'm surprised Hazel has stayed with her this long."

"Oh no, she loves Great-aunt Nettie."

She smirked. My mother always thought the worst of people first. Right now, I was thinking she might be right to be that way.

"Didn't Aunt Nettie say anything sensible?"

"She mentioned your mother occasionally and told me about when you once broke your finger."

"She remembered that?"

"Hazel says she remembers the first fifteen or so years of her life better than yesterday. You never talk that much about your parents," I said. "Especially your father."

"I talked enough about them," she replied, and began to put things away.

I went right up to my room, not even stopping in the living room to say good night to my father. I couldn't remember ever feeling this tired and was happy to sleep in my clean bed with my oversized soft pillows.

No one bothered me the following morning, even though I had slept until nearly noon. When I finally dressed and went down to the kitchen, my mother was already outside with her two best friends, describing my trip and elaborating with her own details. After all, to them, I was headline news.

"Young women today just don't have the common sense we had," I heard her say. "The best thing that could happen to my daughter is someone responsible and decent decides to ask her to be his wife. I swear, she exhausts me, and my husband is just too busy to realize what I endure. Children should be born older so you don't have so much trouble getting them to become responsible adults."

Of course, Louise Francis and Etta Benjamin completely agreed with her and expressed their sympathies. I was sinking into a deep funk and thought I would just spend the whole day in my room with the door shut. But as I was going back upstairs, I heard a knock on our front door. My first, hopeful thought was I was receiving a telegram from Garland, who had discovered I had fled from Charlottesville and was feeling very guilty. I was still debating with myself whether or not I would forgive him.

It was as if there really were good and bad angels, one of each on my left and right shoulders, whispering in my ears. The bad angel told me Garland Foxworth, no matter what his faults, was still the most exciting and best-looking man I had ever met. Whether I had drunk the limoncello or not, I'd have wanted to make love with him, wouldn't I? I just wanted it to be more romantic. Well, couldn't that happen the next time? The good angel stressed I was violated and reminded me how rough the sex had been. That wasn't gentle and loving, but the bad angel said, "You liked it. Deep down, you liked it."

Did I?

Thinking about this caused me to move slower to the door. Whoever it was knocked harder. This had to be important, I thought.

But it was only Elsie Daniels and Emma Lawrence, who had ridden their bikes over to my house. They both were wearing divided skirts, having convinced their parents to buy them for them after they had seen me wearing one.

"What?" I asked instead of saying hello. The sight of them was too much of a letdown.

"We came by to see if you wanted to go with us to Bessie Raymond's house," Elsie said. "Her cousin Arthur is visiting, and we remembered how handsome you thought he was. He's in his first year at Penn State, and he's on the football team. We asked Daisy to come, but her mother has her doing chores in the house."

Emma's smile reminded me of a splattered egg. I imagined how they gossiped about me on the way over to my house. Nevertheless, I pondered the possibility. I had seen Arthur Raymond two years ago, and like most of the boys who first met me, he spent most of the time talking to me. His mother was from Dublin, and he had her striking kelly-green eyes, rust-brown hair, and what I thought was a very sexy smile because of his firm lips. He was easily six feet tall, with very manly shoulders. It wasn't until after he had left that I remarked about him, because I saw how jealous the other girls were of his attention to me.

"He's good-looking," I had said, but made it sound so casual that no one bothered even to attempt to tease me.

"He asked after you almost as soon as he arrived, Bessie says," Elsie said.

"Did he?" I said with almost no enthusiasm.

Their smiles wilted.

"Well, you did say he was good-looking," Emma practically bellowed with frustration.

"Good-looking is not enough as far as I'm concerned. I don't expect to have interest in any boy who isn't. When you realize that there has to be a lot more, you're an adult. Children have crushes; young women have flings with young men, not boys. I haven't thought of Arthur since he left."

One thing I would never need, no matter what had just happened to me, was other girls finding me beaus.

They looked disappointed. They had probably promised him they would bring me over this afternoon. It made them seem more important, and they could enjoy a romance vicariously.

"But I'm bored, so I'll come," I said, rescuing their smiles. "I'll go change."

I closed the door on them so they knew I wasn't going to invite them in and up to my room to watch me get into my cycling clothes, fix my hair, and maybe put some tint on my cheeks. Then again, I thought the bike ride would bring enough of a flush to them. For a little while, this felt like some sort of vengeance I was taking out on Garland. I could easily go on with my life and simply forget him, forget what had happened, and never give it another thought. But then I told myself what my mother often told me: *The easiest person to lie to is yourself.*

When I came down again, my mother had put up some tea for her friends and saw me in my divided skirt.

"And where are you going?"

"With my friends to visit Bessie Raymond. It's only a little over a mile."

"Well, you be home before dark," she said, and was suddenly suspicious. "I thought you were still exhausted from your horrible experience. You complained about the train ride so much the railroad would pay to lock you up and keep you from talking about it."

"Being home has revived me," I said.

She looked at me skeptically but nodded.

Elsie and Emma leaped to their feet when I stepped out. They had been lying on the lawn.

"We were beginning to think you weren't coming," Emma said.

"Well, here I am. I just don't jump into my clothes and go out. Let me get my cycle."

I took it from the shed, and we started cycling. It was a relatively easy ride, with just a few small hills. For most of it, we pedaled side by side, even though they both had trouble keeping up with me.

"Have you seen that man you danced with at the Wexler gala?" Elsie asked.

I saw the way she glanced at Emma. So this was really their motive for coming to get me, I thought, more gossip and more inside information about my love life.

"No," I said. I would never tell these two anything close to the truth. "Nor did I expect to. Men like that are like shooting stars. Now you see them, now you don't. You certainly don't let them break your heart or give them a chance to disappoint you."

"He looked much older than us," Emma said. "That's what surprised us when we saw you together."

"I don't think I look that young, especially not at the Wexler gala."

"You didn't, but he still looked a lot older."

"So what?" I said. "Do older men frighten you? Do they make you squeeze your knees together?"

They both giggled.

"That's not so funny. Older men want to do more with you right away," Elsie said with the authority of someone who had been there.

"Oh, so you've been with older men and know all about their sexual desires?"

"Noooo!" she exclaimed. "I mean, not that much older."

"So, you really will never see him again?" Emma asked.

"Why is that so important to you?"

"Just curious."

"Curiosity killed the cat," I said.

They both giggled again, never sounding more like children.

I felt like turning around and going home.

"What if you did see him again?" Elsie asked. "What would you do if you and he were alone like you were in the Wexlers' garden?"

So this was it, they wanted to live some excitement through me. Why was I not surprised?

"I might say, 'Hello, how are you?' Or 'What took you so long to come calling?'"

Another giggle.

"And then what?" Emma asked.

"I'd make him take me somewhere expensive and spend a lot of his money on me."

"He'd want something in return for that," Elsie said. "Older men don't just flirt."

"So?"

"How far would you go with a man?" Emma asked.

I knew this was the main question. It would make their day to hear the answer.

"How far?" I pedaled silently, as if I was thinking hard about it.

They both were paying so much attention they nearly bumped into each other.

"Yes, how far?" Elsie said.

"I think Charlottesville," I said.

"What?"

The bad angel was laughing on my shoulder.

I sped up, now giggling to myself and leaving them behind in more ways than one.

8

Arthur Raymond had become even better-looking, but it would always be in a pretty-boy way, with his long eyelashes, his perfect but soft lips, and his attractive kelly-green eyes that had never looked as innocent and vulnerable to me. His hair was shaped and shiny like hair just washed, probably for my benefit. It looked like he had spent more time on his coiffure than most of us girls. Since he had begun college, he had manicured fingernails and the posture of a military cadet. He rushed to greet me with a "So pleased to see you again, Corrine. How are you?" He sounded like he had memorized a page out of *The Correct Thing in Good Society*, one of my mother's other bibles.

Ordinarily, a girl like me would appreciate a boy who conducted himself so politely and respectfully, but for a reason I couldn't fathom, his well-mannered way annoyed me at the moment. Maybe I was comparing him to Garland; maybe I would always do that. Maybe every man I met from now until forever would be similarly doomed.

We sat on Bessie Raymond's back porch. Her father, who was a stationmaster, tinkered with carpentry as a hobby and had built a swing seat with a bright blue cushioned bottom and back. Arthur quickly offered it to me, with the obvious intent to sit beside me. None of the other three would have dared taken it anyway. I sat, and Bessie brought out lemonade. I felt my stomach churn at the sight of it. I was the only one who declined and asked for just water.

Emma and Elsie might as well have sat at Arthur's feet, I thought. They were wide-eyed and painfully obvious, exaggerating their "oohs" and "ahs" with every claim Arthur made about his good grades and achievements on the football field. He constantly watched for my reactions, hoping to impress me most of all, but I was sure I looked totally uninterested, because I was.

While Arthur spoke in his silvery perfect English, describing his college classes, his dormitory, and college social events, I found myself drifting back to images of Foxworth Hall, its silhouetted roofline against the night sky, and Garland's firm, arrogant pride about its charm and power. Maybe it was because all the boys I had been with and even the young men I had met at dinners and events with my parents put me on a pedestal, rushing to satisfy my smallest desire. Now Garland's really at times impolite, gruff, and aggressive ways seemed more manly to me and thus, ironically, more attractive. Despite what had happened or maybe because of it, I never felt like he saw me as a young girl instead of a young woman. He had confessed it himself: he thought I was more worldly, which I knew meant more sexually sophisticated. I was; I just wasn't ready for how fast it all happened.

I assumed that any other woman, especially any of these three girls, would probably have concentrated on and emphasized how she was seduced. She would be moaning, "Poor me." Garland would be seen as a criminal, easily a rapist, but I was thinking now that I honestly shared a large part of the blame. In fact, I could see him claiming I had seduced him and not vice versa. Maybe I was straining to find a way to forgive him. Perhaps I was being a fool, but I honestly couldn't help it. I even imagined his response to the accusations.

"She fooled me, tempted me, brought me to the brink, and for a man balancing himself on that cliff, there was no other way to go."

What would be my defense if I really wanted a defense? Hadn't I let him kiss me at the Wexler gala after I had gone into the garden with him unchaperoned, leading him to believe I was more worldly? I did write to him and eagerly await his response. I encouraged him to pursue me, didn't I? When I was there, I did agree to rush off to Foxworth Hall without telling anyone. I did willingly drink the limoncello. I did sneak back into my great-aunt's house, and afterward, I told no one anything. I envisioned a jury made up of

187

all my mother's stiff-faced friends and spinsters scowling at me and pointing their long, bony fingers when they shouted, "Guilty!"

Get over it, Corrine, I told myself. Maybe now you really can claim to be a woman of the world. Isn't that what you always wanted to be? So it came a little sooner than you anticipated and not exactly how you had dreamed it would come—so what? You'll never see Garland again. You can live with it. There'll be other Garlands, won't there? Maybe none will be as wealthy and none will come accompanied by a Foxworth Hall, but there's surely someone out there, rich and powerful, who will want you beside him, and now, now you will know exactly what switches to throw and what levers to pull.

Of course, I still would be successful when it came to romance and marriage. How could I doubt it? I envisioned my own gilded horse and carriage, having miles of closets filled with the latest fashions, and having servants at my beck and call. There would be galas and dinner parties and lots of jewelry. Oh yes, there would be diamonds and gold practically dripping off my neck and wrists and covering my fingers. I'd make Lucy Wexler look like a pauper. I could practically hear the music and feel myself doing that waltz again.

"Corrine?" I heard. The voice sounded far off. "Corrine!"

"What?"

I looked at the others, who were staring at me as if I had done something terrible, as if they had heard my thoughts and knew what had happened at Foxworth. For a moment, I did think I had been speaking aloud. They continued to stare.

"What?" I practically screamed.

"Arthur just asked you how you intended to spend most of your summer," Bessie said, scowling as if ignoring a question from Arthur was akin to treason.

I looked at her, at Emma and Elsie and then at Arthur, who was smiling but more like someone who was embarrassed he had been caught with such interest in me. It was painfully clear to them all that I hadn't heard a word he had just said, maybe none of what he was saying. What was a more recognizable way of telling someone that you had no interest in him than totally disregarding him while he was working so hard at being attractive and interesting to you?

"Oh. I have no idea right now. I'm waiting on an invitation from Queen Victoria to visit her at Windsor," I added.

"What?" Emma said.

Elsie giggled uncomfortably.

Bessie swung her eyes, and Arthur's smile wilted.

I stood up. "I'm sorry, everyone. I've got to go home. Sorry to rush out, but I just remembered that I promised my mother I would sift through

189

my wardrobe today and sort out the clothes I no longer want or need. We're going to present our annual gift to the Salvation Army.

"So," I said, turning to him, "to answer your question, Arthur, I'll probably spend a lot of time this summer replacing things, and we have been talking about a trip to the beach. I've also been thinking about taking private painting lessons, too. My father says I doodle so much that I might as well see if I can sell one."

Arthur stood. "I'd be happy to borrow Bessie's bike and escort you home, Corrine."

"How gallant, but I find I go faster when I don't carry on a conversation while cycling. To most, it's a social event. To me, it's merely another means of transportation and some good exercise. Besides, it would be cruel of me to take you away from your devoted audience. I'll catch up when I see you all again. Good luck with your football, Arthur," I said. I couldn't help but make it sound like something insignificant, even childish.

He looked at the others and then said, "Thank you," but weakly, his disappointment so obvious that it could bring someone more susceptible to it to tears.

" 'Bye."

I hurried around Bessie's house to my bicycle and started away, pedaling more like someone fleeing the scene of a crime than someone merely going home.

I'm changed, I thought. Months ago, I would have loved being the center of attention for my friends, but everything felt different. Was it for the better? A year ago, I would have easily permitted Arthur to escort me, if for no other reason than putting icing on the cake of jealousy the other girls baked. I'd string him along and enjoy watching how hard he was trying to get me to care about him.

Now all that appeared so childish to me. Almost everything I was doing with these friends this afternoon seemed beneath me. I had outgrown them all practically overnight. Conversations with my girlfriends, even my best friend, Daisy, now loomed like clouds stuffed with words of the immature. I would drown in boredom, as I just nearly did moments ago. I wasn't joking when I suggested I might take lessons in art. It was something I could do alone. Right now, there wasn't a friendship or a prospect of one among my peers that appealed to me, even having someone at my side who adored me. All that seemed to be in the very distant past.

I hadn't lied about sorting through my clothes, however. I had returned from Charlottesville years older. I wanted to rid my closet of anything and everything that looked juvenile. I glanced at blouses and skirts, petticoats and stockings, and then tossed on the floor everything I thought was ridiculous. I wasn't left with much and thought I would work on my father to allow me to buy new things for daily life.

Later, when I descended to help my mother prepare our dinner, I decided my wardrobe was going to be the top of our talk. I had all my new arguments prepared, but my father stole the stage by announcing he was starting on the construction of a new house.

"It's going to have all the new modern appliances and be twice the size of this one. I've bought acres of land across from the Fieldings' house on Garden Grove."

"Twice the size?" my mother exclaimed. "And I'm to take care of such a monster?"

"Oh no. We're going to have more household help."

"Can we afford all that?" she asked.

He smiled and looked at me as if I should have known. "Yes. I've made some investments of late that have boosted our net worth, and there is talk about our having a new chairman of the board. I think you might be looking at him. Early indications are that I have the necessary votes."

"You're taking my breath away, Harrington," my mother said.

"No worries, Rosemary. I have a prospective buyer for this house," my father continued. "There are so many new things to modernize our new home. I'll be explaining and describing it all to you, Rosemary."

"Exactly how big will this new house be?"

"You'll be delighted to know it will be at least three thousand square feet bigger than this house. In fact, it will be one of the biggest in Alexandria," he declared proudly.

But not the biggest in Charlottesville, I thought, probably the size of a few closets put together in Foxworth Hall.

Nevertheless, I decided to take advantage of my father's buoyant mood and brought up the subject of my wardrobe.

"You introduced me to society, but I still have the everyday clothing of a little girl."

"Yes, you do need new clothes," he said.

At the moment, I thought I could ask for the moon and he would buy the ladder to reach it.

My mother turned from me to my father and shook her head. She looked like she was going to burst into tears. "All these changes coming so fast. I am losing my breath. It makes my heart palpitate."

"Now, now, Rosemary, nothing is happening overnight. It seems like Corrine has become a young woman in a matter of hours, but we both know it's been happening for some time. I'll set aside some money for a charge account at Hester's. They're one of our best bank customers. I think maybe all of us could use some new everyday things. I can't have my girls looking ordinary with all this on the horizon. Appearances when we step up to this level are very important, as the Wexlers have shown us."

"I was thinking of having some private art lessons this summer, Daddy," I said, deciding to push my advantage. "I'd like to do something sensible with my time."

"Sensible?" my mother said. "You call wasting money on some passing fancy like art sensible? We've been discussing you while you were away on this fruitless, wasteful trip to Charlottesville. Your father has a better suggestion when it comes to your time." She looked to him and nodded, giving him the floor.

I turned to my father. Somehow his talking about me seemed like a betrayal. I was the one with whom he kept secrets, not my mother.

"Which is more reason for you to have an improved wardrobe, Corrine," he said quickly, to lessen the impact of whatever boulder they were launching in my direction.

"What?" I asked, now the one who was taking deep breaths.

"I'd like you to come work at the bank. I have an opening for a receptionist. You'll greet customers looking to open accounts and get loans. My secretary will educate you in the basic information, and you'll direct the prospective customer to the right person. You'll make some money to continue buying yourself some nice things and on the way learn about financial matters. More women are getting involved in the business world today. You might take to it."

"And you'll meet young men who have established themselves," my mother added. "What clearer way to judge than a fat bank account?"

I could feel the blood rising up my neck to my face. This was her true purpose. She, they, would arrange my future after all. My mind raked through the images and memories of young men my father thought were up-and-coming businessmen, sons of well-to-do ones as well. If boring was a color, they'd be dressed in it.

"I don't think I'll like that," I said.

"Of course you will," my mother insisted. "It's your father's livelihood, and from what he's telling us, even more so. Why wouldn't you want to learn more about it?"

I looked at him. She was forcing me into a corner. If I refused to do it, I could hurt my father's feelings. He obviously liked the idea of my being the first face his prospective customers would meet. That was very pleasing to him, especially if he really was in the running to be the new bank board chairman. How could I be so selfish as to not share my natural beauty, use it to his advantage, and thus make a real contribution toward our family?

"You heard him," my mother pressed. "He's building us a new house, and he said he was willing to get you new, more attractive clothes, clothes suited to a young woman with some stature. Are you still a child, or are you ready to do something very adult? Does it scare you, despite how much you claim you've matured, Corrine?"

"I'm not saying I'm afraid," I said. "I just don't know if I'm going to be good enough. I don't want to embarrass Daddy."

"Not possible," he said, beaming.

"I'm horrible at math."

"You don't have to add or subtract a thing, Corrine. You'll just learn the descriptions and the simple information to start the process and pass the customer on. It has nothing to do with running numbers. If someone asks you more detailed questions, you'll simply tell him all his questions will be answered by the officer of the bank he'll meet. I'll take you to work with me every morning and bring you home."

"When?"

"Shall we say in two weeks? You can do your shopping within that time. Your mother will help you again, because she herself will be looking for new things. Rosemary?"

"Yes," she said. "Of course."

Probably none of the new fashion I had envisioned for myself would meet her standards, but the new shirtwaists with high collars and a waist tailored more like a man's shirt were being worn by working women. I had no tight bodice or a skirt gathered at the waist, either. I wanted those clothes, but I didn't want the work that accompanied them.

"I don't understand any of your hesitation. You never stop badgering that you want us to treat you more like a young woman than a young girl," my mother said, sitting in her pool of self-satisfaction. For once, she believed she had successfully manipulated me. "Well, now you will have your wish. Your childhood friends who you always complain are too juvenile will peel away."

She folded her arms across her breasts and sat back. I was losing any resistance, and she knew it.

"Both your father and I were quite impressed with how you handled your short visit with Aunt Nettie. You traveled on your own and managed what you saw as difficulties. We have new confidence in you," she added. It felt like she was throwing me a bone.

Managed? If she only knew, I thought, but I thanked her. To do otherwise would have raised new questions.

"I can't say I'm not saddened to see my little girl fade away. We wish, as you will someday, that children could remain innocent and without the trials and tribulations of adult life, all especially difficult for a woman today with the added baggage of being a good wife and managing a home. But time is a great thief, probably the greatest," she said sadly.

My father looked close to tears himself.

There was no doubt in my mind from where I had inherited my dramatic powers. I was convinced she had been rehearsing this speech in her mind many times for years and probably dreamed of delivering it just like this every night. I looked at my father again. Now he was smiling and nodding. I felt like someone falling with nothing to reach out to and grab to break my descent. At least I would get in some defiance, I thought.

"I'm not going to wear clothes that make me look like some old hag."

"You'd better not," my father said, still smiling. "It's not whom I want new customers to see when they enter my bank."

I glanced at my mother.

The battle was set, at least. I'd make the best of it.

Nevertheless, after dinner, I went up to my room to pout. I started on my diary again. I had so much to tell it, from my visit to my great-aunt to Garland to this. Never did I write with such frenzy. Finally, the words came easily.

When I looked at what I had written, I realized I had mentioned Garland or something about him on almost every page. What, I wondered, would my rendezvous with him at Foxworth Hall have been like if I hadn't drunk much or almost none of that limoncello? Would I have been more coy, fought harder to preserve my innocence? Would he have had more respect for me at the end of the evening? Wouldn't he surely have appeared the following day to continue his courting? Now I felt like nothing more than another one of his romantic castaways adrift on a sea of her own regrets. And look at the future my parents were spreading before me.

I closed my diary and put it in the bottom drawer of my dresser. Why, I wondered, was I bothering with it? Was it because I had no one to confide in but myself? Somehow, as was maybe true for most young women my age, a diary did become the ears of someone else. After a while, it was no longer like talking to yourself. The one thing I remembered my paternal grandfather telling me before he died was "If you talk to yourself, you'll never be lonely."

It was true. The diary took on a life of its own. Every night when I thought about it or looked at the drawer, I imagined it was pondering my words, my confessions, and my dreams. One day I would take it out and there would be pages and pages automatically filled in, all with advice and wisdom. It would tell me things my mother never had and never would. It would be my magic mother.

It would eventually answer the biggest question I had: how do you separate the fantasy wishes of a young girl from the realistic and possible plans of a young woman? Night after night, I tossed and turned, struggling with the answer. I hated the way I looked in the morning. I hated the windows into a troubled mind that my eyes had become. Neither my father nor my mother appeared to notice any difference, however. My father thought I was worried about starting this new job in his bank, and my mother surely thought I was hating the thought of it. She looked so satisfied, which made me feel sicker.

Maybe because of my heavy, joyless demeanor, she didn't argue very much about my choice of everyday clothes. The salesladies reassured her and supported my choices, which obviously helped. I built my new wardrobe with the purpose being that I'd have something new and fresh to wear every workday. I bought new shoes and a fancy new hat to wear to and from work as well. The following week, my father surprised me at dinner with a new watch. It was a Waltham jeweled pocket watch in a gold case. My mother was far more stunned at the sight of it than I was. Watches weren't exactly at the top of my wish list.

"Harrington, what was the cost of such a thing?"

"The cost is a business investment, Rosemary. When Corrine takes out her timepiece to tell a customer the time, I want him to be impressed even more with the quality of our employees. Take good care of it, Corrine," he said, pushing it toward me. "Mark the time. In two days, you'll be opening the bank with me at nine a.m."

"Thank you, Daddy," I said, but not with the enthusiasm my mother wanted to see.

She grimaced, grunted, and rose from the table. "I do hope all this investment in clothes, shoes, and now an expensive watch has the results we expect," she muttered.

"I'm sure it all will," my father said, smiling at me.

I smiled back, but he would have had to be an oaf not to see how empty it was.

Despite what my mother had thought and how I had behaved toward the idea, I wasn't at all afraid of working at the bank. From the way my father had described my duties and reinforced that description in the morning on the way in, I saw myself as nothing more than window dressing. If my father wasn't the president of the bank and a potential candidate for board chairman, this position for me surely wouldn't exist. Actually, as we rode into Alexandria and I sat back in my new clothes with my new and very fashionable small blue bonnet, I grew more excited about my being the prettiest female in the bank. My father said I would sit at a desk quite prominent to anyone entering.

Even those men who had no need to speak to me would find a way to do so, I thought. It would be difficult, but I would try very hard to be modest and sound as if I had been working in banks and similar institutions for years.

Every female employee stopped what she was doing to look at me when we entered. My father's secretary, one of my mother's widowed friends, Mrs. Emma Stone, rushed to greet us, pouring her saccharine welcome over me with embarrassing exaggeration.

"Oh, how nice you look and so grown-up. I confess I couldn't believe it when your father told me his plans for you. I've made sure to have one of our nicest desks brought out for you and, as you can see, placed in a perfect part of our lobby. I'll go over all the options you can suggest and offer new customers with the proper referrals clearly delineated," she said, her eyes moving off me to my father on almost every other word. "You mustn't be afraid to ask me anything. Nothing is too small."

She paused to take a deep breath. I thought she reeked of some heavy rosewater scent. How could my father tolerate it? I wondered. She tried to take my hand to lead me to my desk, but I recoiled so sharply she could only widen her smile, nod at my father, and lead the way.

My nameplate was on the desk, with the words *Bank Receptionist and Information* printed below my name. There were small piles of paper describing different types of loans, savings accounts, and checking accounts. She asked me to sit first. I suspected she was testing to see how I would do so. Would I, like some young girl, slump in my chair or sit up with dignity? I didn't need any lessons. I sat quietly while she reviewed the information. When I didn't ask a question, she asked if she was going too fast.

"Not at all," I said.

I gave her my best false smile, and she continued. She ended just as the bank's doors were opening.

"Good luck," she said, and hurried away. I sat back, aware that everyone in the bank was still looking at me. Some other girl would be intimidated, I thought, but having eyes drawn to my face magnetically was something I was quite accustomed to experiencing.

My only fear was utter boredom.

As it turned out, I had no reason to be afraid of long, empty moments. There was hardly a single male customer who didn't stop by to greet me and be greeted. When I glanced over to my right to where my father sat, I saw his proud smile. Wouldn't it be something, I thought, if Garland Foxworth entered this bank unaware that I would be the first person upon whom he would set sight? Just imagining it brought a softer, happier smile to my face. Many other young men, many who were already married, misinterpreted it as showing romantic interest in them. Those men stopped to talk on the way out as well.

But as good-looking and as obviously established and successful as some were, none caused my heart to flutter the way Garland Foxworth first had that night at the Wexler gala. I guessed what I feared was coming true. I was doomed to judge and compare him to anyone I met forever and maybe never find a man who would satisfy me. Garland would surely think so and be the first to express it with that arrogant smile invading his eyes and his lips. Try as I might, it was a smile I simply could not forget.

Sometimes, as the days went by, I thought my mother was actually upset that I was doing so well. My father never stopped talking about me at dinner, and suddenly, he and I had more to discuss. When he talked about some redesigning for the bank lobby, I could offer an opinion. If he ruminated about things he wanted to change to make the everyday business more efficient when and if he became board chairman, I could explain why I thought this suggestion or that might work out well. It was funny how I never considered the impact my working at my father's bank would have on our father-daughter relationship.

I put it all in my diary.

Any of the girls or boys my age or a little older who saw me working were impressed, too. Daisy came to the bank with her father just to see me at work, and Arthur Raymond came in when he was back for a long weekend and had heard about me. He tried so hard to get me to pay more attention to him, but older, far more sophisticated young businessmen drew my eyes and ears away from him even while he was standing there and talking. Finally, he left the bank like some puppy with its tail between its legs, glancing back at me with disappointment dripping like tears from his eyes. I almost felt sorry for him, but then I thought that years from now, he would thank me for getting him to grow up faster.

I was actually enjoying myself at the bank these days and loved how surprised I was about it. I took more care with my appearance, did just what my father suggested, and spent my earnings on things that would enhance my looks. I bought new handbags, a parasol for almost no reason at all, and another pair of shoes for work, even though I spent very little time on my feet.

With my father, I attended some business lunches, met some interesting men, but no one yet who captured more than some passing interest. Every once in a while, I would think about Garland and expect some letter, an apology, something, but nothing came for the next seven weeks. One day, my father made a reference to him when he talked about the bank's investors planning on a quarterly meeting, a meeting that would lead to the election of a new board chairman. I tried to act uninterested, but I saw the way he was looking at me out of the corners of his eyes and then nodding to himself.

If he only knew it all, I thought, perhaps he wouldn't be so excited every time he mentioned Garland Foxworth, but it wasn't something I would willingly tell him, ever.

Ever is a small word. It doesn't have the strength to be what it claims when it is over-shadowed by the events of the day.

At the beginning of my eighth week at the bank, it suddenly occurred to me that something was wrong. I woke at night with the realization that I had not had my monthly. It was well over two weeks since my due date. Being so occupied had kept me from thinking about it. When I realized it, a rush of blood flowed up my neck. My face became so hot I had to get up and get a cool washcloth to pat my cheeks. While I stood there gazing at myself in the mirror, I felt the way my nightie was making the nipples of my breasts tingle. Maybe it was the way I woke up, with fear slithering up my legs to the small of my stomach and then on into my heart.

Nurse Grace Rose's warning gonged like fire-alarm bells. *This can't be,* I thought. I'd been a virgin. There had been too much blood, surely. The blood would have drowned any of Garland Foxworth's sperm. I was just having some sort of summer cold or something, and that had upset my body clock. I worked on convincing myself, but it never was enough to permit me to fall asleep again.

My parents noticed how quiet I was at breakfast, but both thought it was because I did not have a good night's sleep and was tired. My mother even suggested that I stay home from work this morning.

"You could do that," my father seconded. "You've done swell, Corrine. You've earned yourself a day."

"Are you sure, Daddy? I don't want to look like I'm taking advantage of the bank because you are the president and possibly the new chairman of the board."

That made him laugh. "Not at all," he said. "And what of it? If I can't get my daughter some special favors, what good is being the president of the bank?"

"Still, she's right, Harrington. You shouldn't go out of your way to give her privileges other employees don't enjoy."

"I think I know how to run the bank, Rosemary. No worries there," he said sternly.

"Well, I was the one who suggested she take a day of rest."

"So noted," my father said. "And a good, sensible business suggestion it is. If an employee is not up to his or her usual standards, I always suggest something similar. Take the day off," he told me. "That's an order from your official boss."

"Thank you," I said. I looked at my mother. "Thank you, Mommy."

She looked quite satisfied. It wasn't often that I called her Mommy. There was always so wide a gap of formality between us, but right now, my fear had turned me into a little girl again. I waited for nearly an hour after my father left, dressed in my cycling outfit, and told my mother I needed some fresh air and a little exercise. Before she could protest, I left the house.

I set off quickly.

I knew exactly where I was going.

I knew exactly where I would find Nurse Grace Rose.

9

After I described my concerns, Nurse Rose's words, although spoken softly, were thunderous.

"A woman can lose her virginity and at the same time have one of her eggs fertilized. Losing your virginity has nothing to do with the natural process."

I guess I wore a stunned expression, looking like I either didn't understand or refused to.

"You can get pregnant, yes, Corrine," she emphasized, more like pounded.

"But the first time ever?"

"Nature doesn't know that or care. I explained to you why and when you had to be most careful, when you would be most susceptible. Why didn't you listen? You seemed like a very intelligent young lady. I told you more than I tell most girls when they are your age. I even described methods to ensure you avoided all this. Most women would have simply said, 'Don't have sex until you're married.' I've lived long enough and seen enough to know that's unrealistic."

I sat back, hoping I was in a dream. I'd wake up soon. She wasn't telling me what I had hoped to hear.

We were on the screened front porch of her small Queen Anne home. I had been lucky to catch her there. She was on a night schedule for an elderly lady, Mrs. Louella Woodhouse, whose son was a church deacon. She looked at me with a mixed expression of pity and anger and disappointment.

"It wasn't something I intended to happen," I said dryly, like someone who had just been struck in the face by a gust of heavy, wet wind. "I didn't forget most of what you told me. It wasn't because of remembering all that this morning that I came over here."

Her eyes widened. She was wearing a light-green cotton bathrobe. She had just finished washing her hair and was still wiping it dry when I had cycled up to her house and knocked on the door. She had paused, surprised to see me, and after taking a closer look at my face, had suggested we both sit. Maybe because she was a nurse, she could feel the way my very bones were vibrating.

"Are you saying you were raped?"

"I don't know if I'd put it that way," I replied. "I was offered too much of a unique lemon alcohol drink made in Italy, and I didn't realize how it would affect me. I drank too much of it."

"So someone took advantage of you when you were inebriated?"

Now that this had happened, was I prepared to cast all the dark, black sheet of blame over Garland Foxworth?

"Maybe," I said.

"I don't understand. How can that be maybe? There are no maybes or almosts when it comes to this."

I looked away. The tears felt like they were freezing over my eyes and I was looking at the world through snow. Garland's smile faded in and out. Somewhere on the street, little girls were laughing, and for a moment, I longed to be a child again, free to do anything that didn't make me or my clothes dirty as long as I was where my mother knew I'd be. But I was never an angel, I thought, even then.

"I'm not entirely without fault," I said in a voice barely above a whisper. "I went to Charlottesville deliberately to see him and used visiting a great-aunt as an excuse. When I was there, I willingly went to his home without any chaperone or anyone knowing. My great-aunt and her servant are too old to realize anything. The gentleman didn't force me to drink. I did willingly take it."

"More than one?"

"Yes, and then everything just seemed to happen so fast. I didn't offer any real resistance."

Nurse Rose sat back, the right corner of her mouth tucked in as she thought about what I had just said. "Willingly didn't offer any? Are you saying you led this young man into believing this was all right, that you wanted it to happen?"

"No. Certainly not," I protested. "Not this."

She nodded but didn't look like she completely believed me. "All right, Corrine. How much fault will your young man admit to?" she asked.

I shook my head. Could he blame it all on me? Would he?

"Does he know yet?"

"No."

"And your parents? They know nothing of this yet?"

"Nothing."

"I think that is where you have to begin, Corrine. Have you been nauseated in the morning, unusually tired?"

"Not nauseated, but I have been tired. I was too tired to go to work today. My father has me working in his bank."

"I heard," she said, smiling, and then, as if she realized how insignificant all that was now, her smile flew off her face like a frightened hummingbird. "How much longer you will do that depends on how your body reacts. Some women are lucky; some suffer most of the symptoms early."

"I have often overheard my mother tell her friends how difficult it was for her to have me."

"That doesn't necessarily mean it will be the same for you."

"What else happens? I mean, right now."

"You might soon find yourself going to the bathroom more often, urinating."

I nodded.

"That's begun?"

"Yes."

"You'll gain weight, of course. Some women don't show for quite a while, even into the seventh month. From what you have told me, you're most surely into your second month."

Visions of pregnant women marched by, with me making up the end of the parade, my beautiful figure almost beyond memory. I never imagined myself envying any pregnant women, even though most I had met were happy to be with child. Years and years of overhearing how miserable my mother was should have made me more careful. I was thinking that when I married, I would never get pregnant, even if my husband thought it was the most important thing in the world. I'd do everything possible to prevent it until he finally gave up.

And then I thought, what kind of a marriage would that be without a family? It all twirled in my head. I was still in that state of confusion I expected every young woman experiences as she moves from childhood fantasies to adult reality. But then again, I always wanted the pleasure and satisfaction without having to suffer any effort or pain to get it. Right now, though, it was still difficult for me to believe this was actually happening to me. Perhaps my mother was the same way at my age and that was how I came about. Maybe we were more alike than I or even she cared to admit. But what good would that do me now, even if she confessed it? She loved saying, "Two wrongs don't make a right."

"You can tell your mother I'll be available to help you in any way she or you wish," Grace Rose said, sitting forward to take my hand. "But as I said, your first responsibility now is to talk to your parents. You must make decisions as a family. Of course, I will keep your confidence." She sat back again.

"Thank you," I whispered.

"Unfortunately, you won't be the first to whom I made such a promise."

That didn't make me feel any better. I rose, started to turn, and stopped.

"I heard that sometimes babies just fall out way too soon and no one even knows the woman was pregnant. Can that happen to me?"

Her eyelids narrowed. "Don't keep this a secret from your parents and then do something foolish to yourself, Corrine. Women can bleed to death. I've seen enough of that, too. If too much time goes by and it's clear to me that you haven't told your parents . . ."

"I will. I promise," I said.

"Good."

I took a deep breath, nodded, thanked her, and walked to my bike. She remained sitting on the porch until I was on my way. Just before I made

214

the turn, I looked back. She was still sitting there, looking like she was in deep thought, her hair still wet, the towel dangling from her hand as if she no longer knew what to do with it.

How much of what was happening to me had happened to her? She was yet unmarried and now living alone since both her parents had passed away. Again, I wondered why she didn't marry. Could she have had a baby secretly, a baby someone quickly adopted? Suddenly, every woman's story was important to me, but especially those who did get pregnant too soon while still having wonderful romances. This was one time when I didn't want to be the center of attention. I wanted to listen to others describe how they avoided becoming me.

I pedaled on, my heart pounding all the way home. My mother was busy in the kitchen and didn't hear me return. I went quietly upstairs to my room, feeling like someone drowning in a dream. It hadn't surprised me to hear Nurse Rose ask if I had told my parents and not specifically ask if I had told my mother. Most girls probably would run to their mothers first; it was a woman's crisis. Their fathers would be the ones raging, and their mothers would be embracing them and crying for them. Nurse Rose realized what my mother was like from the very fact that my mother had hired her to do a mother's first important mother-daughter talk.

No, I thought, this was something I had to tell my father first. I dreaded it, dreaded how his face would shatter. All he had planned for me, all that had made him so proud of me, would drop out of his eyes and to his feet like tears formed out of stone. He would never look at me the same way again. I knew how he would take it. I had betrayed him, betrayed his dreams for me and therefore his dreams for himself.

The man I loved and respected, the man who walked with such self-confidence, shoulders back, stride firm, the man who won the admiration of any man who knew him, would suddenly stoop and lower his eyes like a flag dropped to half-mast to mark the death of someone very important. The parasites would come out of the woodwork with their mean and ugly gossip to gnaw at him and our family. Who knew? Maybe he would lose his position at the bank or certainly not be elected chairman of the board. And all this would come raining down on him just when he was so happy about building us a new home, making his star brighten.

I closed my eyes and lay back on my bed. The fatigue Nurse Rose had suggested I might continue to experience appeared to be rushing into my body faster from every angle, up my arms to my neck, up my legs to my stomach and my back. Sleep was like someone on Arthur Raymond's football field calling "Time out." I was grateful. For a while, at least, I would not think about any of this.

When I opened my eyes again, my father was standing there looking down at me. He wore a deeply worried and concerned expression. My first fearful thought was that Nurse Rose, after giving it all more thought and deciding not to have any responsibility, had sent a message to him at the bank and he had come rushing home. But when I glanced at the clock, I saw I had slept away the remainder of the afternoon and he was home when he usually returned.

"How are you, Corrine? Your mother didn't know you had returned from your cycling. When I came into the house, she thought you were still out somewhere. I told her I saw your bike lying by the shed. Why didn't you put it back? Are you all right? Why are you sleeping so much? Does anything hurt?"

I sat up slowly and quickly brought my hands to my face, like someone trying to be sure she was awake or like someone reassuring herself she was still in her body. My father's eyes darkened. It was never easy to tell my father a lie or try to hide my feelings from him. I always believed in my heart that he knew when I was pretending or being overly dramatic to get my way. Sometimes, with things far less important, it amused him. I had to believe that came from a very deep love.

"Corrine?" he said, stepping closer. I was

looking out my window at a passing cloud that had ripples of dark gray across its belly. A tree swallow right outside my window was gossiping with other swallows nearby. For a moment, the sounds were hypnotic. I wished I could rise off my bed and fly out the window.

"Corrine," my father said in a more demanding tone. "What is going on with you?"

"I lied to you," I said. He stared silently, anticipating I would continue, but I felt like I had spent my ability to speak for the rest of my life with just those four words.

"What lie?" he asked. "Well?"

"I did go to Foxworth Hall that night."

He nodded. "I can't tell you I wasn't suspicious, Corrine. I knew how taken with Garland Foxworth you were, and from the way you described your great-aunt Nettie's home and what was happening, the temptation to do something more interesting and exciting was surely there."

"It was more than just that, Daddy."

He nodded again. "Anyway, I'm glad you decided to tell me the truth. I don't want there ever to be gaps of distrust between us. Lies between people who love each other are like cancer."

I could see how eager he was to end with this, to wrap up this uncomfortable moment with only that simple confession. How I wished I could, how I wished I deserved this father who was so forgiving and who loved me too much ever to despise me.

"I was impressed with Garland Foxworth from the moment I met him at the Wexlers'. I can't say I'm not still. He's very good-looking and has traveled so much and . . ."

"And?" His eyes narrowed as he realized I was not finished with my confession. "So you went to his home and . . ."

"He showed me some of Foxworth Hall, and we ended up in a room upstairs, where he had a drink he had discovered during his travels in Italy."

"What drink?"

"He called it limoncello and was so taken with it he wrote down a recipe someone in Italy gave him and had it made here. We talked, and I drank, and—"

My father's eyes darkened. His body stiffened. "You got sick from it?"

"Yes, but—"

"You were alone in this room the entire time?"

"Yes."

He turned like he was going to run out but just stared down at the floor. "How far did it go, Corrine?"

I took the deepest breath of my life first. "Earlier today, I cycled to Nurse Grace Rose's home to ask her some questions about myself."

He looked up quickly, his face sizzling with growing fear and rage.

I was afraid to look at him and looked down at my hands in my lap instead.

"Why?" he asked.

"I thought . . . I was worried that I was pregnant."

He was silent. I could hear his deepening breaths.

The bird outside, as though it had eavesdropped on our conversation, flew away. I heard no other. The whole world seemed to be holding its breath.

"And what did Nurse Rose tell you?"

"She said I was . . . was pregnant."

His legs seemed to go out on him. He sat on the edge of my bed quickly.

"It was the first time I had ever . . . but that doesn't matter," I said. Right now, I felt like I had to keep talking, or I would start screaming and crying. "I thought we were just going to be a little romantic. He was so impressed with me and I with him, right from the first time we met at the Wexler gala."

He folded his hands into fists. They had never looked so big. They were more like mallets. I had never seen my father violent, but from the way his neck tightened, I thought he was on the verge of being just that.

"Who else knows about this?" he asked in a very deliberately controlled voice, punching out

220

each word as if it was a sentence unto itself.

"Just Nurse Rose knows. I haven't told Mother. She doesn't know I went there, went to Foxworth Hall, either, of course."

He shook his head and smacked his lips. His upper body rocked a bit. "I warned you. I told you that you had so many young woman's years yet. I was telling you to be careful. I thought you were smarter than this, wiser for your age."

"I know, Daddy. I'm so sorry and so ashamed," I said, the tears now trickling faster and faster down my cheeks. I flicked them off and sucked in my breath.

He froze and now was simply staring at me. I wondered if he was seeing his little girl again or if he was now seeing someone he didn't recognize or want to acknowledge. Maybe he would send me out of the house, have me taken somewhere so I'd be out of sight and out of mind. I couldn't blame him.

"You're only sixteen," he said. "Garland Foxworth is a man of the world, a man in his twenties. It must have been like fishing in a bathtub for him," he said bitterly.

"It wasn't entirely his fault," I said.

He looked at me askance. "What? You are still fond of this man, a man who had his way with you and seemingly discarded you as so much used goods?"

"If I hadn't drunk so much, maybe—"

"Maybe that was exactly why he brought you to his home."

"I thought . . . he was so charming, and he cared for me."

"Oh, he cared. I'll grant him that."

My father's face hardened in a way I had never seen. His eyes looked like they had frozen, his teeth clenched and the bones of his jaw pressed so hard against his skin that I thought it might tear.

"I'm sorry, Daddy."

"I'll destroy him," he said through his still-clenched teeth. "Every business he has, every investor who had joined any of his enterprises . . ."

He stood up—shot up was more like it.

"But, Daddy . . . maybe you shouldn't."

His eyes softened with confusion. "You really still care about this man?"

"I don't want everyone seeing you so angry and sad because of me."

"And him!"

"Yes, I know, but isn't there some other way? I'll go away until the baby comes."

"Just like that? And no one asking questions? And if someone should find out and the story spreads, what do you think our lives would be like here? Just think how your mother would be."

He paused, nodding.

"For now, I don't want you telling your mother anything. Say you just had some indigestion."

"But . . . what are you going to do?"

"I'll do what I have to do. Say nothing about this to anyone else, Corrine. That's of paramount importance, and I want you to return to work tomorrow."

"You do?"

He started out and stopped to turn back. "I'm sorry for you. I'm upset, but I'm not going to stop loving you."

The moment he was gone, I burst into the worst sobbing I had done since I was a very little girl.

Later, just as he had asked, I complained about indigestion, and my mother said nothing about how I was eating. I had absolutely no appetite, but I forced myself to nibble. My father announced a business trip that had come up at the last minute.

"After I drop you off at the bank, I'll be taking the train," he said. He turned away quickly, but I felt my heart quicken its beat.

I tried to approach him alone, but my mother hovered about us almost as if she sensed there was something going on, so I decided to wait until morning when we rode together to the bank. When I awoke, washed and dressed, and then went down for breakfast, I had another surprise, however.

"Your father left early," she told me the moment I appeared. "Horace Makens will be coming by to take you to the bank."

"Horace Makens? But Daddy said he was going to take me."

"He changed his mind. He didn't sleep well, tossed and turned all night. Something about this business venture has him on pins and needles. He had to leave earlier to make a train. It won't kill you to go with Horace. He's a very nice fifty-year-old man. Sad that he never found a good wife after Leona died of the flu. Well, don't just stand there looking so shocked about something so simple, Corrine. Sit down and eat your breakfast.

"You'll have to be as good at your job as you are when your father is at the bank, too. You don't want people thinking you're only successful because your father is looking over your shoulder and everyone else is afraid to say anything, do you?"

I was half listening to her as she went on and on.

"I must say I'm proud of you, too. I've heard only good things from my friends. Your deportment, knowledge, and efficiency tell me you are probably more like your father. I doubt I'd do as well at your age. It's good to see you have a sensible head on your shoulders.

"A responsible woman attracts only responsible men. And now, with your father building us a new and impressive home and possibly becoming the chairman of the board, you'll be quite the catch."

"What?"

"Haven't you heard a thing I've said?"

"Yes, yes." I looked at my new watch. "I'd better finish eating. Mr. Makens is one of those men who live according to the tick-tock."

"Live according to the tick-tock?" My mother smiled, and then she laughed. "What a clever way to put it."

Most of my life, I craved having compliments from my mother, unbeknownst to her, apparently, but right now, her smiling at me, praising me, made me feel absolutely sick to my stomach. The higher up she held me, the worse my fall in her eyes would be once she knew the truth.

I left the kitchen the moment I took my last bite and then ran upstairs to look at myself closely one more time. Although Nurse Rose's description of the early months assured me no one would guess my condition unless my symptoms suddenly perked up, I was still concerned. What if one of the other women at the bank knew just as much, if not more, about pregnancy? What if one could look at me and see something I could not see in my mirror? All my life, I had been good at hiding or manipulating my feelings. Was this just too much for me to handle? I should have asked my father if I could stop working now. Wasn't he worried I'd be discovered?

I knew that despite my efforts, anyone who was accustomed to my behavior would wonder why I was quieter than usual. Mr. Makens fortunately never shut up all the way from our house to the bank, so I didn't have much chance to talk anyway. I think he was nervous about having a young woman sitting beside him.

Perhaps precisely because my father wasn't present, the other employees were even more attentive. I flashed my smiles, laughed when I could, and treated every new customer as if he would make the bank one of the most important in the country by investing his savings in it or establishing an account. We did seem to be busier than usual, and for that I was grateful. Who wanted to think?

Just before the close of the bank day, my father appeared. He nodded at me and went directly to his office to handle whatever he had missed while away. From the moment he had entered to the moment he began wrapping up to take us home, my heart beat faster and at times fluttered with my anxiety.

"Let's go, Corrine," was all he said until we were in the carriage and on our way.

I sat quietly, my hands in my lap, my eyes lowered, waiting and thinking that the next words he uttered would be the most important of my life. When we rounded the turn to take us out of Alexandria proper and onto the road to our home, he finally looked at me.

"I had a message delivered to your mother before I returned to the bank," he began.

Oh, how I dreaded this, but also how surprised I was that he had chosen such a formal way to reveal it all to her.

"Her heart will break," I said, now feeling more miserable than I had in the morning or even after I had spoken with Nurse Rose.

"Maybe not," he said.

I looked up quickly. "Why not?"

"I wanted her to know that we're having a guest for dinner," he said. He didn't smile. He continued to look forward.

"What guest? Nurse Rose?" I thought immediately.

"No." He turned to me. "Garland Foxworth," he said.

I didn't think he was going to say anything more. We rode on for nearly a minute in silence. Was it because it was painful for him to say any more?

"Why is he coming to our home, Daddy?"

"I always imagined that the big things that happen to us in our lives, the directions we take, are as currents in a stream. Sometimes they are smooth, graceful, and gentle, and sometimes they are raging. Wisdom, whatever I possess, tells me that you have to know what sort of current you are in and what exactly you can do about it.

"If it's the raging current, you can battle it and smash yourself or be smashed against obstacles, boulders, whatever. In the end, the current will have its way anyway, or you can choose to not only let it carry you but swim faster than it can carry you.

"That's the choice you have now, Corrine. Garland Foxworth has the same choice. I confronted him with all my rage, but I don't think he was so intimidated that he would make a decision because of me. Actually, surprisingly, he was more upset. He was in tears."

"Garland was?"

"Yes. I thought at first they were tears of self-pity, but very quickly, they became tears of regret, not for himself but for you. He went on to explain how much he was captivated by your beauty and charm. He confessed to acting like a cad but assured me it was not his intention to put you in this state. He claimed he was himself overwhelmed with too much of his lemon drink, which he says is very subtle but very powerful. Normally, he has only a small amount after dinner.

"That was his defense and his story about your night with him. He then went on to swear on his life that no woman he has met has had the effect on him that you have had. He realizes, of course, how young you are, but he says he's been with women years older who have not as much poise and charm. I think he sees himself as the lord of a castle, and to be sure, Foxworth Hall is one of the most impressive properties I've ever visited. We both know he is quite wealthy, too.

"He claims that he is ready to have a more significant life, a family, and wants to settle down and build on what he has achieved and inherited. Practically going to his knees, he begged me not to do anything to destroy his child or give the baby away after you went on some mysterious journey. He wants the opportunity to convince you and your mother, especially, of his serious intentions and asked for the audience we'll give him this evening.

"However," my father continued, "we both agreed that no mention would be made of your pregnancy. Your mother will not be told of this, nor will anyone else."

"But—"

"If you decide to swim faster in the current because you do have strong feelings for Garland Foxworth, you will, after a honeymoon of sorts, remain basically sequestered at Foxworth Hall, and your birthing will be advertised as premature. He seems quite clever when it comes to such a deception. Perhaps he's had more experience than we imagine or care to know.

"Finally, I want you to understand, Corrine, that I left him with only the promise of having him to dinner. This decision will be yours and yours alone to make. I will not, like most fathers in a similar situation, force my daughter to do something."

Our house came into view.

We were both going to put on an act for my mother, I thought. Whenever we had done it in the past, it was for small, even silly, things. Nothing compared to this.

Lies and half-truths, more than anything else, were what everyone wove between them. We weren't much different after all. Now I wondered, truly wondered. Did I love Garland Foxworth enough to swim faster in the current?

And if I told myself I did, would that be another lie?

If it was, I'd have to live with it for the rest of my life.

10

My mother greeted me with "What magic spell did you cast over this very wealthy and accomplished young man at the Wexler gala to bring him to our doorstep so quickly? Or has this something to do with your run for chairman of the board, Harrington?"

I glanced at my father. Apparently, he had told my mother a great deal more about Garland Foxworth than simply that he was coming to dinner; otherwise, she wouldn't have been sure to say "very wealthy and accomplished." Frankly, I was still quite surprised at my father for being so understanding when it came to Garland. I had nightmares about my father challenging him to a duel. There was surely much about Garland Foxworth when it came to the business and financial world that I didn't know, couldn't have known. Maybe he was very important to my father's run for chairman of the board, but to think my father would make such a compromise, sacrificing me, was out of the question. Other fathers, perhaps, but not mine.

On the other hand, my father's willingness to give him this opportunity to impress my mother caused me to question my share of the responsibility for what had happened. Was this how my father was thinking? Men, I thought, did tend to forgive each other faster than they forgave women.

"Me? Cast a spell?" I said, with my best innocent face.

"Oh, please, Corrine. Spare me the blameless look of a confused young girl. This is the same man with whom you dallied at the Wexler gala every chance you had, is he not?" she asked.

"I didn't dally. We enjoyed each other's company for a short time during the gala, but his appearance here today is just as surprising to me as it is to you, Mother," I replied. There was nothing untrue about that.

I was sure that in her mind, Garland Foxworth was simply someone I did flirt with at the Wexlers' and never saw or heard from again. For a moment, I wondered if my father's insistence that we not tell my mother anything about my pregnancy was due partly to his wanting to avoid her blaming him for any part of what was happening now.

"Is it?" she asked. She glanced at me with a wry smile across her lips before she said, "Come down quickly after you change your clothes, and help set the table." She looked at my father. "We'll be using our best china and silverware. Your father likes to impress his more important business clients and associates, especially those who have a say in his future."

My father's face reddened.

"*Our* future," he corrected.

I hurried up to my room. No matter what I decided later, right now I had to tread over the truth as softly as someone walking over hot beach sand, hotter than the sand Garland had described in Spain. My first challenge was dressing correctly. I didn't want to look like I was trying to overwhelm Garland with my beauty again. My mother would surely notice. Despite my situation, I hoped to avoid looking too anxious, too inclined to accept any offer he made. Even now, I would cause him to wonder if I cared enough about him to become the mother of his child, the mistress of his great house. Was it too late to follow what I thought was my guiding principle, never to let a man take anything for granted? Had I given that up and placed myself helplessly on his doorstep?

Of course, I wanted to see for myself how remorseful he was for what he had done. Despite my father's willingness to permit him to present himself properly, I imagined it still would be difficult for him to come into our home and face my mother and especially me. How much did he believe she knew? Did my father tell him she knew nothing? If she asked either of us any questions about my trip to Charlottesville, we'd have to be very careful with our answers. It would be like walking over broken glass for both of us. We'd be tiptoeing through this dinner, wondering if at any moment he or I was about to blurt something that would set my mother's eyes on fire.

I found myself rehearsing answers to probable questions. It was truly like being in a play. The curtain was soon to be raised, and when it came down at the end, there would either be just thunder or thunderous applause. I think I was still in too much of a daze to realize how much of my future, my life, depended on how this all went.

I brushed my hair and chose a deep-pink blouse to wear with an ebony skirt. The bodice was narrow in the shoulders, with thick gathered pleats over my bosom. I checked myself from all angles and slipped on my newest black shoes. On my way down the stairs, I overheard my mother questioning my father about Garland as if my father was on the witness stand in a courtroom.

"What do you mean, he suggested you invite him to dinner at our home? That sounds quite forward. One doesn't suggest it; one gets invited. Truthfully, I wasn't happy about his spending so much time with Corrine at the gala without first being properly introduced to us. That didn't make a good impression on me, and I am surprised you're not as upset about that. Besides, since when do you jump so quickly at the command of another businessman, Harrington Dixon? No matter what influence he might have on the board of directors?"

"I told you I knew him from previous business

dealings, Rosemary. He's a very successful young man, and all I've heard from businessmen who have anything to do with him are good things. You have a terrible habit of prejudging someone before he has a chance to breathe the same air."

They both turned to me when I entered the kitchen. My mother's eyes flooded with new suspicions.

"Have you had correspondence with this man since the Wexler gala? Don't dare lie to us, Corrine."

I looked at my father, who nodded slightly.

"Yes."

"To what end?"

"I saw him in Charlottesville. He visited me at Great-aunt Nettie's."

Again, I wasn't telling a lie. I was just not telling everything.

My mother slapped her hands together like she would if she was trying to kill a mosquito. "How did he know you were there?" she asked.

"He saw me crossing the street and had his carriage follow me to Great-aunt Nettie's house. Naturally, I invited him in for a cool drink."

Her eyes didn't lose their look of suspicion. "Why is it that I have to dig like a coal miner to get the whole truth out of you, Corrine? It's not natural for a daughter to keep so many secrets from her parents, especially when it comes to men and especially from her mother."

"I'm sorry," I said. "I didn't mean it to seem like a great secret."

She sighed. "So you've given him encouragement? This dinner isn't exactly something plucked out of the blue?"

"We've given each other encouragement," I said. "I can't check every word, every look I've had from every gentleman with you first, Mother. You'd hardly have time for anything else during your day."

That sarcasm she missed. If anything, her day was so empty to me that she really had the time to work a coal miner's shift.

She stared at me a moment, the frustration exhausting her. "This isn't the time for any argument. Let's just get this done properly now. I will not have someone come to dinner in my home and leave with a bad taste in his or her mouth."

"I'm sure it's delicious."

"I don't mean just the food. Don't pretend to be dumb, Corrine. Fold the napkins properly, and be sure whatever you put on the table is immaculate."

"Yes, Mother," I said, and began.

My father slipped out to go change his shirt and suit, gliding away softly like someone escaping a church sermon. At the moment, I was feeling sorrier for him than I was for myself. Eventually, somehow, some way, she'd find reason to place most of the blame at his feet.

At precisely seven p.m., a horse and carriage pulled up to our house, and Garland Foxworth, carrying two gift-wrapped presents, came to the door. My mother and I stepped out of the kitchen to greet him. He was wearing a suit similar to the one he had worn to the Wexlers' gala, only a lighter shade of gray, a beautiful new pair of black leather boots, and a black derby. When he took it off, I saw that he'd had his hair trimmed quite a bit since I had last seen him. His complexion looked ruddier, which emphasized his eyes. Despite my plan to appear as aloof as possible when I first confronted him, I couldn't help thinking he somehow looked even more handsome than the first time I had seen him and since.

"Good evening, Mrs. Dixon. Thank you for your willingness to feed a young man who is unfortunately unaccustomed to real family dinners these days."

"You are welcome," my mother said, not quite sure how to respond to such a nakedly honest confession. "Your own parents?"

"Gone, I'm afraid, but there'll be no sadness brought into your home tonight and hopefully no future night. Instead, permit me to show my gratitude with this small token," he said, handing my mother one of the gift-wrapped boxes. "It's just something I brought back from a recent visit to Paris. It was being auctioned, and when I looked at it now, I thought it would be something unique for your home."

"Oh," my mother said. "Paris."

"Unwrap it. I'd like to see the expression on your face. Be unafraid of not liking it," he said. "I have a terrible habit of deciding what people should and shouldn't like," he added, glancing at me.

My mother carefully peeled away the paper to reveal a statuette in pure white porcelain of a Chinese woman holding flowers. She was dressed in regal garments and wearing a necklace.

"They call it a Guanyin, a Buddhist deity associated with mercy and compassion," he said, glancing at me again. Was that what he wanted me to extend to him, mercy and compassion?

"My," my mother said, not quite sure how overwhelmed she should be or even if she liked it and wanted it displayed in her home. "It is unique." She turned it around in her hands.

"It's supposedly five hundred years old," Garland added. "I don't know for sure if it's that old, of course, but it's old."

My mother nodded, now looking sufficiently impressed. "Thank you," she said.

My father looked pleased.

"And if you'll permit me," Garland said, "another small token for Miss Dixon."

He handed me the other small gift-wrapped box.

I slipped off the pretty paper neatly and then, holding the box in my left hand, opened it. My mother was practically breathing down my neck. I plucked out a hairpin set with six freshwater pearls and what looked like rose-cut diamonds.

My mother gasped. "Are those real?"

"Oh yes," Garland said nonchalantly. "It comes from Scotland. It was my mother's."

My mother looked up with eyes so wide I thought she would rupture her lids. "Your mother's?"

"She had so many nice things, beautiful things. I think leaving them stuffed in drawers does them and my mother's memory an injustice. After all, a beautiful thing is not beautiful if it's never seen. Wouldn't you agree?" He glanced at me and then smiled at my mother.

"Oh yes," she said.

"Thank you," I said, looking at the pin and not him.

"Let's go to my study while the ladies prepare our dinner," my father told Garland.

"Thank you," he said, and followed him.

My mother turned her statuette slowly and then looked at me as if she wanted me to tell her to keep it.

"Surely no one you know has anything like that in her home, Mother."

"Um," she said. She looked more confused than anything.

I gazed after my father and Garland.

"I just don't know where to put such a thing. Still, if it's anything like he described, people will be quite impressed."

"Maybe your friends won't. They are not exposed to such things."

"How would you know that? Don't become snobby, Corrine."

"Of course not, Mother. You're right. How could they not be impressed?"

"Um," she said, still turning the statuette in her hands. "From what he said, he must have spent a pretty penny on it."

"It would be impolite to ask how much," I said, and she looked up sharply.

"Of course it would."

I smiled, and she pulled in the corners of her mouth. My correcting her when it came to social graces was not a flag to fly high in this house. I looked toward the library. Was Garland as sweet and generous as he appeared right now, or was he far better than I was at maneuvering people to do whatever it was he wanted? Or had my father put the fear of hell and brimstone into his heart, and he was here to first be forgiven?

It could be all of the above. Somehow I suspected it would take me much longer to find the honest answers, but that only made me more determined to get them.

My mother and I went to work.

When she thought the table was perfect, she sent me to fetch them. My father rose quickly as soon as I entered. He looked at Garland and then turned to me and said, "Mr. Foxworth asked for a few minutes alone with you. I'll keep your mother entertained," he added, and left us.

Garland rose and approached me slowly. I was sure the expression on my face would frighten anyone, even him.

"I guess I've made a mess of things," he began.

I didn't say anything. I would do nothing to make this easier. He did look quite uncomfortable.

Finally, satisfied I was dangling him long enough, I spoke. "Looks like I'm the one in the mess, however."

"Absolutely not." He seized my hands. "I knew from the moment I saw you that you would be the woman I'd love and the woman who should be mistress of Foxworth Hall. I was determined to court you for as long as it would take. All that's happened to us, I pray, is that fate has decided to speed up our future."

Fate? I thought. We might better blame it on limoncello.

"I'd get down on my knee right now, but I know I have some turning of the earth before planting."

"I think you've already planted, Garland."

I saw his lips tremble as he fought back a smile. "You will be a challenge, Corrine Dixon, but I do welcome it. I do. Most of the women I've met have been so shallow and obvious. Life will be most interesting with you at my side or making me work harder at being a proper husband and, it seems, a proper father. Mine never was, but you have a wonderful father, so you know the standards any man should meet. I hope I can."

"How did my father convince you of this?"

"He had no convincing to do. Believe me. Please."

What choice did I have? What other choice did I want? I had yet to meet another man like him, but truthfully, I had yet to know him. However, from what I understood, witnessed, and heard about so many women pledged to marriages, they really weren't that much more confident of the men they hardly knew. They put all their faith in vows, but if anyone knew how empty words could be, it was I, who used them so well.

"We'd better go to the dining room. My mother is as nervous as I've ever seen her. I haven't told her very much. She knows only that you saw me at my aunt's home. I said nothing about going to Foxworth."

"Leave it to me," he said, and brought my hands to his lips. "If you will so honor me, that is."

I said nothing. I was as dizzy and confused as I was after having drunk his potent lemon drink. Had it put me in a spell that still lasted, or was I really on the brink of a great love and family life?

I led him out to the dining room. We seated him so he would be across from me, and then my mother and I served. For most of the dinner, Garland did what he had done to me, enchanting my mother with tales of his travels, describing the beauty, the people, and the foods he had eaten. My father hadn't been much of a traveler. Neither of my parents had, so she was intrigued and entertained, interrupting occasionally to tell my father she would like to go to this place or that.

"You hate an hour's ride in the carriage and especially a ride on a train, Rosemary," he reminded her with an amused smile.

"What you do," Garland answered for her, "is keep your mind on your destination. When you get there, you realize it was worth the effort."

My mother nodded as if she was so convinced she'd leave tomorrow.

Interspersing his descriptions with comments on the food, Garland carefully wove a cocoon of comfort and ease around my mother. Before the dinner had ended, he had her laughing more than I had ever seen her laugh with a relative stranger. I was truly impressed myself, and when I looked at my father, I saw how rapt he was as well.

Maybe fate had given me a wonderful prize. Maybe I shouldn't hate limoncello after all, I thought, and smiled to myself. Garland caught it and winked at me. When it was time for our coffee and cake, we retired to the study. After my mother and I served, Garland put down his cup, cleared his throat, and stood up with his hands clasped behind his back. I thought he looked quite silly, but he was determined to do this in the most formal and correct manner he could.

"I would like to make a confession," he began, which actually started my heart pounding. What confession? Was he mad? "Ordinarily, I am a particularly careful and studious man. If there was one thing my father left me, it was caution. 'Only rash men,' he told me, 'make unforgivable and uncorrectable errors.' This is obviously something your husband not only knows well, Mrs. Dixon, but has as the guiding principle of his own life and career; otherwise, he would not have been given such an important position in such a prestigious company and be considered for one even higher."

I glanced at my mother. She sat back, listening as if she was seated in front of the president of the United States. My father was looking down at his coffee cup. I sat forward like someone poised to rush out of the room.

"But I am someone who knows he has benefited from his good fortune. Business and travel have educated me enough to confidentially read the hearts of other people. I flatter myself by saying that I have therefore accumulated the wisdom of a man years older than I am. I leave it to others to praise my accomplishments normally, but I'm here now to win your confidence." He turned to my father. "Win the confidence of you both.

"In short, whether it was divine purpose or simple good fortune, I was placed close enough to meet your beautiful daughter. Others will be quick to tell you that we have not spent enough time together even to be merely friends, but they have not experienced what I have, we have. Everything I know and all that I have seen has assured me that I will never do better, that I will never find another woman who can stand as confidently at my side and continue my good fortune, my family's reputation, and complete my life as wonderfully as your daughter will. I believe she feels the same way.

"So, I would formally ask your permission to ask your daughter for her hand in marriage."

He took a breath, and my mother, who was simply sitting there mesmerized, also took a breath but left her mouth wide open.

"Marriage?" she finally said.

"Precisely, and very, very soon. I am involved in many international business ventures and have much of the year planned and scheduled. If you will give me permission to ask for your daughter's hand, and if she should accept as I hope, I would like to propose that you permit me to stage our wedding affair at Foxworth Hall. When you visit, which I hope will be soon, you will see a property unlike most you've seen. Besides the mansion itself, the grounds, the lake, the views will be what most people would think belong in dreams."

He smiled.

"Our marriage ceremony and celebration will be the social event of the year, not only for people from Charlottesville but for people all over Virginia and elsewhere. If I have your permission and Corrine agrees, I will contract a major artist and company to draw up the invitations immediately, all of which will be hand-delivered to each and every guest. It will seem fast, but I do have friends who will come from faraway places and ordinarily schedule their calendars almost a year in advance. Exceptions will be made and postponements issued once they receive the invitations, I assure you.

"Naturally, I would seek your input on and approval of every aspect of the event . . . the flowers—I know you're partial to irises—the menu, the music, everything. There will be no limit on the number of guests you want to invite. I humbly suggest that it will be the most sought-after invitation in Virginia society."

When he paused, it was quiet enough to hear us all breathe. My mother looked like someone had splashed ice water over her face. My father sat back, keenly satisfied. Garland cleared his throat, now looking a bit uneasy at my mother's silence.

"Well, I think I've said enough. If you'll permit, I will retire to your front porch with Corrine, if she agrees, and give you and Mr. Dixon time to discuss my proposal."

"Tonight?" my mother asked, now even more astounded. "We're to decide this tonight?"

"Should you need more time after you begin your discussion, of course, take it." He looked at his watch as if to communicate his demand for a decision this very evening, however. He smiled at me and held out his hand. "Corrine."

I rose and, without looking at either of my parents, took his hand and left the room. We walked out, and he nodded at the bench.

"How did I do?" he asked as soon as I sat.

"I'm waiting for my breath to return."

He laughed and took out a thin cigar.

"How much of what you just said was true?" I asked.

"What? All of it." He leaned against a post. "Since you left, I haven't spent an hour without thoughts of you and regrets about how awkward our parting was. I did have pressing business, however. That was not an untruth."

I scowled at him.

"Dear me," he said. "Don't peel off my skin."

"Did my father threaten you?"

"Threaten?" He shrugged. "He did what any father would do at first, but that isn't and never would be a concern of mine. I sincerely am sorry for the way I treated you." He smiled. "I've put away all the remaining limoncello. It's under lock and key, in fact."

"Unless it does have some magical powers, we can't blame it all on that. It's just some fancy alcoholic drink," I said.

"Not that fancy, but I agree."

"I wouldn't light that cigar," I said. "My mother loathes the scent but especially indoors. And it doesn't inspire good memories for me."

He looked at it. "Oh, right, right. Sorry."

He put it away quickly.

"So, if your parents agree tonight . . ."

"Don't," I said quickly.

"Don't what?"

"Don't make any promises until we say our vows. I hate promises."

"Why?"

"You can't be disappointed without them, and there's nothing I hate or fear more than disappointment."

"Okay," he said, widening his smile. "I promise never to make promises."

"It may not be possible for me to love you the way you anticipate," I said. It sounded more like a warning.

He laughed. "I completely understand. It's chancy for any woman to think she could love me as a wife should, I'll admit it, but if anyone can do it, you can. I really believe it. And I wasn't kidding in there when I spoke to you alone. If not now, then surely soon, I'd be knocking on this door. You wouldn't have gotten away, Corrine Dixon, not easily anyway."

I smiled. *Does this handsome man who lives like a prince really love me? Can I tell myself that dating other men and working my way back to him would have been a colossal waste of time?*

"It's such a nice night," he said. "Why don't we go for a short walk? Give them more time." He held out his hand. "Mrs. Soon-to-be-I-hope Foxworth?"

I stood and took his hand. Was my father right? Did I still have choice, the choice of swimming faster in this current that was sweeping me quickly into my adult life? Or was I holding the hand of the man who had trapped me? Some women, my mother probably being one of them, believed love put a woman in a cage. She lost all her freedom, because love led to marriage, which was full of chains. The choices a woman had left as a wife were usually about things of little significance, yet even the dinner menu, the house furnishings, and her own clothes still had the heavy hand of her husband pressing her to go this way and that.

When women said they had "fallen in love," I thought, they didn't realize it, but they literally meant they had fallen into something out of which they would find it nearly impossible to escape.

I had taken away the one decision I believed I owned, or perhaps, as I had always feared might happen, I had suffered it being taken away from me: the decision about whom to marry. I realized, as we walked under the partially cloudy sky with its peekaboo stars, that I would have to either be extremely happy or learn how to believe the delusions.

"I wasn't exaggerating in there to impress your mother," Garland said. "I intend to make this wedding an event people will talk about for years. I will spare no expense. Queen Victoria would be jealous."

I stopped walking. "This is not about a gala wedding, Garland. It's about a gala life."

The shadows spilled over him, but I could feel the way he was looking at me. The air was so still, not even a slight breeze. Perhaps it was only in the darkness that people truly saw each other. We could momentarily be distracted by the glitter of stars, the cry of an owl, or, when they were stirred, the whisper of the leaves, but darkness has a way of undressing you. It lifts off false faces. Only your voice reveals what's truly in your heart.

"Of course," he said. There was just a hint of surprise. I was determined that he would believe he was going to marry a woman who clearly was no longer a girl. I would not be dazzled. I would be cherished. "We'll have a great life. I promise. Oops. I wasn't supposed to say that."

He laughed and then moved closer so he could kiss me.

"Some men think that in the dark, all women are the same, but I would never say that about you, Corrine Dixon."

"I hope not."

He took my hand again, and we turned back toward the house.

"Let's think about a honeymoon."

"Let's wait to see what my mother says."

"I doubt she'll oppose what your father wants for you."

I wanted to say probably not, but not because she was an obedient wife. She was more likely seeing my marriage as lifting a burden off her shoulders. She'd rationalize and think she had to send me off eventually, so why not now?

As soon as we entered the house, my father called to us. I could see from the opened bottle of his highly prized port and the four glasses that the decision had been confirmed.

"Let us be the first to toast the future Mr. and Mrs. Garland Foxworth," he said, and handed a glassful to Garland and one to me.

"Oh, then, in that case," Garland said, reaching into his pocket to produce a ring. "Another of my mother's beautiful jewels, her engagement ring."

He held it out to me. It was a three-diamond gold ring.

"Will you have me, Corrine Dixon?"

251

I looked at my mother. She wasn't smiling, and she wasn't gloating.

I held out my hand, and Garland slipped the ring onto my finger.

"As I suspected, a perfect fit. My mother was remarkably similar to you in so many of her features. It's uncanny."

I gazed at the ring and then looked again at my mother. For the first time I could recall since I was a little girl, she looked frightened.

But not for herself.

For me.

11

I never fully appreciated what the word *whirl-wind* meant until my upcoming marriage to Garland Foxworth was confirmed. On an almost daily basis for a week afterward, something was delivered to our house for my mother to consider: menu items, flower arrangements that featured irises, and the biography of the minister whom Garland had chosen to perform the ceremony. He hoped that was all right, because this minister had married Garland's parents. My mother thought that was sweet and illustrated how respectful of his parents' memory Garland was. How could a man like that be anything but a devoted husband?

And then, the following weekend, Garland invited us all to Foxworth Hall. He even sent along our train tickets. My mother was all in a fluster, suddenly deciding that maybe her wardrobe indeed needed to be updated. After all, she was going to be constantly in the eyes of society now. Insecure about shopping for herself, she took Etta Benjamin and Louise Francis along on her search for new and appropriate clothes. For me, that was truly the blind leading the blind.

Even my father was surprised at how many new things she bought. We needed an extra suitcase, and only for a weekend. I wondered if we would visit Great-aunt Nettie. I was afraid Hazel might slip and tell my parents how Garland had upset me.

"Not this trip," my mother said quickly. "We don't want any unnecessary distractions. I can't imagine inviting her to the wedding, but of course, we will."

"And Hazel," I said.

I didn't mention Great-aunt Nettie's dislike of the Foxworth family. If she thought about it, she probably wouldn't want to attend, but Hazel would probably convince her she must. She'd keep her from saying nasty things. At least, I hoped she would.

My mother made a face but reluctantly agreed, saying she wouldn't want the responsibility of looking after Nettie. She would certainly be too busy entertaining the guests. I looked at my father, who had just the slight imprint of a smile on his lips. My wedding was suddenly, probably as he and Garland had planned, becoming more important to my mother than anything or anyone.

She talked about it almost the entire train trip to Charlottesville, reminding my father about weddings they'd attended that lacked the proper attention to detail. Sometimes it sounded like she was talking more about her own wedding than mine. Parents did live vicariously through their children, I thought. That was why they wished everything would be better for them.

Lucas was waiting for us at the railroad station with the same fancy carriage in which I had been taken to Foxworth Hall that life-changing night.

"Mr. Foxworth is taking so much extra care with preparations for your visit," Lucas said, "that he begs to be forgiven for not being here in person to greet you. He's personally inspecting the grounds work, the cleaning of the manor house, and your chambers."

"Is that so?" my mother asked. "Our chambers?"

It was clearly a question and not a simple acknowledgment, which surprised poor Lucas. How would he answer? He fluttered about, loading our luggage, and then assisted both my mother and me into the carriage.

"This is a beautiful carriage, Harrington," my mother said, running her hands over the new leather seats. "We should get a new one, perhaps. Perhaps something similar."

"I forget the name of this one," my father said, "but I know it's from England."

"It's a brougham," I said, speaking before thinking.

My mother looked at me. "How would you know that?"

"When he visited me at Great-aunt Nettie's, he showed it to me."

She nodded but remained suspicious rather than impressed that I would have paid attention to such a detail. Had I said too much? I glanced at my father, who gently shook his head. I said nothing else until Foxworth Hall came into view. I was seeing it for the first time in the daytime, and it did look quite different. Garland was right. It changed its personality and appeared to be more austere, older, but still quite beautiful, resting in its stunning natural settings with the rolling hills behind it and the manicured lawns and flowers around it. He wasn't overstating by telling me he had far more than the Wexlers when it came to his gardens.

When I was here at night, I hadn't seen all the windows on the two main floors, either, and now noticed the windows above the second floor, too, windows of what surely was that attic he had described. It seemed to go the length of the mansion. The driveway widened more than I had thought, and from this height in the daytime, the houses below looked like ones in a toy village.

"Well, I do declare," my mother said at first sight. "It's so big. Is that lake part of his property?" she asked, nodding to our left.

"Oh yes," my father said. "And soon to be your daughter's, too."

My mother gaped out the side window and then turned to me as if it wasn't until that moment that she understood what was happening.

"I don't know how you'll manage being the mistress of such a mansion. You hardly know enough to take care of your bedroom. A busy husband like yours will certainly be dependent on you to look after your domicile. I'm sure you won't have the hours and hours to dote on yourself, Corrine. Now, finally, you'll understand what I've carried on my shoulders all these years."

How could she compare our lives to this? I wanted to tell her that there would be servants, maids, cooks, grounds people, and drivers all at my beck and call. If she thought I hardly lifted a finger to care for myself and my things now, she'd be even more astounded at how much would be done for me after I was married.

However, I did admit to myself that I was quite frightened about it as I looked out and was able to see so much more than I had anticipated after being here at night only once. To me, it looked like it needed a small army to maintain it. How would I begin life here? What was the proper etiquette for speaking to and ordering servants about to do this and that? Exactly what would my responsibilities be, what would Garland leave up to me to do? What, if anything, could I change, would Garland permit me to change? It almost felt like a rebirth into a totally new world. Maybe my mother was right; maybe I was being naive thinking I could successfully be the mistress of Foxworth Hall.

Garland, having seen his carriage approaching, awaited us at the front entrance, wearing a riding jacket, cloth breeches, and a soft felt hat with black jackboots. He looked like he was dressed to go foxhunting on an English estate.

Myrtle Steiner stood beside him in her plain blue housekeeper's dress. It hadn't occurred to me until just now that she might greet me in a way that clearly demonstrated I had been here, that she knew me. What should I do? Would she handle it as well as Lucas had? Surely my mother would see the panic in my face the moment we stepped out of the carriage, but as it turned out, I had no reason to fear. Garland had set the scene. He introduced the three of us to her. Obviously, he had ordered her how to react.

"Mrs. Steiner has an assistant we will introduce you all to later. She is someone she has been training herself, her niece Dora Clifford. She's seeing to your chambers right now, especially yours, Corrine."

"Thank you," I said. If my mother wasn't standing right beside me, I probably would have said nothing. I would have taken that for granted, and I wasn't going to thank my future husband for every little thing he did for me anyway. My tongue would collapse with fatigue.

"After you settle in, Mrs. Dixon, I'd like to show you where we will set the entire affair, the altar, the chairs, and the tables. There will be bars on four ends and at least fifty people serving and caring for our guests. I have three different service uniforms on a table in the Foxworth ballroom from which you can choose. Afterward, perhaps at dinner, I'd like to discuss the music and complete the menu with you.

"That banging and knocking you hear is coming from the area for the wedding. I'm having a stage constructed and painted. As to the supervision of the food preparation, I have a wonderful cook, Marion Wilson, whom"—he leaned in to whisper—"I stole away from an English lord. She's quite familiar with planning large events, and she will have an army of assistants.

"Mrs. Steiner, who has been with me a while now, will escort you to your chambers, and Lucas will see to your luggage."

He finally stopped to take a breath, but before my mother could utter a word, he turned to my father and said, "Aren't we lucky to have so fine a day for all this, Harrington?"

"You mean you didn't arrange it?" my father said, and Garland laughed.

He shifted his eyes. "Of course, I should offer you something to help you relax a bit first, Harrington. The women can see to the chambers. Better than we can, I'm sure," he added, laughing. "My mother used to tell me I could sleep in a pigsty. Sometimes, when you do as much traveling as I do, you don't sleep in quarters much better than that, but you're too exhausted to care.

"So? We can go to my study and wait for them before touring the grounds? Talk a little bank business, perhaps. Mrs. Dixon wouldn't mind?"

"No. I'm sure it's fine," my father said before my mother could reply.

My mother smirked. I thought she was going to complain, but when we entered and she saw the art, the family portraits, the impressive stairways, the ceilings, and the vastness of it all, she was struck speechless. Mrs. Steiner barely glanced at me and led us up to our bedrooms. My mother gasped at the height of the bedroom ceiling. Her eyes were scanning everything like someone who had been kept in the dark for years. Not a single work of art, sculpture, sconce, or chandelier escaped her interest and questions. Just before Mrs. Steiner brought her to what would be her and my father's room, she turned to me.

"Have you even an iota of an idea of the wealth displayed just in this part of the house?"

I shrugged. I had had a similar reaction but kept that under lock and key, of course. "No, but I'm sure Garland will explain it eventually," I said, as if money was the very last thing that moved me.

She shook her head. "How will you survive? You're still a child," she muttered, and entered the bedroom.

Dora Clifford was brushing down a chair and turned. She didn't look a day older than me. I thought she was very pretty with her rich strawberry-blond hair pinned in a bun and startlingly unusual greenish-blue eyes. Her skin was creamy, with a splash of freckles on the crests of both cheeks. She was a little taller than I was, with a bigger bosom straining the buttons of her uniform, the hem of which was shorter than any maid's skirt I ever had seen.

"This is my niece," Mrs. Steiner said. "She, as well as I, will attend to all your needs."

Dora smiled and curtsied.

I smiled back and then waited in the hallway while Mrs. Steiner explained everything about the room to my mother, including the bathroom, closets, and lights. Of course, my mother followed her out to see what my room would be. As we walked farther down the hallway, I glanced back in the direction of the Swan Room. I wondered if Garland would show it to my parents, not that it mattered. My mother certainly would think it quite odd.

Dora came out of my parents' bedroom, and after glancing at us, she turned and walked in the opposite direction. It wasn't until then that I noticed she had a slight limp, as if her left leg was shorter than her right.

"Quaint," was my mother's comment about the room I would have. It was half the size of hers and my father's. The bed was as long and as wide, which made the room seem crowded. The windows were smaller than those in my

261

parents' room; however, there was an impressive Persian area rug with a floral medallion woven in a brilliant crimson. I thought it was too big for the room as well. Before I could mention it, my mother did.

"This rug would fit better in the room we're occupying," she told Mrs. Steiner.

"Everything in this house is designed and organized the way Mr. Foxworth's mother had decided. Nothing's been changed, and I doubt it ever will be."

My mother glanced at me, her face full of silent criticism but also anticipating my insistence that it would be. I didn't really care about some guest room. There were so many others anyway. Once Garland and I were married, I'd probably never even glance at this room. And I didn't think it wise to start an argument with Mrs. Steiner at the moment over what power I would or would not have.

"How many bedrooms are there?" my mother asked Mrs. Steiner.

"In this, the southern wing, the family wing, there are fourteen," she replied. "We don't open the rooms in the other wing unless there are guests."

"Well, we're guests," my mother said, a little too sharply, I thought.

"Mr. Foxworth considers you more family than guests."

"I see," my mother said.

She then peppered Mrs. Steiner with many other questions about the house, silly things, I thought, like the size of the pantries and linen closets. Again, how many rooms in total? Where did Garland sleep? Where had his parents slept? At least she had the restraint not to ask to see those rooms immediately.

Lucas brought in my bag, smiled at me when my mother wasn't looking, and then hurried out.

"Garland is waiting to show you the grounds for the ceremony, Mother," I said.

I thought she'd keep us here forever with her cross-examination of Mrs. Steiner, who looked grateful for my interrupting.

"What? Oh yes. I would like to see more of the house, of course. But first things first. Besides, if we give them too much time, your father will drink himself into a stupor before dinner."

Mrs. Steiner shifted her eyes quickly to look away. It wasn't that long ago that I was in a stupor in Foxworth Hall. I was anxious to move on to other things.

However, it really wasn't until we were on the way down the stairs that I realized Garland hadn't included me in his invitation to inspect the area for our wedding ceremony and party. Now that I thought more about it, it occurred to me that I hadn't been asked for my opinion about anything, not even the menu. Was that because he was so intent on pleasing my mother and, along with my father, keeping my pregnancy still a grand secret? Get her so excited about the event that even if she learned the truth, she might not care? Right now, I couldn't imagine that, but how much should I protest? I wondered. What was the proper role for the bride, especially one with my disadvantages?

The moment we entered the study, Garland suggested my mother follow him and my father out through the French doors he had recently installed. He said he was determined to do even more modernizing. "Especially now that I'm getting a wife," he added. It sounded like a wife was something he had ordered from a catalog.

Before my mother could respond, she paused to look at the head of a tiger that was so well stuffed and preserved it appeared as though it was just peering at us through the wall on our right and might leap in our direction at any moment.

"My Lord," she said, stepping back with her hand over her heart.

Garland laughed. "Wait until later, after dinner, when we all retire for the evening," he said. "Perhaps I'll take you first to my father's trophy room. This one," he said, nodding at the tiger, "was his, but I've added a few up there."

My mother looked at him and then turned to me. I could read her mind as well as I could if I were inside her head.

Are you another trophy?

Funny, I thought, until this moment, I had never considered that possibility. Foxworth Hall was filled with things Garland and his father had collected. They seemed to be the lifeblood of the mansion. It consumed paintings, statues, vases, and jewels. Why not people, too? Now that the idea hovered in the air, I wondered if courting women was simply another form of hunting to Garland. More important, of course, if that had been true until now, would it stop?

In one of our very rare mother-daughter talks, as short as it was, my mother had told me marriage either changes a man or reinforces who and what he is. She meant my father was a very responsible and organized person, and marriage not only fit nicely into that but emphasized it. It was one of the few times she bragged about winning him before any other woman could.

Of course, right now, I was worried more that this marriage would change me in ways I wouldn't want. That was what probably made every soon-to-be bride nervous, although most of the girls I knew would likely be concerned their fiancés would discover something terrible about them right before the wedding and cancel.

We all walked out, and Garland immediately began explaining how he envisioned the event's layout. It was all far too much for my mother or me to comprehend, with "this squared with that and that at right angles to this." He and my father were quite into it, however. Like two emperors surveying their kingdom, they walked ahead of us, gesturing to each other as if we were no longer there. We saw the stage being constructed on our right. While Garland and my father were talking, a bulky, thick-necked young man, stocky and with hands that looked too big for his short arms, quickly approached.

"This is Olsen, my head gardener," Garland said, turning back to us. "He's going to have a lot to do with the setup out here. Olsen, this is my fiancée, Corrine, and her parents, Mr. and Mrs. Dixon."

He nodded and struggled to say, "Plea . . . sed to . . . m . . . eet you."

Garland smiled. "Olsen was in a bad accident when he was twelve. The buggy his father was driving turned over. He was under it for hours, with the heavy weight on his chest, but he's overcome all that when it comes to running my grounds. He's a genius at it. I hired him when he was only fourteen, three years ago, right, Olsen?"

"Ye . . . yes, sir," Olsen said.

"I've been said to have a good eye for help," Garland bragged.

"Can't be a leader without that ability," my father said.

They walked on, with Olsen trailing behind and nodding at every suggestion and command either

Garland or my father uttered about the grounds preparation.

"I think I need some rest," my mother called to them after a while. She never liked walking in the sun without an umbrella, but she did look tired, even aged, by our journey.

They stopped and turned.

"By all means, Rosemary," my father said. "We're here two days. There's time to learn it all."

"I doubt that," my mother muttered under her breath. She looked at me.

"Go on," I said. "I'm not tired yet, Mother."

She was probably returning to the house to get more of a tour and information anyway, I thought. Poor Mrs. Steiner.

I watched her return to the French doors, and then, seeing that my father and Garland were in a deep conversation with Olsen beside them, his head down, all of them continuing on, I turned and started in the opposite direction. This was my wedding, too, I thought again. I should be at their side, and they should be looking to hear my opinions. Right now, it was as if I wasn't here.

Rather than chase after them, I decided to see the lake.

It really hadn't struck me yet that this was all to be my new home and I would be the mistress of it. I wasn't even thinking about my pregnancy anymore, either. Since the early days, I had been

267

lucky and experienced little, if any, discomfort, certainly nothing that my mother would notice. Being lazy and tired was my middle name, according to her.

But could I be lazy and indifferent here, even with a small army of servants? Actually, like my mother, I still had most of the house to explore. I was hoping that Garland would reserve time for some of that when we were alone. As we walked about the rooms and outside together, he would spin the story of his youth and his family, and I would truly get to know him. It was something I had to do very quickly now. At the moment, long romances were fables only recited in novels. My hope was that our marriage would be a long romance.

Today was a perfect day for romance. I wished that Garland and I were alone, that my parents weren't here, and we perhaps could picnic somewhere on the property that was always special to him, perhaps down here by this lake. I was eager to hear what it was like to grow up among all this.

I found a little knoll and sat to look out over the water, where two wood ducks were waddling up and down a dead log. A rowboat was tied to the small dock, and two sparrows were posing on the edges as if they owned it all, the boat, the lake, and the property. It made me smile.

I leaned back to let the warm sun wash over

my face. The grass felt cool on my neck. It was a nearly cloudless sky, with just a gentle breeze barely stirring the leaves on the trees. A flock of geese was flying farther north. I rarely appreciated my natural surroundings, I thought. Here, perhaps, it was staring me in the face, daring me to ignore it. *You can't embrace Foxworth Hall if you don't embrace me,* Mother Nature was saying.

Really, where am I? I wondered. *What has happened to me? Am I going to wake up tomorrow morning in my own bedroom back in Alexandria and realize it's all been a long dream?* Too many wishes can get knotted up and make it impossible for any to come true.

I closed my eyes.

I think I fell asleep for quite a while, because when I opened my eyes, Garland was standing there, smiling down at me, his hands on his hips and a wide smile over his lips. I sat up quickly, expecting my father to be nearby, too, but he wasn't.

"You looked so peaceful I didn't want to wake you. I caught a glimpse of you walking in this direction," he said. "But I couldn't just leave your father. He is definitely a details man. He went in for a nap, too. Thankfully."

"I could have helped you with him, but you didn't seem to care whether I was there or not," I said.

"Of course I care, we care. I know how over-whelmed you can get, and I don't want you to be extra nervous. After all," he said, his voice dropping to a whisper, which, seeing where we were, was overly dramatic, "you're in a very deli-cate state at the moment, Corrine. However . . ."

"What?"

"I saved this to show you first."

He unbuttoned his shirt, reached in, and came out with a pink envelope. He handed it to me and sat beside me.

I opened it slowly and took out the wedding invitation.

The words *YOU ARE INVITED* were written over the Foxworth crest he had shown me in the carriage that first night. I opened it and read: *Mr. and Mrs. Harrington Dixon and Garland Foxworth invite you to the marriage of Garland Neal Foxworth to Corrine Beatrice Dixon on the twelfth of August, one thousand eight hundred and ninety, at 2 o'clock p.m., Foxworth Hall, Charlottesville, Virginia. Reception to follow.*

"Simple but sweet, huh?" he asked.

"It's only ten days from now!"

"They are being hand-delivered to the guests on the list as we speak. Most will have them by late today. Whoever can't come will be sorry," he said. "As you know too well, we can't wait much longer."

"But my wedding dress?"

"You'll be measured for it tomorrow. The dressmaker has been summoned to Foxworth Hall."

"Measured? I haven't chosen one."

"My mother's will be perfect. It's still quite in style, and as I have said, you are remarkably similar. Besides, why bother you with such details now, Corrine? It's the dress I've always envisioned for my bride anyway. You will look absolutely beautiful."

"But—"

"Besides, I've always thought wedding dresses were silly. You wear it only once and then put it in some carton or hang it way back in a closet and never look at it again. My mother's was quite expensive. It is very similar to the wedding dress Queen Victoria wore when she married Prince Albert, a white satin dress. I'll give you my mother's jewelry to wear, and if I'm not mistaken, you are about the same shoe size."

"That's not going to be a fashionable dress, a dress in today's style," I said.

"It will be perfect, and you'll look beautiful," he declared, his voice raised. He sounded like some Moses announcing commandments.

I simply stared at him. He looked away and then turned back, smiling.

"Anyone would think you'd be grateful to have all this taken care of for you so quickly, especially in light of the time we have. I don't want you worrying about anything for the entire period of this pregnancy. I didn't want to say it in front of your parents, but I hired Dora Clifford to be your personal maid from now on."

"What do you mean? We don't want someone hovering over me right now."

"No worries. She knows about your . . . condition, as does Mrs. Steiner. It would be the height of folly to try to fool my servants who will see you daily. Now, I know how concerned you'll be about your figure, your looks. My mother was the same. So I've arranged for you to have a wet nurse when the baby is born." He smiled. "I don't want those beautiful breasts toyed with, even by my own child.

"I've also arranged for the doctor who will come out here to deliver our baby when the time arrives. He'll visit periodically to be sure you're doing well. Also, when it's no longer possible to hide what you have in store from anyone who visits, we'll get you the prettiest maternity clothes made, even if we have to travel to New York City to get them. Okay?"

"I suppose," I said. Did I have a moment to take a breath? I was back in that rushing stream, that current my father had described. I couldn't decide to swim faster, because I couldn't go any faster.

"Now, I've spoken with your father about your leaving, and he agrees you shouldn't. There's too much to do here."

"What? Shouldn't I leave?"

"Your parents will leave the day after tomorrow, and you'll stay. Don't worry about clothes. I will open my mother's closets to you, and the same dressmaker who does your wedding gown will come out to adjust anything you want."

"But her clothes are . . ."

"What?"

"Old," I said.

He laughed.

"She's been dead for years, hasn't she?"

"Some of the garments were worn only once. Most of it looks brand new. I think there are things with tags still on them, in fact."

"But it's not today's fashion."

"Oh, again with fashion. Don't worry about it. After you give birth, we'll buy you an entire new wardrobe, and you can buy some new clothes now, too. That's a . . . a given truth," he said, and stood. "It will be so wonderful having this time alone before our wedding. It will be like an early honeymoon, and what better place to enjoy one than Foxworth Hall?"

He didn't give me a chance to offer an opinion.

"We should start back. You'll want to freshen up for tonight's dinner."

He reached for me, and I gave him my hand. When he pulled me up, he embraced me and then kissed me. Smiling wryly, he said in a loud whisper, "Once your parents are gone . . . don't

273

worry. No limoncello," he said, and laughed.

He held my hand all the way back to the house, describing what he and my father had discussed about my wedding. I couldn't help feeling like I'd be one of the guests. Not once did he ask, "How's that sound?" or "Is that okay with you?" The only choice I could think was left to me was who, if anyone, would be a bridesmaid. Of course, I thought about Daisy first and then wondered how she would react to learning I was going to be married in ten days. People, if Garland was right, were receiving the invitations this very moment and would soon be talking about it. Everyone at home would know. If I remained here, Daisy wouldn't be able to ask me any questions. Maybe that was good.

"I want to send a telegram to my best girlfriend and ask her to be my bridesmaid," I said.

He paused and thought, as if what I was asking was a very big thing.

"What?" I said.

"I'm not putting up any guests at Foxworth Hall, not even distant cousins. I'm arranging for carriages to be available at the train station on the day of our wedding, and your father and I will have a special train scheduled to leave at ten in the evening for Alexandria so your parents' guests can easily attend and go home. It's expensive, so we have contracted for only two passenger cars for this special edition."

"What does that have to do with my maid of honor?"

"We'll have to check to see how many guests they have invited so no one will be without a seat."

"I should have a maid of honor, Garland."

"And that will mean her parents, I'm sure. That's three people, three more seats."

"Who else would be my bridesmaid? Daisy Herman is my best friend."

"Another sixteen-year-old? You don't look your age, but surrounding yourself with girls that age . . . think of the way that will look. Why have people wondering and gossiping about us?"

"But no maid of honor?"

"I was thinking Dora would be quite honored to do it," he said. "You understand what I'm saying. You want to leave your childhood friends behind now anyway, Corrine, don't you? You'll probably rarely, if ever, see them again, and you're far more sophisticated. It will be years before any of them will have things in common with you again, if ever."

"But Dora's a servant."

"No one really knows who she is, which is good. She can handle it. No worries. Mrs. Steiner will see to her needs so she looks proper."

There wasn't a cloud in the sky, but I turned to look back as if I had heard a roll of thunder. All the birds had left the lake, and the shadows from the sun dropping in the west had grown and widened, casting a dark silver sheet over the water. It looked like ice.

He tugged on my hand. "C'mon. I want to tell you more about the plans for the wedding reception. Guess what we're going to have to practice?" he said, as we entered through the French doors.

"The waltz?"

"Exactly. It's an important wedding dance. See? That's another reason I want you to stay until the wedding and, of course, forever after that. We'll practice in the ballroom. I bought a brand-new Edison phonograph with a cylinder that has waltz music so we don't have to have an audience watch us practice. And occasionally, I'll have a pianist on my new piano playing for us. How's that?"

I nodded. He did seem to be thinking of every little thing.

He opened the study door and stepped back. "Now, go get some rest, my darling girl. Look at all you've done today, and we're going to have a wonderful dinner. Mrs. Wilson has prepared your parents' favorite, larded sweetbreads with peas."

"I detest that," I said.

He stared at me. "Your mother never said . . ." He grimaced. "Don't worry. I'll have her prepare some chicken for you. Now, as I said, with all you've done today . . ."

"All I've done?"

"The traveling in your condition and . . ." He looked to his left, as if he wanted to be sure no one was listening. "And the act we both performed for your mother. I know you were tense throughout. That's why you fell asleep on the grass back at the lake," he said, as confident as someone who knew everything. "Now, go rest and freshen up. Dora will be attending you, and there will be a surprise in the room for tonight."

I looked at him suspiciously. "Surprise?"

"Just go up and see," he said. He stepped back and, even before I took a step in the hallway, closed the door.

For a few moments, alone in this still strange, immense house, I froze. When would this feel like home to me? Could this ever feel like home to me? Foxworth Hall was filled with rugs and drapes, bedrooms with comforters and blankets, but as I looked about at the tall ceilings, angry ancestors peering down as if anyone who entered was violating their sanctity, and the cold statues, I thought about my own bedroom at home, in which I slept so comfortably, feeling safe and cuddled by its warm walls and familiar scents.

Yes, I was about to become the wife of one of the wealthiest young men in Virginia, and I would live in and be mistress of a home big enough to be called a castle, but would I be happy? I couldn't even brag to my best friend. As far as she would be concerned, I had disappeared off the face of the earth. Was I about to?

I walked slowly to the stairway. Somewhere deep inside the manor house, someone was making noise that sounded like the movement of furniture. Every sound echoed in this home, I thought. I heard the clanking of pots and pans off to my right, and through an opened window, I caught the sound of men talking as they worked on the stage. Everything that was happening here now was happening because of me. And yet I didn't feel proud or smug about it. I felt a little frightened, and I didn't really know why.

In fact, as I headed up the stairway, I could sense the trembling inside me. Was that simply because I was pregnant? When I turned to head toward my "quaint" bedroom, I listened for my parents talking but heard nothing. They were both probably asleep. I did need a good rest and then, hopefully, a warm bath. Dora would see to it, I was sure.

I turned into my bedroom. She was standing there by the closet, stroking a dress that hung in the doorway as if she was stroking soft, beautiful hair. At her feet was a bustle. She turned quickly when I entered and smiled. She started to curtsy, too.

"Stop that," I said. "I'm not some princess."

She instantly lost her smile.

"What is that . . . thing?"

"It's the dress Mr. Foxworth wanted me to prepare for you tonight."

I approached it slowly, and she stepped away.

"There's enough material here for four dresses," I said. I nodded at the bustle. "I've never worn one of those. They're not in style now."

She looked at it and then at me with a blank expression.

"I think I'd suffocate in this," I added, lifting the material. "It weighs a ton."

The dress had an overskirt draped to an apron front and a full flounced underskirt with full petticoats. There were multiple layers of ruffles and flounces.

"I'll wear something else, one of my own things. Take it out of here, and that thing, too," I said. "Actually, they smell like clothes stored for ages in some dank closet."

"Mr. Foxworth was keen on your wearing it," she said. It sounded like a warning.

"Dora, is it?" Of course, I knew her name, but I wanted to impress her with my clarity and demand.

"Yes, ma'am."

"Let me say it in stark, clear English. Take it out. I'm not wearing it."

She moved quickly to gather it up. Carrying out the bustle as well made it awkward. I almost laughed when she looked back. The moment she stepped out, I closed the door.

What was it Garland had said? "You want to leave your childhood friends behind"? They had nothing in common with me now?

Well, maybe that's true.

I will be the mistress of Foxworth Hall. I will especially surprise my mother.

I lay down on the bed to get some rest, with defiance embracing me.

But when I closed my eyes, I didn't see myself strutting like a peacock through the halls of the manor house.

I saw myself embracing my soft, oversized pillow and, as a little girl, falling to sleep with a smile on my face in my bedroom at home.

I drifted off, driving down the thought that I would see that warm comfort again only in my dreams.

12

Garland woke me, not by shaking or touching me but simply with his overbearing presence, a shadow moving over me. I had the feeling he had been standing there beside the bed staring down at me for a while. Was I always to awaken with him looming?

The impishness in his eyes that had teased and drawn me to him was smothered by the dark intensity of a man who looked like he had no memory of me. Who was this girl sleeping in one of his beds?

I ground the sleep out of my eyes and sat up.

"What's happening?" I asked. "Have I overslept?"

He stepped back, his arms folded across his chest. The expression on his face was so firm that it looked chiseled out of granite, the face of one of the statues in the halls. It drew away all the warmth in his eyes, turning them into cold glass. His silence was the most disturbing thing of all. Did I imagine myself speaking? Hadn't he heard me?

"What is it, Garland? Why are you just staring at me?"

"Is this your way of getting some subtle revenge?" he replied in a voice I didn't recognize, a voice that seemed to echo from a darkness deep inside of him. He resembled one of his austere, grim ancestors frozen in a portrait hung high enough in the hallway to glare down with disapproval at anyone who dared enter Foxworth Hall. It was as though his family's ancient anger and madness had been passed down from generation to generation wrapped in a ball of fire and was now emerging in him.

"What?" I asked in a voice barely above a whisper. "Why do you ask such a thing?"

"You chased Dora out with my mother's dress, my mother's dress, balled and crushed in her arms!"

"I didn't chase her."

"I'm trying to make our first dinner as a family special, unforgettable. I thought by bringing back some of the Foxworth history together, we'd have fun, too. You frightened the poor girl so badly she's been crying in her quarters. Mrs. Steiner came running to tell me. She was quite upset herself."

He stepped closer, his hands on his hips, his face softening as I felt my own begin to crumble into sobbing.

"I know you didn't mean to do it. I'm sure it was because you were tired, and being tired makes anyone a little irritable. But we have to remember that if we don't treat our servants properly, we won't get the best out of them. People are just as much an investment as anything, any land, any business, anything, and when you put something in, you want to get the most out. Now, about the dress . . ."

"I'd look like an idiot in that dress," I said as firmly as I could.

I never could tolerate a lecture from my mother, and I wouldn't start tolerating his. Too many young women simply shifted their parents' authority over them to their husbands almost before their vows were spoken. Not me. I had made up my mind about that long ago.

"An idiot? In my mother's dress?"

"I'd be swimming in that dress. And a bustle? I've avoided wearing one, Garland. I'd feel so silly starting to do so now."

"My mother never felt silly wearing it."

"That was because it was highly fashionable then. It's fallen out of style. I've studied fashion closely. Remember the beautiful dress I wore at the Wexlers'? I chose that myself. I know what is the rage now and what is passé. Besides, as I recall, you were quite impressed with how I looked, weren't you?"

"Yes, yes," he said, waving his right hand as if he wanted to chase my words away as he would an annoying fly.

"I had my father take me to the department store as soon as we received your invitation for the weekend, and I have something very much up-to-date that is quite proper for a family dinner.

I thought you'd be proud of me, proud that I had the knowledge and the taste, and that despite my age, you'd never be ashamed or . . ."

I stopped because I felt myself choking up. Where was the gentle, loving man who had come begging for my hand in marriage? I felt myself flinch with anxiety. Was there something about this grand house with its yet-to-be-explored shadowy corridors and rooms, its attic and its closets that harbored the ghosts of unhappy and dreadful times? Was all the natural beauty I had seen surrounding it forbidden entrance? Was my soon-to-be husband one man to the world outside of it and another when the grand doors closed behind him? Could something similar happen to me?

He looked down, shook his head, and sighed before he looked up. "Wear what you brought tonight. Tomorrow I'll have Dora show you my mother's entire wardrobe, and you can choose whatever you think can be updated, altered."

"But—"

"It would mean a lot to me if you could bring some of her beautiful things back to life," he said sharply, and then smiled. "At least try. Please. Besides, Corrine, you can't look foolish in anything. You're far too attractive. Gorgeous clothes, even expensive jewels, will only embellish what is already there, provided by generous Nature herself, Nature who has given me a great gift."

His gentle, handsome smile returned, rushed into his cheeks and his eyes, and softened his beautiful, perfect, and manly lips. This was the face that had captured me so quickly at the Wexler gala. I felt the chill and dread recede.

"As long as I don't have to wear a bustle," I said, relenting.

"Whatever. I so want this to be a memorable evening for you, for everyone. It's important to me that you are comfortable and happy at Foxworth Hall. Embrace it, and it will embrace you."

He stepped forward to kiss me. He wanted it to be short, a father's kiss, but I held on to his shoulders so firmly that he laughed and then kissed me the way a man should kiss a woman, his lips letting me clearly know that he wanted to touch me deeply in my sex. I was moved and even moaned. Did we have time? He heard my thoughts.

"Later," he whispered, with the seductive eyes of someone proposing a secret assignation. He stepped back. "I'll have Dora return to help you prepare yourself. She's very good at attending to the needs of another woman. You'll see. Only, be a little nicer to her. You might have noticed that she's a little fragile."

"She has a limp."

"Born with one leg shorter than the other," he said. "But she can do all she has to and more. See you in a while."

He left, and I realized what he had just said.

She's very good at attending to the needs of another woman. How would he know that? What other woman? Where?

Minutes later, there was a knock on my door. Realizing the size of this house and how far off the carriage stables were, I suspected Dora had been hovering in the wings somewhere nearby, nervously awaiting Garland's assurance that all would be fine. I felt a mix of sorrow and power. Having authority over other young women wasn't something new to me. They sprawled at my feet during my womanly talks and later hoped for some acknowledgment when they saw me. Something my father once told me rose to the surface of my thoughts, however. "Kings and queens have power," he'd said, "but it doesn't take them long to realize that power traps them." I didn't quite understand it when he said it, but I thought I did now. It adds responsibility and widens the reach of your conscience.

"Yes?"

Dora peered in gingerly. "Ma'am?"

"Please, just come in," I said. "I'm sorry I raised my voice."

She smiled and entered. "You're wanting a bath after such a long day, I'm sure. I have the water ready for you," she said. "My aunt gave me some powders to soften the water and give it a scent. It's very nice."

"Where are you from, Dora?" I asked, rising.

"Richmond, ma'am."

"Do you have brothers and sisters?"

"An older brother. He works in one of Mr. Foxworth's factories. He lived with my parents, who were both quite sickly. They had us late in life. My mother was in her mid-thirties, and my father was forty."

"I see," I said. Although she answered shyly, her eyes down, I thought if I continued to ask her some personal questions, she would relax and not be as afraid of me. "Do you have a boyfriend?"

"Oh no, ma'am," she said, actually blanching at the idea.

"You can't be much younger than me."

She looked confused.

"What?" I asked.

"I'm almost five years older," she said. It sounded like a reluctant confession. "But unlike most girls my age," she continued, "I had to spend most of my time caring for my parents."

"You weren't a servant for any other family?"

"No, ma'am. Until most of last year, I was at home. When my mother passed, I cared for my father, and then when he passed, my aunt told Mr. Foxworth about me. I was at home, caring for my brother's needs."

"I thought you were only just hired. How long have you been here?"

She thought a moment. "Since October tenth of last year, ma'am."

I stared at her. Why didn't I see her when I was

287

here? Surely she knew I had been here that night. Why hadn't Garland mentioned her?

"You stay in the carriage house?"

"In rooms above it, yes, ma'am."

"Your brother never brought a young man home to meet you?"

"No, ma'am."

I nodded, but in the back of my mind, I was thinking that despite her good looks, her limping might have driven some romances away before they had a chance to start. Or worse yet, her brother might not have wanted to lose his personal maid, her future be damned. My mother would say that just like any other selfish man, he wasn't at all concerned about her needs, her dreams, only his own comfort.

"I mean," she quickly added, "I wouldn't count Mr. Foxworth that way."

"Your brother brought him to your house?"

She nodded. "When he was visiting his factory, he mentioned that my aunt had recommended me, and he asked to meet me. I suppose my brother couldn't refuse him. When Mr. Foxworth came, it was like an interview for a job. It was a surprise, but I had our home in good order."

"Yes, I suppose it was quite the surprise."

I wanted to ask more questions, but I was afraid of the answers I might be given. I couldn't imagine any young woman not having a crush on Garland the moment she saw him.

"I'll take that bath," I said.

I went to my suitcase and took out the dress I had bought just for this night. It had a flared and gored skirt and a tiny boned bodice with elbow-length sleeves. My hourglass figure wouldn't be well hidden. I doubted Garland's mother's wardrobe had anything like it.

"I'll be wearing this."

She nodded and smiled. "Very pretty, indeed, ma'am."

I considered her a moment. I didn't like her calling me ma'am even though I realized a servant should address the mistress of the house this way, but somehow, even though I was younger, the way she said it made me sound much older. There was too much forced deference. I was more comfortable with girls who were envious. I guessed I'd have to get used to it and let it go. I imagined Garland would not approve of her calling me Corrine. Soon she could call me Mrs. Foxworth anyway.

It was curious how I hadn't thought of that until this very moment. Could I get used to it, to being known as Mrs. Foxworth? Right now, it seemed more like a shoe that wouldn't quite fit, a shoe that squeezed my toes. I supposed it was the same for any young girl about to change not only her name but her whole life.

Dora surprised me by remaining in the bathroom preparing washcloths and towels. I looked at the filled tub. It had a sawn-oak trim rail and sat on a cast-iron frame and legs. There was a decorative scroll design on the legs.

"Are all the bathrooms this nice?" I asked.

"All I've seen, ma'am."

"You mean, you've been here since October and there is still a lot more for you to see of this house?"

"Oh yes, ma'am. Mr. Foxworth doesn't like anyone wandering about the house. We do what we have to where we are sent, and that is that."

I wondered if she had ever seen the Swan Room, but I didn't ask. I started to get into the tub, conscious of the way she was looking at me when I disrobed.

"Oh, please be careful, ma'am," she said, moving to help me sit in the water.

The water was a light-blue color and did have a delightful, fresh sweet scent. As soon as I sat, she moved quickly to begin washing my back with a soft washcloth. I turned and looked at her, her face so close. Except for those freckles, she had a complexion that definitely rivaled mine, and her lips, which were straight and full, had a natural orange-red tone. I admired her teeth as well, because they were so straight and white.

"You've taken good care of yourself, Dora," I said.

"I had to," she said. "I couldn't get sick with my parents as they were."

"I meant more than health," I said. "Your beauty."

"Oh. Thank you, ma'am, but I've done nothing special."

I studied her a moment, my suspicions triggered by how carefully she touched me and how concerned she was.

"You know about me, right, Dora? You know about my current state?"

She was silent. According to Garland, all the servants knew about me, so I assumed she did, but she had also obviously been told to keep it so buried in her mind that it was as if it wasn't true. That was fine for now, I thought. Servants gossiped, and the gossip could leak out and find its way to my mother's ears during these two days.

I closed my eyes and let her massage my neck and shoulders. She ran the washcloth gently over my shoulders and down my arms. When she reached around and glided them over my breasts, I was a little shocked, but she continued as if she was washing the tub and not me in it. I lay back so she could go farther down my stomach, and then she came around and gently lifted each of my legs separately to softly scrub over my calves and thighs. I looked at her face as she washed my body. She wore a soft, simple smile, as if she was washing the body of an infant, a baby, but I didn't complain. This, I thought, was a life I might very well enjoy, the life filled with pampering and comfort.

When she was done, she stood there with a towel in her hands, quickly wrapping it around my shoulders. Even before I could think of it, she was drying me. As she knelt to dry my rear and reached in and between my thighs, I felt a part of me wanted her to stop. It made me feel ridiculous to be treated like real royalty, but another, stronger part of me settled back to enjoy it. I think I even moaned. My eyes were closed.

"You are very beautiful, ma'am," she suddenly said, when she was on her knees wiping my legs and looking up at me.

"Thank you," I said. I had never been good at saying that so it sounded like I meant it and had not expected it, but the appreciation I heard in her voice touched me.

She began to attend to my underthings, dressing me. I might as well be a storefront mannequin, I thought. So this was what Garland meant when he said she was good at looking after the needs of a young woman. I wondered for a moment if that grew out of her having to care for her mother, who was probably incapable of dressing herself at one point. I didn't want to think that; it made her seem more like a nurse than a servant. Would she tell me more about her past? I wondered how truthful she would be, how revealing. Were we far from trusting each other? How long would it take?

"You've attended to other women guests here at

Foxworth since October, haven't you?" I asked.

For a moment, she looked like she was going to choke on the answer.

"It's all right," I said. "I'm quite aware of the fact that I'm not Mr. Garland's first woman friend."

"Yes, ma'am," she said.

I thought about it for a moment. "Were any of them permitted to sleep in the Swan Room?"

Her whole body seemed to freeze.

"Don't be surprised I know about it. Surely you're aware that I was here at Foxworth."

"Yes, ma'am."

"Mr. Foxworth showed me the Swan Room. Haven't you seen it?"

She shook her head. I thought she would start trembling and run out.

"But you know about it?"

"Yes, ma'am. My aunt told me. She had to prepare it after . . . I mean . . ."

I quickly smiled. "That's quite all right, Dora. It's nice for me to know that Mr. Foxworth shows that room only to someone for whom he has some regard. Maybe after the wedding, I'll show it to you myself. I might even sleep in it occasionally, since no one else ever will."

She nodded, looking grateful and astonished.

"Let's go finish my preparations for dinner," I said.

After I had put on my dress, she brushed my

hair. I looked at the perfume on the vanity table and realized it was not there before I had taken my bath.

"Did you bring this?" I asked, holding up the small bottle.

"No, ma'am."

"Well . . . perhaps your aunt."

"Oh no, ma'am. She is very busy working with Mrs. Wilson on dinner preparations and looking after your mother's needs."

I smelled it. It was interesting but not exactly appealing.

"Have you seen this anywhere in the house?" I looked at her in the vanity mirror.

Why was it that some of my questions put such fear in her eyes?

"Have you?" I demanded forcefully. I was growing tired of all this hesitation. Either she was *my* personal assistant or she wasn't. She would come to know things about me that I didn't want shared; the same had to be true for her.

"Yes, ma'am. I believe that is from Mr. Foxworth's mother's possessions. His parents' bedrooms are unchanged from how they were before they passed. The brushes still have his mother's hair in them. There is even a scarf on the floor where his mother dropped it years ago."

"And no one will pick it up?"

"No, ma'am."

I thought a moment. "Did you say 'bedrooms'?"

"Yes, ma'am."

"So, Mr. Foxworth's mother slept in a separate room from her husband?"

She stared at me, probably wondering why I knew so little about the Foxworth family and Foxworth Hall.

"I don't really know all that much about the Foxworths, either," she said, trying to sound more like an equal. We were suddenly resembling roommates in some boarding school, whispering about the other girls. "No one asks questions about them in this house."

"This house is built on a foundation of secrets," I muttered.

She didn't nod. She looked like she was holding her breath to keep herself from having any reaction. It was clear to me, however, that she thought I was right. What was even clearer was the thought that secrets here were born almost daily. After all, if I was honest about it, I'd have to admit that I was probably the latest in a long line. I was carrying the heir whose existence had to be kept hidden for a while. I almost laughed aloud when I envisioned Garland bringing his mother's ugly clothes to me with the excuse that they would be better than any fashionable maternity clothes. Why, if I was cooperative and wore those clothes, we could hide my pregnancy until I gave birth.

My baby suddenly would appear one day like

some immaculate conception, a new Foxworth born out of the very air trapped in this mansion. The sperm had floated through the house and found me sleeping in one of the bedrooms, perhaps the Swan Room. Of course the house knew; it knew all the Foxworth secrets. It was whispering about me in every dark corner. I actually shuddered for a moment thinking about it having a throbbing heart, the walls pulsating and the ancestors growling in their portraits.

"Are you all right, ma'am?" Dora asked. My thoughts surely made me look a fright.

"Yes, yes," I said, and dabbed Garland's mother's perfume on my neck and between the tops of my breasts. Later, as he had promised, he would come to me, and he would be so pleased. Of course, now I realized that was why he had brought it here, another dark secret.

But there had to be some very good ones, too, didn't there?

I rose. Dora stepped forward to brush something off my dress and then smiled. "I'll straighten up your room, ma'am," she said. "And be down to help with dinner."

"Thank you," I said.

She started to curtsy.

"Don't do that," I snapped. She looked confused. I smiled. "Some things just make me feel too old, and I'm not ready for that." Thinking about things I had overheard my mother say about her pregnancy, I added, "And I will not permit my being a mother to age me a day more than I would anyway."

She nodded. I thought she was fighting a smile. Did she know more than I did? Did she think I was being naive? Perhaps she liked my self-confidence, wishing that she had an iota of it herself. In the back of my mind, I harbored the thought that I might just help her achieve it. Despite her being older than I was, she was like a new project for me, a challenge, almost as if she was all the silly little girls who folded their legs under them and listened to my wisdom at my womanly talks.

"We've got to trust each other," I said, reaching for her hand. "Even with our own secrets. That way, we can become more to each other than simply a servant and a mistress. Okay?" I asked.

Garland's own words had come back to me. We needed to treat our servants like any other investment. I'd invest everything I could, everything I knew about being a woman, and in return, she would give me her loyalty.

Pleased, now she smiled and nodded. I thought she intended to curtsy again but saw the no in my eyes and stopped. I glanced at myself one more time in the mirror and then started for the door.

"Wish me luck," I said, as if my going to dinner was equivalent to being in the Roman Coliseum to fight for survival.

She widened her eyes, and I walked out and down the hallway, proudly defying every ancestor in every framed portrait along the walls. I paused at the stairway when I heard laughter below. Was that my mother's voice? What had Garland done to charm her so quickly? I wondered, and started down with more enthusiasm.

They were all waiting for me in the study. My mother, to my surprise, was having a martini, something I rarely saw her do in the presence of anyone but my father. All three were drinking the same thing. My mother looked embarrassed by it, especially because of the expression on my face.

"These two fools insisted I imbibe," she said.

"We all should," Garland said, pouring one for me.

My mother was about to say something when it must have suddenly occurred to her that I was going to marry this man. The door to my childhood had been slammed shut. And so, too, apparently was her mouth. She sat back when I took the filled martini glass. It wasn't something I was used to drinking; in fact, I had barely tasted one once.

"Shall I make a toast?" Garland asked.

"I should be the one to do that," my father said.

"At dinner. Permit me this one first," Garland said, raising his glass. "To my new family, who I hope will merge so smoothly with mine that there will truly seem to be no differences between the House of Foxworth and the House of Dixon."

"Hear, hear," my father said, and we all sipped our drinks.

"I'd like you all to be as familiar with Foxworth Hall as I am. Tomorrow we shall tour the house and then, depending on the weather, of course, take one of my carriages to traverse the property. We could even take rowboats, Harrington and I at the oars, of course, and have a spin around the lake. I hope that's all to your liking," he said, directing himself to my mother.

"Very much," she said. How quickly he was charming her, I thought.

He smiled at me as if to say, *See? This will be easy.*

Maybe it was already the effect of the martini. Maybe it was simply all that I had done, seen, and heard in so short a time, but I laughed a bit too loudly. My mother's eyes widened, and my father smiled.

"Only one of those for her," my mother said.

"Absolutely only one," Garland agreed. He winked. For the moment, at least, he looked like he was enjoying keeping our secret hidden from my mother. He expected I did, too. Did he know me that well already?

I looked from one to the other to my father. They were all staring at me and smiling like parents enjoying their child. The realization rolled about under my heart.

I was feeling more like a ward of my husband

and not an independent, mature woman who was his wife, and my parents looked like they approved of it.

Most frightening of all, I realized that I was doomed to be a prisoner of Foxworth Hall once I began to show my pregnancy, at least until after the baby was born. The chains and the bars would be invisible, but nevertheless, they were there.

Maybe I'm wrong, I hoped. Maybe it was all just a silly young girl's reaction because everything was happening so quickly.

Garland's love for me was too strong for him to permit a drop of unhappy rain.

He put down his empty glass and stepped forward to take my arm. "The future Mr. and Mrs. Garland Foxworth will lead you both to dinner," he said, and took my glass from my hand, even though I had drunk less than half, and put it on a table. "Mrs. Foxworth," he said, and gestured at the door. "Shall we?"

I stepped forward quicker than he did. I was in my father's stream, and I was swimming faster than the current, clinging to what was left of myself.

13

Garland wanted the house to look exceptionally festive for our first family dinner. We all descended into the well-lit foyer.

Garland held out his arm for my mother. My father and I followed them.

"You're marrying quite the charmer, Corrine," he whispered.

"Should I be worried, Daddy?"

He raised his eyebrows and then smiled and said, "But you're quite the charmer, too, daughter."

When I have to be, I thought, *when I have to be.*

My mother hadn't ever drunk as much wine at any dinner, but Garland was pouring and insisted he had the best wines imported from France. He had four bottles out, each from a different region, and wanted my parents to try every one. He was hesitant to pour me any and gave me barely a taste. The talk was quite spirited about our wedding ceremony, and the more Garland described something else he had added or something else that would entertain our guests, like portrait photographs celebrating our occasion, the more excited I became. He hadn't exaggerated when he declared that I was going to be the center of one of the biggest social events in Virginia.

As I listened to him, especially when he talked about me, I thought he was doing a good job of covering up what led to our being here. Even if later on my mother found out why we were moving so quickly on our marriage, I didn't think she would be upset. Despite how efficiently and how fast the details of our ceremony and reception were being spun, this had no resemblance to what some people might call a shotgun marriage. There wasn't the hint of any arm twisting. Even my mother was overwhelmed with how much Garland loved and respected me. I could see how she was looking at me when he talked about me, elaborating on our first meeting each other, to the point where she began to wonder if he was still talking about me. It was as if my mother's eyes had been opened to see a new daughter.

I read her mind. Was I really that sophisticated? Could I really be that charming? As far as she could tell, I had completely won this worldly man's heart instantly. She even looked a little jealous. Perhaps in her mind, my romance, as short as it was, was ten times as romantic as hers and my father's had been. By the end of the evening, Garland had certainly succeeded in wining and dining my parents. At our nuptials, there would be no hint of anything but his and my love for each other and my parents' joy.

How pleased my father looked. It was, in fact,

his acceptance of how strong Garland's love for me was and his belief in Garland's remorse over nearly losing me that helped convince me I wasn't making a mistake. My father rarely made significant errors, and in my heart of hearts, I still believed he only wanted not only what was best for me but what would make me happy.

Mrs. Steiner and Dora had served us so well my mother compared our dinner service to the service at the best restaurant in Alexandria. When we were up to dessert, Garland asked Mrs. Steiner to bring out his cook, Marion Wilson, to be introduced. She was a very pleasant-looking, tall, light-brown-haired woman with a soft-spoken English accent. Her hair was severely pulled and pinned back and tight into a bun. Her cheeks were crimson, perhaps from the heat of the kitchen, but they made her large hazel eyes dazzling. I didn't think she was much more than thirty years old, if that. Wisely, she directed herself mainly to my mother.

"Very pleased to meet you, mum," she said, and nodded at my father, barely glancing at me. I supposed she thought she and I would have a lifetime to get to know each other.

Garland suggested a return to the study for a cordial after dinner, but my mother, who had eaten too much and had way too much wine, protested her fatigue. She looked to my father, who quickly agreed.

"Yes," Garland said. "Very wise for us all to get some rest. We have a big day tomorrow."

"Well, then," my father said, standing and helping my mother with her chair, "we will bid you good night and thank you for your hospitality."

"And please confer my appreciation to your cook. I suppose I should call her a chef. Is it Miss or Mrs. Wilson?" my mother asked.

"It's Mrs. Her husband looks after my horses and carriages, but I think she's more married to her kitchen."

My mother laughed loudly. The wine had reddened her face and brightened her eyes until they looked like the hearts of tiny candle flames.

"It was a wonderful dinner. Don't let her get a divorce," she added, which for my mother was quite witty.

Both my father and Garland laughed.

"Little chance. No worries. And you'll always be invited to dinner, Mrs. Dixon."

"That's very kind," my mother said. Suddenly, her eyes were drooping as if the whole day had hit her like a pillow in the face.

"To bed, my dear," my father said. "Good night."

He took her arm. I could see how she was leaning on him for support. He threw me an amused glance.

Garland nodded and then gave me a conspiratorial look as my parents started out to go to their room, my mother now complaining how my father was rushing her away. Frankly, I had never seen her as funny and as talkative. But strangely, as I saw them walking arm in arm toward the stairway, I felt an unexpected pang of sadness. It was the first time I really thought of them as older. So much of my life seemed like a pull and tug with them, but suddenly, the thought of leaving them, even for all this, was disturbing.

As soon as they were gone, Garland reached for my hand.

"How tired are you?" he asked.

"Pleasantly but not totally exhausted."

"Then let's continue in the fumes of this wonderful evening."

My parents were up to the bedroom floor. My father was hurrying her along. Could it be with the goal of sex? Maybe this house brought the lust out in people. Garland ascribed so much magic to it.

He paused at the foot of the stairs. "Although I am ecstatic over the results from your first night here, which I realize wasn't pleasant for you, of course, I want to be sure I make this second night much, much different. Shall we?" he asked.

We started up the stairway, his arm around my waist, brushing his lips over my neck, tickling me as we ascended, giggling. When we reached the top landing, I anticipated his turning toward the guest room I was occupying, but instead, he turned right, and we walked quietly past my parents' room, him putting his finger over his lips so we tiptoed silently deeper into the house. My body tightened as we drew closer to what I was doomed to call the Limoncello Room. I wouldn't go back in there for some time. Maybe he felt my body stiffen. He never paused, leading me on until we reached his bedroom.

"Now that I got your parents asleep . . ."

He opened the door. His lamps were lit dimly, casting a romantic glow over his bed. I suspected either Lucas or Dora had, at his order, prepared it while we were all at dinner.

"Got to practice," he said, and then he lifted me gracefully into his arms, kicked the door closed behind us, and carried me to his bed. He held me while we kissed and then lowered me tenderly, carefully, as if I was made of thin china. For a moment, he just stood there looking down at me. "You are so beautiful," he said.

"Grace Rose, who is a nurse and a friend of my mother's, told me women blossom when they are pregnant."

"Are you pregnant?" he joked. "Might be a false alarm."

"Is that what you wish?"

"Hey, it would have happened sooner or later. Might as well be sooner. I wasn't going to let you get away," he said, and lowered himself to his knees beside the bed, where he began to undress me like a little boy unwrapping his Christmas or birthday present slowly, luxuriating in the expectation. I moved only to make it easier for him.

When I was totally naked, he paused and just looked at me without touching me. In my mind, I felt his fingers exploring. I saw him lean in to kiss my breasts and then work his way down over my stomach, his lips on the insides of my thighs. I moaned and heard him laugh.

When I opened my eyes, I saw he hadn't moved.

"Maybe you don't need me," he said, with that irritating arrogant smile.

"Maybe I don't." I put my hands over my breasts.

"Like hell you don't," he said, and pounced to do everything I had envisioned.

He began ravenously, but suddenly, probably recalling his promise to make this night dramatically different from my "limoncello night," paused and became far more gentle, moving like a man unsure about how far he should go, anticipating my command to stop. Instead, I closed my eyes and reached for his shoulders, clearly urging him to enter me and begin our climb toward ecstasy.

I smiled to myself, remembering how I had once described it, described what I imagined it to be, to

Daisy and two others at one of my womanly talks. "It's like climbing a steep mountain at first. You warn yourself to stop, to turn back, but the top looks so inviting, and soon it becomes effortless. It's more like sliding down now until . . ."

"Until what?" Faith Grover had asked in a breathless voice.

I had opened my eyes and looked from her to the others. Even Daisy was holding her breath now.

"Until you explode and explode until you think you're going to die and love it all the way."

"How can you love it if you think you're going to die?" Mildred Petersen had asked.

"That's the mystery. You'll see. Someday maybe," I'd added.

"How did you know all that?" Daisy had asked after the other two left. "You made it sound so real."

"It's not hard to imagine if you're doing it right," I'd said. Her eyes had looked like they were spinning. I'd smiled. "Don't ask me to show you. Practice," I'd said, and she had laughed the nervous laugh of a virgin, someone who had to first conquer fear to settle into pleasure. Whether it was evil of me or not, I had never had the fear.

I certainly didn't now, even after making the cardinal mistake mostly made by foolish women, who, despite all they knew and all the warnings, thought, *It won't happen to me.* Now that I was beyond caring, past that point of no return, I didn't hold back. Yes, this was going to be different tonight, but there was nothing tentative about my lovemaking. If anything, I was so demanding Garland was the one to rush to finish. He looked like he thought he would die in my arms if he didn't.

When he rolled over, he was laughing but also exclaiming how I might kill him with love.

"And to think you were a virgin," he said.

"Only technically," I replied. He thought that was very funny.

After a while, we were both quiet, clearly both exhausted.

"You had better get back to your room, or you'll fall asleep beside me and shock your mother in the morning."

"You just want to be sure I don't come back at you," I said, and he raised his hands in surrender.

"Now I'm happy that you will have your own bedroom after we're married."

"What? Why my own bedroom?"

"I like the idea of your being in your own room. I'll have the room your parents are now in prepared as soon as they leave. It's quite nice."

"But why?"

"It will make our marriage more romantic and more exciting. Just like we just were because we're doing this surreptitiously tonight. Don't you see?

"Besides, a woman has so many other needs. I'd be underfoot with my things and constantly stumble over yours. Your bedroom will be your world, solely your world. I'll come to it only when I want you or when you ask me to come."

"But we'll be married."

"Oh, I know about married people. Sex becomes something mechanical after a while. You know, carried on Tuesdays and Thursdays or something. Lovemaking should be spontaneous, even after years and years of marriage. It will be like the first time every time."

From the expression on his face, I understood that he wanted me to see this idea as tender and amorous, but it struck me as just the opposite of spontaneous. It was more like forbidden lovers planning affairs, trysts, and not people in a marriage. In a way, he made it all sound illicit, like we'd be sneaking love in the mansion.

I dreamed of a different set of circumstances. In mine, I would often turn to him in our bed, my eyes filled with desire, which would immediately light up his. That was spontaneous, too, wasn't it? Alone, busy with my clothes and hair, pins and scents, I wouldn't feel his presence, his breath, and be touching his body with the tips of my fingers the way he would touch mine. Then our lovemaking would seem fitting, fulfilling. Wasn't that all far more romantic?

"Your bedroom is so large," I said. "How can

there not be room for the two of us? I don't understand. Why can't we share your room?"

"Your parents don't share a room, do they?" he asked. How did he know that? Why would my father confide such a thing in him. Did he just look at them and surmise? "Well?"

"I don't want to be my mother," I said as sharply and firmly as I could.

He smiled. "Oh, you won't be. I know so little of her, but even in my wildest imagination, I wouldn't call your mother an exceptionally passionate woman, would you?"

I didn't disagree about her. She wasn't my touchstone when it came to marriage anyway. "But . . ."

"You should return to your room now. We have so much to do with your parents tomorrow. Don't forget, the tailor is arriving in the morning to adjust your wedding dress. Best we both get some sleep."

I sat up and began to dress.

"Dora will be waiting for you in the guest room to attend to any of your needs before sleep."

"I don't have any needs," I said petulantly.

"Don't be angry. Just think about what I'm saying. You're going to be into your pregnancy in a short while, and you'll want more privacy then. You'll see. I'm right about the separate bedroom," he continued as I dressed.

When I was finished, I turned to him. "I'm not

angry. I was just thinking about it, that's all. And I've made a decision."

"Oh?"

"I agree."

"Oh, good," he said, smiling.

"But I don't want to move into the bedroom my parents are using."

"Why not?"

"I want to move into the Swan Room," I said. "In fact, that is the only room I'd move into if not sharing yours."

He sat up, staring at me. "No one's ever slept in it," he said.

"Exactly. Why waste something that beautiful? Have done whatever has to be done. I'll move in right after my parents leave."

I walked to the doorway and then turned back to him.

"And I'll look at your mother's wardrobe sometime tomorrow after the tailor works on my wedding dress. If there's anything to rescue, I'd like to do it now. Okay?"

"Sure," he said, but he still looked a little dazed.

"Good night, my love. I'm very excited about all you're doing to make our wedding practically a historic event."

I blew him a kiss and left.

I walked to my room and entered. Dora was there, just as Garland had said she would be, but she had fallen asleep in the chair by the bed.

I started to undress. She heard me and quickly rose to help.

"I'm fine," I said, feeling quite annoyed now. "I don't need help with this. I'm not an invalid."

She looked devastated.

"It's all right," I said with less annoyance. "Thank you."

She smiled with relief. Obviously, Garland had warned her never to do anything that would displease me.

"I put out your nightgown," she said, nodding at the bed.

I looked at it and shook my head. It was a dull-gray gown with a square neckline and a capelike collar, puffed sleeves, and a pleated front bodice. The neckline had elaborate embroidery.

"That's not my nightgown. Where did you get it?"

"Mr. Foxworth had me fetch it from his mother's things and told me to lay it out for you."

"Take it back to whatever old chest it was stored in."

"I washed it, and it's scented."

"I don't care. I'm not sleeping in that. I'm going to the bathroom, where I will put on my own nightgown. I'll be going right to sleep afterward, so go get some sleep yourself, Dora."

She stood there like someone afraid to move.

"Go," I nearly shouted.

She jerked herself to the right, carefully

gathered up the nightgown, and started out. "I'll bring up some warm milk."

"I don't want any warm milk. Go to sleep," I ordered, and went for my own nightgown. She was still standing in the doorway when I turned back. "What?"

She looked absolutely frightened. "Can I just leave this here, maybe in the closet?"

"You're afraid Mr. Foxworth would blame you for my not wearing that?"

She didn't answer, but she didn't have to.

"Just leave it and go," I said.

She hurriedly brought it to the closet, hung it up carefully, and then left. If I had the slightest doubt before, it was gone. I was marrying a man who ruled his mansion like a king ruled his palace. It wasn't a total surprise, but I did believe he was enchanted with me. And after all, I was not coming here to be another servant; I was coming to be his wife, his queen, if he liked. Our wedding was certainly being organized as if it was a royal event.

Besides, as I once told some girls at one of my womanly talks, a man is not unlike any other wild animal. Once you corral him in marriage, capture him with your beauty and charm, you lead him to the belief that he exists now for only one thing: pleasing you.

"How do you do that?" Bethany Sue Andersen had asked skeptically.

"You lasso him like a wild horse."

They had all laughed.

"With what, a rope of steel?" Mabel Warren had said, smiling, thinking she was so clever. The girls had laughed again.

"No, Mabel. With a rope of sex," I'd said, and everyone had stopped laughing.

Maybe a woman couldn't vote, couldn't run a company, couldn't be an executive like my father or do half the things a man was permitted to do.

But that didn't mean she couldn't get a man to do everything she wanted him to do for her.

In the end, he would.

It was that confidence, after all, that brought me to Foxworth Hall and soon to the altar to promise my obedience to Garland.

Few who would attend would know my opinion of promises, but Garland certainly did, and if he didn't, he would.

I was tired. I hurried to the bathroom and then to bed, snuggling up comfortably in my own confidence, unafraid of anything, even a nightmare. I decided instead to relive the lovemaking we had just enjoyed, and for a few moments, I even forgot I was pregnant.

14

Garland wasn't exaggerating about how full the following day would be.

Right after breakfast, the tailor arrived. My mother accompanied him to my room and, with me, waited for Dora to bring in what would surely be known as "the Foxworth wedding gown." Even my mother thought that passing it down from one generation to another was a wonderful idea.

My mother said it was quite elegant, nicer than her own. It was an ivory satin with an attached wide gathered skirt. The neckline was trimmed with a handmade lace ruffle, and the bodice featured a black-laced closing. Underneath, I would wear a corset over an embroidered chemise. Layers of full petticoats would be worn with a crinoline hoop, creating a full bellowed skirt. The Limerick lace veil was edged with a nine-inch border of floral motifs.

The tailor took my measurements and then announced he would have little to adjust. He kept saying, "Remarkable," after each measurement. "It's as if the dress was already made just for you, Miss Dixon."

"Maybe it was," my mother quipped, and they both nodded and smiled.

Not if I had anything to do with it, I wanted to say, but I swallowed back my thoughts and impatiently waited for him to finish. What he had to do would take no time. Garland had asked him to return in a couple of days to help with what I would choose from his mother's wardrobe. There wasn't time for it today.

As soon as the tailor left, Garland began the tour of Foxworth Hall. I had really seen so little of it, perhaps a third of the tapestries, art, and statuary. Soon I would be the mistress of this mansion and part of the Foxworth legacy, but for now, it felt like I was visiting a famous museum and should be taking notes. How would I remember what artist did what painting or sculpture and where each originated? Someday in the not-so-distant future, perhaps, I would be taking a visitor through Foxworth Hall, and Garland would expect me to be familiar with and proud of what we possessed.

Because my mother had cross-examined Mrs. Steiner so much, she already knew many of the details, like how old the house was, who were the first Foxworths, how they had acquired so much land, and how the children of some distant cousins had been moved in for a while during a smallpox epidemic.

"They hired a tutor and homeschooled them in the attic," she told my father, as we followed Garland down the hallway.

He overheard her whispering. "Education, books, have always been important to the Foxworth family," Garland said. "Especially first editions."

My father was quite impressed with Garland's library and envied him for his private office in his house. That gave him some ideas for the new house he was contemplating.

"A man should have a private place for his business homework," my father said.

My mother looked at me and rolled her eyes. "I'm for that. Right now, the whole house is his private office," she said, and Garland laughed.

Perhaps the most impressive part of the house was the grand ballroom. Garland had obviously had it prepared for a dramatic viewing. The curtains were closed so that the room was made brilliant with all five tiers of the four crystal and gold chandeliers fitted with candles that had been lit. The light that spilled from the chandeliers reflected off the grand crystal fountain, weaving threads of radiance over the walls. Mirrors captured it and carried it further, illuminating everything silver and gold. The room was dazzling.

"It's a veritable wonderland," my mother said. I spun to look at her when she added, "This house is filled with magic."

Did she actually feel that?

The ballroom was so large that our footsteps

echoed, because there wasn't anything much in it at the moment, except for the long table with samples of service uniforms with different color combinations and the new piano. The hardwood floor looked as new as the day it was installed. A corridor in the house ran above the far wall. It was difficult to make out too much because it was dark. Would I ever get to know every nook and cranny? How does anyone call such a vast residence home?

"In the horrid event that it rains on our wedding day, we can, as you see, hold the ceremony and reception in here and not feel crowded at all," Garland told my parents. "My family has held many a big event in this ballroom, including a reception for Robert E. Lee, among other famous people like senators and congressmen. There's an extension to the kitchen with an additional stove, sinks, and storage when we have to service a large number of people."

"Have you had such a big event here recently?" my mother asked.

"No, not recently," Garland said. He thought a moment and then smiled to add, "Not since my father was alive."

"Hopefully, you will have many now," my mother said wistfully.

"Oh, without doubt, Mrs. Dixon, without doubt. In the meantime, shall we choose the uniforms for the reception?"

The two of them started for the table. I looked at my father. Wasn't my opinion important for this, at least?

He stepped up beside me to whisper, "Let her get totally involved, Corrine. The deeper she's invested herself, the more she'll accept any surprising news if we have to reveal it beforehand for some reason."

At this point, I almost didn't care whether or not she accepted anything, but I took his point and held back. Garland cast a satisfied, conniving glance at me while my mother debated this color or that. She never asked for my opinion or my father's.

When they were finished, we walked out to another one of Garland's carriages, driven now by Mrs. Wilson's husband, John, a tall, lanky, light-brown-haired man who turned out to be quite the expert when it came to Civil War stories.

"Gretta Foxworth, Mr. Foxworth's grandmother, took in war wounded at one point toward the end of the war," he said. "Both Union and Confederate wounded. There was a battle not two miles from the Foxworth estate. The Union Army outgunned the rebels. Dozens died, and they said the field was an ocean of red. I can take you to see the battlefield if you like."

"It isn't still red, is it?" my mother asked.

"Stained forever in other ways," John suggested.

"There are skeletons all over this property," Garland added, just to tease my mother, who looked like she would faint. He and my father laughed.

The ride to the border of the Foxworth property took so long that my father joked we had just entered another state. He continually put value on everything he saw, from lumber to possible housing sites.

"My hope," Garland said, "is never having to sell anything and certainly never to break up this property."

My father nodded as if he agreed, but I could see in his eyes that he didn't. "Bankers," Garland would tell me later on, "see only the monetary value in everything. The only time they're emotionally involved with a dollar is when they lose it. Do you know a romantic banker?"

I didn't like thinking or saying anything negative about my father, so I was silent.

When we reached the lake, another carriage arrived behind us, this one carrying our picnic lunch, blankets, and cool drinks. Both Dora and Mrs. Steiner began to set up.

"Perhaps you'd like to take Mrs. Dixon for a bit of a row before we have lunch," Garland said to my father. "Build your appetite."

"Rosemary?"

My mother glanced at me and then smiled. "We haven't done that since—"

"Since Adam," my father quickly inserted, and everyone laughed.

Garland helped them into the boat, and then my father pushed off with surprisingly strong and graceful strokes. We watched them go farther and farther, and then we sat on the blanket and drank some lemonade.

"You are a charmer, Garland Neal Foxworth," I said. "Right now, my mother would say you can do no wrong."

"Isn't she right?"

I just looked at him skeptically, and he laughed.

"So, are you really serious about wanting the Swan Room to be your room?"

"Why shouldn't I be? It's beautiful, isn't it? I look forward to making love to you while embraced by the wings of a swan."

He nodded and looked away.

"Dr. Ross will be here to examine you in the afternoon tomorrow."

"Oh, that reminds me. I'd like to hire my mother's friend, Nurse Grace Rose."

"Let's wait for Dr. Ross's examination. If all is good, you might not need anyone else until the time comes. I'm sure Dora could ably assist anyway."

I didn't want to tell him how frightened I was because of how difficult my mother's pregnancy with me had been. He sensed my nervousness, put his arm around me, and kissed my cheek.

"I won't wait for our nuptials to begin protecting you, Corrine. Worry not," he said.

I relaxed against him. My parents disappeared around a corner.

"Hope your father doesn't get too rambunctious out there," he quipped, his meaning in his coy smile.

"My father? Doubt it."

"I would," he whispered. "But I don't want to exhaust myself before the evening starts."

I glanced back at Mrs. Steiner and Dora, who were sitting in the carriage, waiting to serve us. It didn't seem right to have servants at a picnic watching our every move to anticipate something we might want. I imagined most women, especially young women my age, would be jealous of me, but I couldn't help but wonder if I'd ever get used to this life.

"I have a great idea. Later, let's practice the waltz for your parents. Your mother claims she never saw us dancing at the Wexlers'. I bet we can get them up and dancing, too. Great rehearsal for our wedding reception, us dancing alongside your parents. I can hear the applause now."

He smiled and then kissed me softly.

"You are so lovely, no matter what time of day," he said.

Would I ever be happier than this?

Close to an hour later, my parents returned, my father looking hot under the collar from the effort to cross the lake or, as Garland was suggesting with his laughing eyes, something else.

"Shall we call it midday delight?" he whispered.

I quickly covered the expression on my face. My parents? In broad daylight? On someone else's property? However, I did look at them with some suspicion. My mother appeared a bit guilty. Perhaps Foxworth Hall could be magical, I thought, especially when it came to love.

After lunch, Garland suggested we all take a nap. He had planned another big dinner and sent for a violinist from Charlottesville to entertain us while we dined.

"And Mrs. Wilson has made us one of her wonderful golden rod cakes," Garland said. I wondered if it would be half as good as Hazel's. "After dinner, Corrine and I will have a surprise for you in the ballroom."

When we returned to the house, Mrs. Steiner sent Dora up to my room immediately to help me out of my clothes, take them all to be washed, and, when I was ready, set out my evening dress. She made no attempt to bring in another of Garland's mother's. She folded back the top sheet of my bed and fluffed the pillow. I couldn't imagine myself doing things like this for another woman, especially one younger. She closed the curtains so I wouldn't be bothered by the afternoon sunlight and then, after I got into bed, blew out the candles.

"Wake me in an hour," I said when she opened the door.

"Yes, ma'am."

I think she curtsied, but I was too dozy to care. In minutes, I was asleep. Taking naps in the daytime was not something I usually did, but I did know that many women, even girls my age or a little older, too, thought a nap during the day kept them looking younger. When Dora did wake me, I was sorry I hadn't told her two hours, but there wasn't that much time before we would all gather for dinner.

"I have your bath drawn," Dora said when I groaned and covered my eyes after she opened the curtains. "We haven't put out what you wish to wear."

We? I thought. She made it sound like she was now an indelible part of my life and would be as close as my shadow.

"I have a new skirt and bodice to wear tonight."

This outfit I had brought was a startlingly new fashion with a pastel tulip of bell skirt that was smooth and tight over my hips down to its wide hem. The white bodice was cut narrow over my shoulders with gathers of pleats and full over my bosom. Dora looked quite surprised when she laid it all out.

"I doubt you'll find anything like it in Mr. Foxworth's mother's closet," I said.

She turned to me but kept her face frozen,

clearly unsure how she should react. She was afraid to say anything that might be critical of Garland's mother's clothes, but she was also afraid of offending me. Instead of feeling sorry for her, though, I was annoyed. If she was going to become part of a *we,* she had better learn to like what I liked, and quickly, too, I thought petulantly, and then regretted it. What did the poor girl have, really? Certainly not much of a future here. It suddenly occurred to me that she was not much better off than she had been when she was her brother's caretaker. At least then there had been the slim possibility of meeting someone who could steal her away. Whom could she meet here besides some Foxworth ghost?

After I bathed and dressed, Dora brushed my hair. For a moment, I felt like a doll she was playing with, her face in my vanity mirror soaked in some fantasy like someday caring for her own daughter. I put my hand over hers to stop what were becoming unnecessary strokes.

"Enough," I said. "You've done a lovely job of preparing me. I fear I might become too dependent on you, Dora."

"No fear, ma'am," she said. "I doubt you could become too dependent on anyone."

She almost bit her own lip after saying that, trembling at what my reaction might be. I looked at her in the mirror and then burst into laughter.

"So quickly," I said.

"What, ma'am?" she asked fearfully.

"You've gotten to know me so quickly," I said, and she smiled with relief.

Our second dinner went even better than the first. My mother was really a different person, laughing at every joke my father and Garland made, complimenting Garland on how well he managed such a big estate, and then giving me an unexpected compliment by saying, "Corrine knows how to protect beautiful things. I didn't have to teach her anything when it comes to that."

"Perhaps she's inherited so much more from you, Mrs. Dixon, than she realizes now. But in time, she will, I'm sure," Garland said.

With all the wine he had drunk and my mother's good spirits, my father looked happier than I had seen him in years. He even looked younger to me. Was it the afternoon delight?

Garland's violinist, a tall strawberry-blond-haired man, was placed far enough from our table and played so softly that he soon became part of the setting. Every once in a while, my father would toast him. Toward the end of the dinner, Garland called him over and whispered something to him. He returned to his place and continued to play. After we had our golden rod cake, which wasn't as good as Hazel's, we all went to the ballroom. I noticed the violinist following us. Garland had that impish twinkle in his eyes.

The room seemed even brighter and more dazzling than previously. Mrs. Steiner and Dora followed us, too, and when Garland signaled to them, they took our glasses of dessert wine. He nodded at the violinist, who began to play a Viennese waltz by Johann Strauss. I was very nervous about it, but I surprised myself, remembering his instruction. My parents were clapping.

"Join us," Garland called, and they did.

We were all dancing. Were these two really the parents I had known all my life?

When the evening ended, everyone was talking at once, my father reminding my mother that I was remaining at Foxworth Hall.

"It makes so much sense. There's so much for her to do in so short a time," he said.

My mother agreed. "And I have so much to do at home," she declared.

My father and Garland met in the morning to finish discussing the wedding details. My parents then left a little after breakfast. Lucas brought the beautiful carriage to the front, and Garland and I said our good-byes.

My mother was glowing when she turned to me. "Never in my wildest dreams, my wildest wishes for you, would I have imagined this, Corrine. I am sorry I didn't have more faith in you. My darling daughter," she said, and hugged me.

I felt more deceptive and low and nearly

confessed, but my father's glance awash in warnings kept me silent. *This isn't so terrible,* I thought as they started for the carriage. *After all, I am in love, and Garland is so in love with me.* He held my hand as we watched the carriage turn and start away.

"Dr. Ross will be here in a few hours," he said. "Dora has been preparing the Swan Room for you. She will show you my mother's things, and you can choose to keep anything you wish. You know from the way he adjusted your wedding gown that we have the best tailor in Charlottesville here tomorrow to adjust and fit whatever you choose. And yes, as I promised, Lucas will take you to Charlottesville the day after to shop for whatever else you need in your wardrobe. I have an account set up for you at Miller and Rhoads."

I looked at the carriage disappearing, and despite everything Garland was saying, his love, the servants, Dora, the wealth and size of Foxworth Hall, I suddenly had a sense of deep, dark foreboding. *There's no reason for it,* I told myself, but it followed me back into the grand house. Garland kissed me and went into his office, and for a moment, I stood there alone in the large foyer, with every ancestor glaring down at me. All were asking the same question, or at least it was what I heard in my mind.

How dare you?

Dora appeared on the stairway as if she had materialized out of thin air.

"Ma'am," she said. "Your new room is ready, and I can take you to Mrs. Foxworth's wardrobe."

Mrs. Foxworth's wardrobe. *Oh, get this over with,* I thought, and walked up after her.

I had no idea how big Garland's mother's wardrobe was. In what was her bedroom, the two walk-in closets were filled with her things, including shelves of shoes and hats. Almost all of it was something my mother would love to own. I wondered if he would mind my giving most of it to her. Finally, knowing how important this was to Garland, I culled four skirts and bodices, a coat, and a half dozen petticoats. It was hardly anything compared to what was there, but it was something, hopefully enough to satisfy him.

"I'll bring it all to your room for the tailor to adjust tomorrow," Dora said, and started to carry out the garments.

Later that afternoon, Dr. Ross arrived. Garland accompanied him to the doorway of the Swan Room and introduced him. He was a short man, only a few inches taller than I was, with very thin gray hair on the sides and back, crowning a bald head peppered with brown age spots. He had thick gray eyebrows and a narrow face with a sharp nose. His small shoulders and upper back were raised so that he resembled someone in a constant cringe. Garland added that he was the family doctor for years and had delivered him. I had no doubt.

After the introduction, Garland left us, but Dora came right in and stood off to the side. Dr. Ross stood gazing at me as if he had forgotten why he had come.

"Well now," he said. "Let's see what we have here." He asked me to lie flat on the bed and then seemed to turn his hands loose like someone releasing two canaries.

The examination was embarrassing. I kept asking, "Do you have to do that?"

"Oh yes, yes," he said.

When he was finished, he stepped back and said, "I've never had a healthier specimen."

"Specimen?"

He smiled, patted me on the thigh, and left to report to Garland.

I could see from Dora's expression that she sympathized with my discomfort. I made up my mind to again ask Garland to hire Nurse Rose. She was better than any midwife, but when I went to look for him, Mrs. Steiner told me he had gone to Charlottesville to work on arrangements for our wedding and reception. He had told her he wouldn't be back for lunch. Later in the afternoon, a messenger arrived to tell us—me, mainly—that he wouldn't be back in time for dinner, either. I spent the day exploring more of the house. Dora hovered behind and around me as if she would lunge to pick up anything I dropped. I finally told her to go take a rest or help Mrs. Steiner with her duties, whatever they were.

So much of the house was dark, unused. I made my way slowly with a candle and found the hallway that looked down on the ballroom. Every time I paused, I thought I heard footsteps. I suspected that either Mrs. Steiner or Dora was shadowing me, worried that I might in some way hurt myself. A pregnant woman should be concerned about tripping and falling, especially in these dark areas of the mansion. But I was bored enough to be courageous and found myself opening the door of another upstairs bedroom. It was so far from everything I wondered who would have used it. There was no doubt it hadn't been used for years. A doorway inside it opened to another, narrower stairway. Surely, I thought, it led up to the attic, but right now, I had no interest in going up there.

Since Garland wasn't returning for dinner and there would be no one but me, I didn't bother to change. I took a short rest in the Swan Room, what was now my room, admiring everything in it. I so wanted to show it to Daisy. Wasn't it a bit cruel to just forget her the way Garland wanted me to? I understood his logic, but maybe I could figure out a way to get her to come visit. If she did so before my pregnancy was obvious, why would Garland oppose it?

When I was in Charlottesville to shop, I would find that telegram office and send her one inviting her next Monday. But then I thought, what if it really upset Garland so close to our wedding? Maybe later, I reasoned, while there was still time before my pregnancy was obvious.

Dora came to tell me dinner was ready. The prospect of eating at that big dining-room table alone discouraged my appetite, but Mrs. Wilson had prepared a turkey breast with cranberries and yam, which was one of my favorite meals. Apparently, my mother had left her a list of things I liked. Dora served me and stood behind me while I ate, until I told her she was making me nervous. If something fell, I promised, I'd call her. Afterward, I went to the library to wait for Garland and plucked a book off the shelf because of its title, *Wired Love.* When I opened the cover, I saw there was an inscription.

For Garland . . . this could have been about us.

Love, Claudette

Of course, I wondered why and began reading. It was the story of a telegraph operator who began a flirtation with another telegraph operator fifty miles away, neither knowing what the other looked like. I became so involved in the story that I didn't realize how much time had passed until I finally looked up at the grandfather clock and saw how late it was. Could Garland have returned and not known I was waiting for him? But then why wouldn't he come looking for me?

I hurried out with the book, and, perhaps waiting for the sound of my footsteps, Dora came rushing from the kitchen to greet me.

"Ready for bed, ma'am?"

"Has Mr. Foxworth returned?"

"Not yet, ma'am."

"Are there any more messages?"

"No, ma'am."

I stood thinking and then decided I should go to bed. He'd most surely come to me when he arrived, I thought. Snuggled comfortably under the swan, I tried to read a little more but found my eyelids too heavy to keep open. When I did open them again, the light of morning had already begun to tiptoe its way into the room. I rang for Dora, who came so quickly I wondered if she had fallen asleep in the hallway right outside my door.

I assumed Garland must have stopped by and found me in a dead sleep. I decided to throw on a robe and go surprise him, wake him by crawling in beside him. First, of course, with Dora's assistance, I washed and brushed my hair.

"What should you wear this morning?" she asked.

"I'll choose something in a while. You can go

help set the table for breakfast," I told her. "Mr. Foxworth and I will be down in a while."

She looked confused, like she wanted to say something.

"What is it, Dora?"

"Mr. Foxworth didn't come home last night," she said, and then fled the room as if she had accidentally set it on fire.

15

Garland didn't arrive until a good hour or so after I had eaten some breakfast. Because it was a cloudless, warm day, I sat outside with a second cup of coffee and my novel, but before I continued reading, I simply stared at the lake, mesmerized by the rolling beauty of the hills beyond it. The surrounding forest, now fully bloomed, looked like an artist had made long brushstrokes of dark green over it all. I did feel like I was captured in a painting. Someday I might hang on the walls inside and someone who was first brought to Foxworth Hall would look up and wonder how such a young, beautiful girl in full bloom herself ended up beside so many grim-looking ancestors.

The great house loomed above and behind me, casting a thick, wide, and long shadow. It was probably my imagination, but birds seemed to be careful about entering it. Eating my dinner and breakfast alone had left me with an unexpected feeling of doom and depression. I should be feeling just the opposite, but I felt everyone's eyes on me and thought they were soaked in pity. What were they thinking? *This could be your life now, Corrine Dixon? Get used to the hollow sound of footsteps, the long, dark shadows flowing out of corners, and the smell of faded flowers?*

I could hear the workers off to my right completing the work for the wedding and reception. Mrs. Wilson told me at breakfast that one of the older gardeners who predicted weather based on his old aches and pains assured her that we'd have a perfect day. Did a perfect wedding day guarantee a perfect life? Were vows made before a minister more powerful and lasting than promises followed by "cross my heart and hope to die"?

But at the moment, I wasn't thinking of our gala wedding so much as I was thinking about Daisy and the other girls, imagining what they might do today. Maybe they all had gone cycling together, some of the boys coming along. I was sure I had become the biggest topic of discussion. I could hear Daisy saying, "Didn't I tell you Corrine would be the first to marry?" The parents of some of them surely had been invited. I was probably quite the celebrity, but I wasn't feeling as happy, as successful, and as important as I had imagined I would.

Who would be my new friends here? Would they all be older women, wives of Garland's business associates? Suddenly, I was seeing the world from my mother's point of view. She had faced the same sort of future when she married my father. My father wasn't as rich, of course, but his world and Garland's ran on the same tracks, powered by engines fed by the same sort of ambition. When did ambition become greed and the greed become stronger than any other motive, even love? Who could answer these questions for me?

How would I find a new best friend? one voice inside me asked. Another quickly answered, shouldn't I be more excited about the future balls and dinners I would attend with Garland than worrying about girlfriends? Think of the parties Garland and I would have. He'd be too busy for the details. I'd be in control of all that. The great house would echo with my footsteps as I pointed to something and ordered that it be changed, dressed in a brighter color, or simply removed. I would shop and travel, even after the baby was born. I'd have a nanny and wouldn't be tied down with any of the responsibilities most other mothers would have, those my mother had. Wasn't this always my plan, my dream?

What I was feeling at the moment was surely simply the normal nervousness any woman would feel on the threshold of a new life. Despite the confidence I had displayed until now, I was afraid of this future that had come so quickly upon me. How could I navigate so many new pathways successfully? I had to adjust to the moods of a man who, unlike my father, wouldn't necessarily put me, my pleasure and satisfaction, above his own. My own happiness depended on how well I did persuade him. Every day would bring new feelings, new fears.

I surprised myself by wishing my mother had remained behind with me. Suddenly, confiding in her and having her oversee every choice I made wasn't so terrible. I couldn't unburden my feelings with Dora or Mrs. Steiner. I certainly couldn't discuss them with Garland. A man wouldn't understand. I was going to make many mistakes, maybe tragic ones. To rid myself of these dark thoughts, I shook my whole body like a dog would shake off water.

"Get hold of yourself, Corrine Dixon. Don't be such a . . . such a little girl," I muttered.

"Hi," I heard, and turned to see Garland. Had he heard me chastise myself?

"Hi."

"Sorry about yesterday and last night," he said, hurrying over to kiss me. "Were you all right? I sent Lucas back to check on you."

"Lucas? I never saw him."

"I guess everything was fine, then."

"Where have you been? Why didn't you come home?"

"You have no idea what planning all this involves. I certainly didn't. I was with providers until dinner, and then I had this very important investment dinner meeting I had nearly forgotten. It went on and on, with a little too many toasts to our success, so I finally decided to stay over at the Caroline House. It was recently built, and I thought I should see what one of these modern hotels is like anyway. Someone is trying to get me to invest in a hotel chain all over the United States.

"Most important of all, however, is everything is falling into place. Just as I promised, we will have quite the gala wedding, my dear." He looked at the book on the table. "What are you reading?"

I turned it over to show him and opened the cover to display the inscription.

"Who was Claudette?"

"Ah, Claudette." He smiled. "She wasn't much older than you. Someone I met in Paris." He looked at the book. "We did exchange telegrams. I really never read the book, though. Is it good?"

"Did you love her?" I asked.

"Maybe for a minute," he said. "That was at least three years ago. Now, don't go searching Foxworth Hall for love letters and notes. What was in the past remains in the past. We are the future," he declared, took a deep breath, and looked out at his property. "What a beautiful day. Lucas will take you to Charlottesville to shop when you are ready. I was very pleased to hear you're making use of some of my mother's wardrobe."

"How did you find out? Did Dora send you a telegram?"

He laughed. "She was downstairs when I came in. Perhaps in time, you'll choose other things as well."

"I doubt it," I said.

He glanced at me, his eyes cold for a moment, and then he laughed. "We'll see. Right now, I had better check on the construction of our stage. I promised your mother there wouldn't be a single blemish on this spectacle."

He kissed me again.

"Don't bankrupt me today at the department store," he joked.

"Garland?"

"Yes?" He paused.

"I want you to show me the attic one day."

"The attic? Why?"

"You told me a little about it, but I discovered a bedroom with a stairway that goes up to it. I thought that was odd."

He shrugged. "It's not that interesting. Maybe a skeleton or two is all."

"Nevertheless, I want to know everything about this house."

"Do you? Good. That will take decades. We'll have a long, wonderful marriage. I'll be like Scheherazade and tell you a different story about something in the house every day. That way, you won't chop off my head to marry another handsome young man."

He laughed, turned, and left.

It was the king who was cutting off heads, not his bride, I thought. I decided to skip lunch and go right to my shopping. Visiting a department store with my unlimited budget to buy whatever I chose would surely cheer me up. I rose, hurried in, and told Dora not to have any lunch prepared for me.

"But Mrs. Wilson already prepared some egg salad the way you like it," she said.

"You eat it," I told her. "You'll like it, too. But first, go tell Lucas I'm coming out in ten minutes."

I hurried up the stairs and checked myself at the vanity table before sweeping up a shawl that had been Garland's mother's, conveniently left there, and hurried down and out to the waiting carriage. It was on the tip of my tongue to ask Lucas about Garland's escapades last night, but I was sure whatever I said would quickly find its way to Garland's ears. When we approached my great-aunt Nettie's house on our way to the department store, I was tempted to have Lucas stop, but then I thought it would only be a waste of time. She wouldn't recall my having been there, and even if she did, I wasn't in the mood to hear her rant about how terrible Garland's father was.

When we arrived at the department store, the salesladies at Miller and Rhoads were primed and ready for me, having heard from Garland that I had carte blanche. I spent hours trying on the newest fashions, shoes, and hats. I thought I should have something different for every day of the week and then special weekend clothes. Not once did anyone mention a price, nor did I ask. My father would have had heart failure, I thought, but what I wanted to ensure was not having the slightest need to wear anything more from Garland's mother's wardrobe than necessary. I was still dreading getting into that wedding dress.

Lucas looked shocked at the number of bags and boxes when I was finished. There was barely room for me, and some had to be put above with him. I sat back, imagining myself even more spoiled than Kate in *The Taming of the Shrew*. Garland was determined I would be. Was that out of love or guilt? Then again, I thought, what difference did it make as long as I got what I wanted?

But look what happened to Kate, I reminded myself when we started back to Foxworth Hall. Maybe my world would come crumbling down, too, but until then . . .

I loved the look on Dora's face when she came out to help bring my new things to the Swan Room. Lucas, feeling sorry for her, rushed to help. Garland was sequestered in his private office and didn't come out to see the parade up the stairway until it was almost over.

"Is there anything left for anyone else to

buy?" he asked when he walked up to see Dora unwrapping everything and hanging up clothes, organizing my new shoes and my hats.

"Not much," I said. "But I will need some of this for our honeymoon."

"Oh, that," he said. "I'm afraid we'll have to postpone it."

"Postpone it? Until when?"

"I've just completed the plans and the investments for a new textile factory in Charlottesville. The construction will begin this coming week. To keep the cost under control, we have to meet deadlines. I simply must be here to oversee it all. It could cost me tens of thousands more than it should."

"How long will it take?"

"Four months," he said.

"Four months! According to Dr. Ross, I'm well past two. That will be six or so. How can I go on a honeymoon if I look so pregnant?"

"We'll go where no one sees us or . . ."

"No one sees us? What would that be? A cabin in the woods?"

He laughed. "Okay. We'll go as soon as you're able to go after giving birth. How's that?"

"What will we tell people now when they ask where we're going?"

"The truth. I'm too busy at the moment, but I couldn't wait to make you my wife. I was afraid someone else would sweep you off."

He kissed me and stood back, smiling.

I didn't smile. The gossips who were coming would have reason to say mean things about me. *She married a man like her father and will become her mother.*

"Hey, hey, hey. We have a whole life to spend together, Corrine. Let's not worry about a ten-day holiday. There'll be plenty of those."

"Not if you're anything like my father," I muttered.

"Oh, I'm not. You can bet Foxworth Hall on it," he said.

But later, at dinner, his conversation was all about his new textile factory, the markets, both domestic and international, and what he would like to see politically to help build his business. The talk was as boring as my father's dinner conversation could be. Where were the romantic and dramatic descriptions of faraway places, the awe-inspiring sights he wanted me to see? The only part that seemed at all interesting was his plan for us to go to London, partly, probably mostly, to set up some new markets for his factories and do some sightseeing. But that was at least a year or so off. Finally, seeing how bored I was, he talked about the musicians he had hired to play at our wedding reception.

"We're paying top dollar for the best."

After dinner, he went to his office for some "last-minute business details," and I sat in the living room reading the novel this Claudette had given him. At least, I tried to read it. Every once in a while, I recalled what he had told me about being in love with her for a minute. Visions of him with some French girl kept coming between me and the words. I finally cast it aside, rose, and went to his office. He was scribbling on some chart and didn't even hear me enter.

"I'm going up to bed," I said.

He turned and looked at me with the oddest expression. It was as if he had forgotten who I was or that I was here.

"Oh," he said after a moment. "I'll stop in," he added, with that coy, sexy smile I loved.

"Good," I said, and left.

As I expected, Dora was waiting for me. She had probably been listening for my footsteps on the stairway.

"Where do you keep yourself up here?" I asked when she stepped out of the shadows.

"Mr. Foxworth told me to take his mother's bedroom while I tended to your needs, ma'am. I hope that's all right."

"Why wouldn't it be? I want nothing to do with that bedroom or any more of the clothes left in it," I emphasized.

She nodded and followed me to the Swan Room. After I prepared for bed, wearing one of my dozen new nightgowns, I lay back under the swan and waited anxiously for Garland. Perhaps he would spend the entire night with me. If we couldn't have a honeymoon right away, at least I could pretend to be having one here.

The bed was as soft as I imagined it would be, the pillows like balls of cotton, pieces of a cloud. I recognized the scent, too. His mother's scent, dabbed on the bed earlier, perhaps. How could it last that long otherwise?

So much time went by, I nearly fell asleep. Every time my eyes closed, I snapped them open, fearing he would peek in, see me asleep, and go to bed in his room, claiming he didn't have the heart to wake me. When he finally did open the door and peered in, I sat up quickly, folding my arms under my breasts. Why had he waited so long? Where was that romantic desire? Were we doomed to become another boring married couple after all? I could see his reaction to my look. As my father often told my mother, "The expression on your face could stop a clock."

"I can see you need more proof, more assurance, that I'm not simply the man who brought you here and ravished you."

"I am hoping you can't keep yourself away from me," I said, lowering my nightgown off my shoulders.

I saw his eyes go from me to the swan.

"It won't bite you, but I will," I said.

His smile looked timid, which for him was quite unusual. He stepped forward and closed the door softly behind him. He didn't move toward me, however.

"What is it?" I asked.

"It's just . . . so unexpected for me to see someone in that bed."

"Good. It gives me confidence that you brought no one else to it and makes it more my bed."

He nodded but didn't move.

"At this rate, I think I'd rather be ravished," I said, finally bringing a smile to his face.

"Oh no. It will always be different now. I promise," he said, walked to the bed, and leaned over to kiss me.

I seized his shoulders when he started to pull back.

He sat beside me to stamp smaller kisses on my cheeks and my closed eyes, holding me confidently in his arms. I lowered my head against his chest, and he kissed my neck before he rose, pulled back the thin blanket, and undid his pants. Naked from the waist down, he slipped in beside me.

"My swan," he whispered. "My own precious swan."

"Yes, yes," I said. This was what I had waited all day to hear, to feel.

As he carefully removed my nightgown, taking his time to kiss and stroke me, pausing to kiss my neck and whisper his love, I glanced up at the swan. Its red ruby eye seemed fixed on us.

I felt as if we were making love under its wing. His gaze followed mine, and suddenly, I felt his hesitation.

"What's wrong?"

"Dr. Ross told me to be careful," he whispered.

"Graceful, not careful," I said, and he laughed and then kissed me the way I wanted him to kiss me, romantically, lovingly, his lips wet with passion, his tongue grazing mine.

Nevertheless, he hovered above me and moved almost like someone I imagined doing this for the first time, tentative all the way. I didn't sense that overly self-confident manner. For a moment, I thought he was in some pain. He looked like he was frightened, agonized. Instead of looking at me and bringing himself closer to kiss me, he gazed up at the swan, pausing and seemingly mesmerized. For a few moments, I felt as if it didn't matter if I was there or not.

"Garland," I whispered.

A puzzled look came onto his face. He looked like he had just realized what he had been doing. I could feel his hardness softening. It was an odd feeling, like his phallus was losing air.

"What's wrong?"

"Oh, I'm sorry," he said. He started to pull away.

"No, I'm not complaining," I said, my hands reaching for him. I seized his arms. "There's nothing wrong, no pain."

He continued to retreat, breaking my grip. "It's all right. I understand," he said.

"Understand what? What did I do?"

He nodded as if he had heard a different voice, different words. "We'll be fine. I need to give you some time. I understand."

"What? No. There was no discomfort. It was exactly the opposite."

He wasn't listening. Instead, he was dressing quickly.

"What are you doing? Where are you going?"

"It's all right. I'll let you sleep. You need your sleep. My mother had a miscarriage, you know, after I was born. They worried about her getting pregnant again."

I sat up, holding my nightgown against my naked body. "But there was nothing wrong," I said. "I had no pain. You were so calm. It was becoming wonderful."

He nodded. "And it will be. You'll see. I'm just a bit nervous and afraid that I might not be as careful and calm if I continued. I did drink too much wine while I worked tonight. My head's spinning a little. I want no more problems between us. Never," he said, getting his shoes on. "Get some rest. The minister is coming over tomorrow afternoon to meet you, Reverend Chase. He likes to make his ceremonies personal."

He stood.

"And he doesn't know you're pregnant, so no

worries about being embarrassed or anything."

He glanced again at the swan, flashed a smile at what was surely my expression of total confusion, nodded, and left without looking back.

"Garland?" I cried when the door closed behind him. I anticipated his opening it again, but he didn't. There was only silence.

I was stunned. What had just happened? Why did he retreat just as we were reaching a climax? At least, I was. What had I done to frighten him? I didn't even moan. Maybe he did drink too much wine. Maybe he was having trouble, man trouble, caused by too much alcohol, and it had embarrassed him. A man like my soon-to-be husband could never tolerate any criticism of his manhood. Did he think I was going to do that? I had to tell him, make him understand I wasn't, that nothing like that had even occurred to me.

I slipped on my nightgown and went to the door. By the time I stepped into the hallway, Garland was gone. It was deathly quiet. The shadows down the hallway looked like they were moving toward me. The lamps flickered, the light more like sparks falling against the walls and the corridor floor. He had rushed away so quickly. *He is ashamed,* I decided. Should I stop by his room to see if he was all right?

I paused at his door and listened. It was very quiet. I knocked softly and waited, but nothing happened. I tried the doorknob. It was unlocked, so I entered. The room was pitch dark. Even the curtains were still drawn shut. Only the dim glow from the hallway cast any illumination, but it was enough for me to see he wasn't standing by his bed or lying in it. I heard nothing coming from the bathroom. Where was he?

I stepped back and looked down the hallway.

"Garland?" I called. "Garland, where are you?"

Only silence replied. He must have gone back downstairs, I thought. I returned to the Swan Room, put on one of my new robes, and walked out and down the stairs slowly. The lights were very dim. When I reached the bottom, I paused to listen, but the sounds I heard came from the heavier winds that were piercing every crack and crevice in the great house. I heard footsteps way up, the sound surely coming from what had to be that attic, but it might have just been my imagination, I thought when it grew still again, that or the wind, which surely found it easier to invade those walls and windows.

I could see there were no lights on in the library. None of the downstairs rooms looked occupied. Why would he come down here to sit in the dark? It was stupid of me to think so. I turned to go back up to the Swan Room. I decided that I might as well just go to sleep and talk to him in the morning.

I paused when I reached the first landing. There was the distinct sound of a door closing.

"Garland?" I cried. When there was no response, I hurried up the remaining steps and stopped at the top.

At first, I thought it was my imagination or the wind again, but when I looked to my left, Garland came out of the shadows. His hair looked like he had been running his fingers through it repeatedly, and his shirt was unbuttoned.

"What are you doing?" he asked when he saw me.

"Where were you? Why did you leave me like that? I called for you and went downstairs to look for you."

"Oh. I'm sorry," he said. He paused and looked down, shaking his head. "I was overwhelmed with the memory of my mother's miscarriage. I was there when it happened, not a nice sight. I still have nightmares occasionally, and then," he continued, looking up at me, "you know my younger sister died in childbirth. I don't talk about it all. Mr. Bravado. So there you have it, another Foxworth secret revealed."

He smiled and reached for my hand.

"I'm so sorry for frightening you," he said. "C'mon. Spend the night beside me, but in my bedroom. I'll make it up to you."

He started us away. I glanced back once. That was where his mother's and father's bedrooms were. I walked past the Swan Room with him but turned when I heard what sounded like footsteps behind us.

It was just a flash, almost no more than a shadow, but it looked like a woman wearing one of Garland's mother's night dresses, one I was supposed to wear. She seemed to float into another shadow. I stopped, and he turned.

"I thought I just saw someone, Garland."

He looked back, too. "Where?"

"Just for a moment . . . wearing . . ." I hesitated to say.

"Oh, probably just a Foxworth ghost," he said, smiling. "Ignore them."

I knew I looked shocked.

He laughed. "I'm so sorry about all this." He opened his bedroom door. "In a few minutes, it will all fade away, maybe in a few seconds. Believe me," he said, with the confidence I was far more used to seeing. He had his arm around my waist, and then, in one swift move, he lifted me into his arms and carried me to his bed.

For a while, at least, he was right.

It all faded away.

EPILOGUE

When I awoke in his bed in the morning, Garland was already dressed and gone. I left his bedroom and returned to the Swan Room, where I found Dora waiting, sprawled on the rose-colored velvet chaise longue. She sat up instantly when I stepped in.

"Oh, sorry, ma'am. I just dozed."

"Didn't you sleep well last night?" I asked, going to the clothing she had laid out for me. She didn't reply, so I turned. "Did you hear anything, see anything?"

"I don't know what you mean, ma'am."

She sounded guilty to me, guilty of something, or afraid to admit to something. I stepped toward her, and she actually backed up.

"Were you wearing something that belonged to Mr. Foxworth's mother last night? Don't lie. I saw you," I said sharply.

Her eyes widened.

"If you don't tell me the truth, Dora, I will see to it that you are sent home, and I will have my husband fire your brother. Well?"

She started to cry. "If I tell you, he will send me away anyway and hurt my brother."

"Not if I don't tell him what you've said. We need to trust each other, Dora. I have to trust you

355

with so many personal secrets, don't I? You have to trust me with yours. Well?"

She looked down, took a deep breath, and looked up slowly, the tears making her eyes look more like glass.

"I put on his mother's clothes and lie still in her bed."

"Why?"

"I don't know exactly, ma'am. He comes during the night and lies beside me. He doesn't touch me," she quickly added, "but sometimes he cries, and then, before he leaves, he says, 'Please, please forgive me.' I don't know if he means me or . . ."

"Or?"

"Maybe his mother. I don't know. If you tell him . . ."

I shook my head. "I won't tell him," I said, but I felt a little numb. There were ghosts in this house. *When you don't let go of the dead, you turn them into ghosts,* I thought. Maybe my father had told me that. I couldn't remember. No, I wouldn't tell him what Dora had revealed. Someday perhaps he would trust and love me enough to tell me it all, including why he wanted his mother to forgive him. I took a deep breath.

"Okay. I'll wear what you put out, but I want to wash and fix my hair. The minister is coming today to talk to us."

"Yes, ma'am," she said, and curtsied.

This time, I let her. Maybe I would always let her. Why did Garland trust her enough to keep such a deeply emotional secret? Was there more she wasn't telling me?

I started out and then turned, stopping her from following. "If I find out he does touch you and you're lying about that, I will tell him you've betrayed his secret, Dora."

She shook her head.

"The moment he does, if he does, you will tell me."

"Yes, ma'am."

She lowered her eyes the way a lady in waiting might lower them for a queen. I didn't want to be a queen. I wanted to be a wife and eventually a mother. I wanted this great house that truly seemed above all the troubles in the world to protect me and my child, my children. Of course, I wanted to be rich, too.

When I looked at myself in the bathroom mirror, I saw a new firmness come into my eyes. *I will have my place in Foxworth Hall. I will have my portrait on that wall, and with my beauty, I will drown out and silence the bleak, dark chorus of ancestors that have ruled it so firmly for so long.*

Maybe a marriage shouldn't be this much of a challenge, I thought, but I was prepared for it. Garland Foxworth would see my self-confidence. I was determined about that.

Later, we sat with the minister and talked about ourselves. Garland held my hand the entire time and repeatedly pledged his love. Reverend Chase, a man close to seventy, with silvery gray hair and charming, soft blue eyes, smiled.

"I feel like I'm sitting with your parents, Garland, and such a beautiful wife at your side. As they say, this is a match made in heaven."

"Yes, it is, Reverend."

"I kept your parents' wedding words, and I think I will, with your permission, use them for you two."

"Of course," Garland said. He looked at me.

"Yes," I said. "It would be an honor."

"Well, then, it's all fixed and perfect," Reverend Chase said.

I looked at Garland. "Why don't we make our first toast now with Reverend Chase?" I said.

Garland widened his eyes with surprise and smiled. "Really?"

"Yes. And why don't you take out that bottle of limoncello you're hiding somewhere in this office?"

"What? Are you serious?"

"Have you ever had any, Reverend?"

"Never heard of it," he said.

"Garland?"

He rose, his eyes on me, and then pulled out two books on a shelf and revealed the bottle.

"You sure?" he asked, going toward the glasses.

"We have to overcome our demons, or we'll never be truly happy, right, Reverend Chase?"

"I couldn't have said it better."

We made our toast and then walked him out to the carriage. Lucas had brought him. As they went off, we watched.

"I think you're going to be quite a surprise, Corrine," Garland said.

"Even to myself," I said.

He laughed, and we walked around the house to watch the finishing touches being made on our wedding site.

I knew now how this would begin.

I had no idea how this would end.

Books are
produced in the
United States
using U.S.-based
materials

Books are printed
using a revolutionary
new process called
THINKtech™ that
lowers energy usage
by 70% and increases
overall quality

Books are
durable and
flexible
because of
Smyth-sewing

Paper is
sourced using
environmentally
responsible
foresting methods
and the
paper is acid-free

Center Point Large Print
600 Brooks Road / PO Box 1
Thorndike, ME 04986-0001 USA

(207) 568-3717

US & Canada:
1 800 929-9108
www.centerpointlargeprint.com